An unforgettable Hollywood princess in a small southern town, Divine Matthews-Hardison lights up the novels of Jacquelin Thomas's

DIVINE CONFIDENTIAL

"There's something compelling about Divine and her amusing take on life."

—*Booklist*

SIMPLY DIVINE

"A page-turning story that's sure to touch lives."

—ReShonda Tate Billingsley, *Essence* bestselling author of *The Pastor's Wife*

"*Simply Divine* is down to earth and heavenly minded all at the same time. . . . It made me laugh and tear up."

—Nicole C. Mullen, Grammy-nominated and Dove Award–winning vocalist

MORE ACCLAIM FOR THE WONDERFUL FAITH-BASED FICTION OF JACQUELIN THOMAS

"Touching and refreshing."

—*Publishers Weekly*

"Bravo! . . . Sizzles with the glamour of the entertainment industry and real people who struggle to find that precious balance between their drive for success and God's plan for their lives."

—Victoria Christopher Murray

"A fast-paced, engrossing love story . . . [with] Christian principles."

—*School Library Journal*

"Entertaining."

—*Booklist*

***Divine Match-Up* is also available as an eBook**

Also by Jacquelin Thomas

Simply Divine
Divine Confidential
Divine Secrets

divine **match-up**

Jacquelin Thomas

POCKET BOOKS
New York London Toronto Sydney

Pocket Books
A Division of Simon & Schuster, Inc.
1230 Avenue of the Americas
New York, NY 10020

First Pocket Books trade paperback edition June 2008

POCKET and colophon are registered trademarks of Simon & Schuster, Inc.

For information about special discounts for bulk purchases, please contact Simon & Schuster Special Sales at 1-800-456-6798 or business@simonandschuster.com

Manufactured in the United States of America

10 9 8 7 6 5 4 3 2 1

Library of Congress Cataloging-in-Publication Data

Thomas, Jacquelin.
Divine match-up / Jacquelin Thomas.
p. cm.
Summary: Living in Georgia with her devoutly Christian uncle and his family, glamorous Hollywood teenager Divine Matthews-Hardison learns important lessons about marriage, relationships, and responsibility.
[1. Marriage—Fiction. 2. Interpersonal relations—Fiction. 3. Responsibility—Fiction. 4. Dating (Social customs)—Fiction. 5. African Americans—Fiction. 6. Christian life—Fiction. 7. Georgia—Fiction.] I. Title.
PZ7.T366932Df 2008
[Fic]—dc22 2007051173

ISBN-13: 978-1-4165-5145-4
ISBN-10: 1-4165-5145-X

To my children, who have always inspired me to do great things . . .

acknowledgments

I'd like to thank all of the readers for your support of my teen series featuring Divine Matthews-Hardison. I really appreciate you!

Bernard, I'd also like to thank you for your never-ending support. You are my best friend and a wonderful role model. I could never do what I do without you.

chapter 1

"Madison and I got married last night . . ." I announce as Alyssa and I walk down a grassy hill to the sidewalk.

Caught off guard, my clumsy cousin nearly topples to the ground in a spill that you know would've embarrassed her. I reach out to help her while I struggle to keep from cracking up in her face.

Alyssa straightens up, then stops just a couple of feet from her house. "Y'all did what?"

"Girl, you heard me. Madison and I are married." She stands there and looks at me as if I'm wearing bright pink eye shadow or something equally not cool. "I wish you could see the expression on your face." I chew my bottom lip to avoid laughing.

"Divine, stop lying! First of all, you're only sixteen years old, and second, you were home last night with us. I know you didn't sneak out 'cause you're not crazy. You know my parents would chop your head off and mail it back to Los Angeles." She shifts her backpack from one side to the other. "By the way, April Fools' Day was yesterday."

Her metal braces gleam in the morning sun, drawing my attention to them. Alyssa is such a know-it-all sometimes but I'm not about to let her faze me today. I'm on my honeymoon. *Some honeymoon.* Going to school is not my idea of a romantic wedding trip. At least Madison and I have nights in our private chat room.

"I can't believe you gon' try and lie about something like that," Alyssa continues to fuss. "Like I'ma believe some stupid crap like that."

We navigate away from the brick ranch-style house, making sure that we're out of earshot just in case Chance or Aunt Phoebe comes outside. Alyssa's right about her mom—my aunt is straight-up crazy. I moved in with them almost three years ago when my dad went to jail and my mom went to rehab. I never thought I'd call any place other than Los Angeles home, but Temple, Georgia, has become very special to me. All my friends think it's just because I'm with Madison. The truth is that I truly love being with my family. Even Aunt Phoebe can be cool at times.

"That's what this is all about," Alyssa is saying. "Right?"

I shake my head. "This has nothing to do with April Fools' Day. I'm telling you the truth, Alyssa. Madison and I are married. We had a virtual wedding ceremony." I take out a piece of paper from my backpack and hand it to her. "See . . . this is our wedding certificate. I told you. We're husband and wife."

"So how did you do it? How did you get married so quickly?" Alyssa asks. Her dark brown eyes look like they're about to pop out her head. She pushes a curling black tendril away from her face. Her hair is getting longer and longer, and it's thick. A flash of envy courses through my veins. I wish my own head of hair was thick like that. "C'mon, Divine . . . tell me."

"There are several places on the Web that will allow you to have a wedding, a reception—even a honeymoon suite. Madison and I have a suite for two weeks as part of our wedding package. You can get married for free on some sites but girl, you know me—I have to do it diva style. So I paid fifty dollars for our wedding."

Alyssa gasps. "You paid fifty dollars? I would've just gotten married on one of the free ones."

"Hmmph! I wanted a nice wedding. Besides, it was only fifty dollars. That's really not a lot of money."

"Well, it's a lot of money to me." Alyssa looks at me with a look of surprise on her face. "I can't believe you did it. You and Madison actually got married."

I take a quick look over my shoulder to make sure Chance isn't sneaking up on us. He'll do that sometimes trying to scare us. Lately, he's been big on pranks even though I keep telling him I don't have a sense of humor when it comes to stupid stuff. "Alyssa, you can't tell anyone. Madison and I are keeping it a secret."

"You better hope my parents don't hear about this. I know Mama will lose her mind if she finds out." She shakes her head in disbelief. "You're the only person I know who skipped dating and went straight to marriage. I guess you really meant it when you said you don't half-step."

"I already know he's the person I want to be with, Alyssa. That's all dating is for—to find your Mr. Right. Well, I've done all that."

"If my parents find out, it'll be the only wedding you'll ever have," Alyssa warns. "Better enjoy it while you can."

"That's why you can't tell anyone. I don't want Aunt Phoebe or Uncle Reed to find out and I especially don't want my mom to know." Alyssa's not only my cousin; she's also my best friend and I tell her all of my secrets.

"I'm not saying nothing," Alyssa vows. "But I do want to know what y'all plan to do. Are you going to try and get your own apartment? Or are you going to keep your marriage a secret until you graduate?"

She actually believes Madison and I are married! I hold back my laughter before deciding to let her in on the real deal. "Even if they do find out, it's not like the end of the world. Alyssa, it's a game. We're role-playing. Our marriage isn't really legal."

Alyssa places a hand over her chest and releases a short sigh of relief. "Girl, you had me thinking you were truly married." We stroll down the street as if we have nowhere to be at any particular time.

"We had a ceremony performed by Preacher David at a cyber-wedding chapel," I explain.

"Divine, how did you find out about this stuff? I've never heard of anybody getting married on the Internet."

"You can find anything on the Internet. I was looking up marriage ceremonies in different cultures for math and came across an article on online marriages in China. They call it *wanghun.* I was curious so I visited some websites for more information. I think it's pretty cool."

"Why were you doing that for a math class?"

"We had to establish how weddings are celebrated in different cultures, then figure out mathematical problems like how many guests should be seated at a table if only eight tables are available, but ninety guests are expected, or which food a person could buy for one hundred twenty-five guests if the budget's like a thousand dollars. Mr. Monroe doesn't have you all doing that?"

Alyssa shakes her head. "Not yet, anyway. But back to this wedding stuff. I've never heard of waygum . . . whatever you call it."

"It's pronounced *wang-hun.* I'm not surprised you haven't heard of it. It's not like you live in a metropolis."

"I know what that means. It means big city."

"You went and subscribed to Word-A-Day, didn't you, copy-cat?"

"Yeah, but I already knew what it meant. You're not the only smart one in the family."

I check my Louis Vuitton watch. We only have about fifteen minutes to get to school before the first bell so Alyssa and I pick up our pace. I'm hoping to see my *husband* before first period. Normally, I wear pants to school but I'm wearing a dress just for him. Today is special.

"I can't wait for prom," Alyssa says. Our prom is scheduled for the last Saturday in May. Seven weeks away. Mom's already ordered our dresses and we have our shoes and accessories thanks to Aunt Phoebe. I'm still waiting on Madison to order his tuxedo. He's such a slowpoke sometimes.

"I hope Stephen and I win Prom King and Queen," Alyssa continues. "We're gonna look so good—If that boy ever gets his tux. I don't know what he's waiting on."

Shaking my head, I say, "Hate to tell you this, Alyssa, but it'll be me and Madison looking fierce that night. I—"

Chance comes running up behind us. "Hey! Why didn't y'all wait on me?"

"You were on the phone with Trina so we didn't want to mess around and be late," explains Alyssa.

She's right about her brother. When he and his girlfriend are on the telephone, they don't know how to get off. I know I'm being hypocritical, especially since Alyssa and I spend hours gabbing on the phone too! I don't see why Chance doesn't just wait to talk to Trina on the way to school. He goes to her house every morning to see Joshua. But oh well . . .

"I wasn't on the phone that long. Trina was just telling me the time of Joshua's doctor appointment. I had to wait for Mom to give me a note so I can leave school early."

"Daddy duty," I mutter. "Aren't you just loving it?"

"It's okay," Chance states honestly. "I love my son so I'll do whatever I have to do."

"Is Trina still trying to get you to marry her after graduation?" Alyssa asks.

"She says little things," Chance replies. The silence between us says what we all know. Trina really wants to get married and has been bugging Chance about it a lot. She's scared he's going to find someone else when he goes off to college in the fall. Chance loves Joshua, but he would've preferred to wait until he was married before having a child.

I guess I can understand why Trina's worried. Chance is a cutie. His new-penny coloring, acne-free complexion, deep dimples and big brown eyes will draw girls to him like a magnet. He's not just cute—he's smart too. I'd never say any of this to him, but my cousin is a great catch.

"I want to marry her eventually. Just not right now." Chance stops walking long enough to adjust the bulging backpack on his shoulders. "We need to get college degrees so that we're able to take care of Joshua. I sho' don't make no real money working at Wendy's."

Chance is the type of person who doesn't complain about anything. Like I said, he's a good catch, and it makes me angry when I see Trina trying to use the baby to manipulate him. I don't like nobody playing my cousin.

I still talk to her but Trina's gone down a few notches on my friend list. She's lucky to have a boyfriend who stuck around while she was pregnant. Aunt Phoebe would say she's blessed and don't even know it.

Alyssa brags to Chance that she's subscribed to Word-A-Day.

"I signed up too," he responds.

"Haters," I mutter. "You and Alyssa just can't stand the fact that

I'm beating you at Scrabble so now you're copying me. Don't y'all have an original bone in your bodies?"

"Don't go around thinking that you are a Scrabble world champ, just because you've won a couple of games. You were lucky, that's all."

"Don't hate, Chance," I reply with a chuckle. "Everybody can't be like me. You can learn all the new words you want—I'll still beat you and Alyssa. Not only am I cute, but I'm smart too."

"Divine, keep dreaming." Alyssa laughs. "You're a legend in your own mind."

"I see you had some haterade for breakfast this morning." I chuckle. "I guess I wouldn't be happy losing all the time either."

Chance shakes his head and laughs. "Girl, you going down . . ."

"Me? Never," I respond. "Divine Matthews-Hardison's not going out as a loser. It's totally not my style."

chapter 2

My heart leaps with joy and my lips turn upward when I locate the tall, lean and fine Madison Hartford. Today he's wearing a black-and-white Rocawear polo shirt over a pair of black jeans.

I immediately kick Alyssa and Chance to the curb. "I'll see y'all later. I need to go over there to talk to my boo."

Alyssa opens her mouth to speak, but I stop her by sending a quick glance in Chance's direction. I don't want her slipping up and saying anything around her brother. He has a big mouth and will tell Aunt Phoebe everything. He's been trying to get back on her good side since he got Trina pregnant.

Alyssa spies Penny and Stacy a few yards away and takes off in their direction. "See you later, Divine."

I nearly sag in relief. I'm going to have a serious talk with Alyssa when I see her during lunch. I want to make sure she understands that my virtual marriage to Madison is a total secret. I don't want her telling Penny and Stacy either. Penny is Alyssa's cousin on her mother's side so she's family, and Stacy is another friend of ours. We're pretty close but I classify them as semi–best friends. At this level, they're not entitled to know all the secrets I share with my B.F.F.s.

My attention is so focused on my girls that I trip over a backpack left lying in the grass and feel myself falling.

Madison's instantly at my side, catching me before I totally embarrass myself. My cheeks warm and my pride bruised, I look away in humiliation when I hear his soft chuckle. I'm so ready to die right on this spot.

"It's not funny," I say.

"It was, kinda," he responds. "You know you'd be laughing at me."

I give Madison a sidelong glance. "No, I wouldn't."

"C'mon, baby . . . don't be mad."

"I'm not mad," I tell him. "Why were you standing over here? I figured you'd be hanging with your boys over on the basketball court." Madison and his friends usually gather there in the mornings just to hang out and brag about their girlfriends and who's doing what to whom.

"I'm waiting on my bride," he whispers in my ear. "I couldn't wait to see you this morning with your fine self." Madison's eyes travel down my body.

My boo knows exactly what I need to hear. He's so sweet to me and he makes me happy. He's almost forgiven for laughing earlier.

I take his hand in mine and say, "It's never a good thing to laugh at my near falls, just so you know."

Madison kisses me on the cheek. "I'm crazy about you even if you are clumsy."

I give him a playful shove.

We walk over to the huge oak tree on campus and sit down on one of the concrete benches. "Did you tell Alyssa about us?"

"Yeah, but she's not going to tell anyone."

He chuckles. "See? I knew you were gonna tell her. Girl, you can't keep nothing to yourself."

"You're not mad, are you?" I ask.

Madison and I had promised each other not to tell anyone about our marriage, but I couldn't help myself. I had to share my happiness with Alyssa. "You know my cousin's not going to go off and run her mouth."

"I'm not mad. But Divine, you just can't be telling Alyssa all our business, though. We need to keep some things private."

"Madison, are you trying to say I talk too much?" I'm hurt by his words.

"Do you?"

"No," I respond coolly. "I don't tell Alyssa everything, if that's what you're implying."

Madison's ex-girlfriend, Brittany Wilkes, strolls by, staring my boo down like he's a piece of chocolate and halting our conversation.

I'm not about to be disrespected so I say, "You might want to just take a picture of him—it'll last longer."

Brittany stops walking. "If I was you, I wouldn't be getting too comfortable. Madison's not who you think he is. Believe me, I know that firsthand."

"Whatever . . ." I dismiss Brittany's words with a wave of my hand. That girl's just jealous because Madison had the good sense to leave her and come back to me. She'll just have to get over it, though. They were only together for a few months after Madison lost his mind and broke up with me. As soon as he realized it was me he really wanted he dropped her.

Madison takes me by the hand and stands. "C'mon, Divine . . .

let's get out of here. That girl ain't nothing but a troublemaker."

"You won't get an argument out of me." I totally can't stand Brittany Wilkes. She's been up in Madison's face a lot lately. Probably trying to get him to break up with me again. Oh yeah, I heard all about it. I have eyes all around this school. I don't know why she can't get it in her head that Madison doesn't want to be with her. Brittany's making a fool out of herself. No boy wants to be with a strumpet. Mom's cook, Miss Eula, says "strumpet" is what they call a girl who goes around having sex with different boys.

Actually, Miss Eula is more than just the cook. We consider her family and love her to death. Miss Eula and my dad's grandmother used to work together back in Tennessee for some rich family. When my great-grandmother died, she took in my dad, Jerome. When I was six or seven, Miss Eula's house burned down. My dad was going to have a new one built for her but she wanted to come live with us. She and Mom travel when Miss Eula's up to it but she enjoys cooking. She always says she was born in a kitchen. Miss Eula's so funny.

The bell rings.

"I hate leaving you right now," Madison says. "We don't even have lunch together anymore."

He gives me this little puppy dog look and I just want to melt.

"I know . . . I hate it too."

We hug, and then go our separate ways. My first-period class is on one end of the school while Madison's is in the opposite direction.

Instead of taking notes in my AP Chemistry class, I spend my time doodling *Mrs. Madison Hartford* all over my notebook and daydreaming of a life with my boo.

I breathe a sigh of relief when the bell rings at nine thirty. First period is finally over. I normally enjoy my chemistry class but today my mind is on other things.

My next three periods go by in a blur: A test in second period that I'm pretty sure I passed. Nothing much happens in my third-period P. E. class; we run around outside trying to swat a little yellow ball and trying not to sweat. I'm testing for my brown belt in tae kwon do soon and I'd rather be preparing for that instead of standing out here swinging a tennis racket. I can't wait to wash up and get out of my gym clothes. They're totally not me.

I enjoy my fourth-period Spanish I class. I want to learn to speak at least two more languages.

My stomach growls loud enough to catch the attention of the boy sitting across from me. He looks over at me and grins. I'm so ready to just go through the floor. As if I'm not humiliated enough, it does it again.

This time he reaches into his backpack and pulls out a granola bar, offering it to me. Talk about totally embarrassing.

I shake my head, turning down his offer. I scribble *thanks* on a piece of paper and hold it up for him to read. Lunch is right after this class so I silently urge my stomach to keep quiet until then.

The bell rings, prompting me to send up a quick prayer of thanks to the Lord. I'm starving.

My hunger is quickly forgotten when I see my boo in the busy student-infested hallway.

I stop and talk to Madison for a few minutes before meeting Alyssa, Stacy and Penny in the cafeteria.

They're already in line by the time I arrive. I wade through a crowd of hungry students to get to them.

"Where were you?" Alyssa asks. There's so much noise in the cafeteria that she has to talk loud enough to be heard. "You're usually the first one here."

"I saw Madison when I was leaving Mrs. Rodriguez's class." I bust into a grin. "You know I had to talk to my boo." My smile disappears when I look at the salad bar. "Look at the lettuce," I tell

Alyssa. "They need to throw that mess away. It's all brown and gross."

One of the workers walks over wearing a stern expression.

"Excuse me," I say. "Can we please get some fresh lettuce? This stuff right here is changing colors right before our eyes."

She takes a long look, shrugs and says. "Honey, just give me a few minutes. I've got to bring some more food from the back. I'll be right back."

I read her name on her badge. "Thanks, Miss Betty. I really like your hair that way. You should wear it down more often."

Her grim expression is replaced by a tiny smile. "Thank you, dear. I felt like I needed a change."

"Look at you working Miss Betty," Alyssa whispers.

"She looked like she needed a kind word today." I shrug. "It's not a big deal."

Miss Betty returns with crisp-looking lettuce. We talk for a few minutes while I fix my salad. Turns out, she's a big fan of my mom's. "Miss Betty, I'll get her to sign a picture to you," I promise. "Thanks so much."

I add a slice of pepperoni pizza and a chocolate-chip cookie to my meal. I make my way up to the register, stopping briefly to pick up a soda.

"What's up with you, Divine?" Penny questions after we find a table. "You seem like you're in a really good mood. You even chatting up the cafeteria workers. That's not like you."

"Yeah," Stacy agrees. "You look happy about something."

"I am," I reply with a big grin.

"Y'all not gon' believe wh—" My cousin shuts up quick when I cut my gaze to her, silently urging her to keep quiet. I'm still not ready to share my news with anybody else. Sometimes Stacy talks too much.

Alyssa picks up a carton of milk. "Y'all not gon' believe what's on the history test. I hope you studied 'cause it's not an easy test," she says instead.

I give her a grateful smile.

Penny squeezes a packet of sour cream on her baked potato. "So, what's up with you, Divine? Did you win some money or something?"

I shake my head. "Nope. Why would I need to win money? I'm already rich."

"Your mom's rich, Divine," Alyssa states. "Not you."

"Like whatever," I mutter.

Stacy picks up her hamburger. "Okay, now I know something's up—c'mon, just tell us," she pleads.

"It's nothing, Stacy." I take a sip of my soda. My eyes travel to her micro-braids. "Whoever did your hair really did an awesome job."

"Thank you, girl. My aunt did them. You know she works at a hair salon in Villa Rica."

Penny points at me. "Divine, don't try to change the subject. I know you lying. You got something going on."

My mouth drops open. "No, you didn't just call me a liar."

"I call a spade a spade," Penny responds. "I thought we was your girls, but I guess I was wrong."

"Yeah," Stacy says. "We know that Alyssa knows what's going on. Be like that."

"Y'all my girls," I assure them. "But there's nothing to tell. Just thinking about Madison makes me happy."

Penny scoops up a forkful of potato and sticks it in her mouth. She chews and swallows before saying, "You two make a cute couple."

"Yeah, we do." I finish off my salad.

"Don't go getting the big head, Divine. I said y'all looked cute together but y'all ain't all that. Now me and *my* boo . . . can't touch perfection."

"Only in your mind," I mutter. "Madison and I are the perfect couple."

Alyssa laughs before taking a bite of her chili dog. "Y'all crazy. Stephen and I are the *perfect* couple. We never have any drama in our relationship."

Trina comes to our table carrying a tray laden with French fries and a couple of chili-cheese dogs. "Y'all mind if I sit with you?"

Alyssa wipes her hand on a paper napkin, then moves her backpack out of the way to make room for her.

"Where's Chance?" I ask, surprised that she's joining us. Trina and Chance usually eat lunch together. Mostly they eat away from school because seniors have the privilege to eat off campus.

"He went to lunch with some of his friends. He's been complaining that he doesn't get to spend any time with his boys anymore, so I told him to go on. I got tired of his whining." Trina picks up a French fry and sticks it into her mouth. "The fries are nice and hot. Mmm . . ."

"You do know that we're related to Chance, right?" I inquire. "It's not too cool trashing him to family."

Trina seems surprised by my words. "Divine, what are you talking about? I'm not trashing him."

"When are y'all leaving for the doctor's appointment?" Alyssa asks. She's probably trying to keep my temper in check by changing the subject.

"Right after lunch. He's going to meet me back here soon. I drove today." She glances over at me. "What's up, Divine?"

"Nothing," I respond.

"You okay?"

"I'm fine." I paste on a smile. I promised Alyssa that I'd try to keep the peace between me and Trina, but the girl is truly getting on my nerves. She doesn't own my cousin. They have a baby together. That's all. I check my watch, then get up to empty the contents of my tray before the bell rings.

"Divine, can I talk to you for a minute?" Trina asks, stepping into my path.

"Sure."

She walks with me to the trash can where I empty my tray. We take a seat on a bench a few yards away.

My eyes take in my surroundings, noting the trees with bright green leaves, couples sitting beneath them having lunch together, clusters of friends dotted all around and students just walking around in their own world. "What's up, Trina?"

"Have I done something to you? You've been acting funny around me lately."

I meet her gaze straight on. "Trina, we've had this discussion before. I don't like the way you treat Chance sometimes. I think you use Joshua to manipulate him and that's totally not cool."

"I'm not using my son like that," she counters with attitude. "I really don't appreciate you saying that."

"I'm not going to debate this with you," I state. "You may not be conscious of it, Trina . . . I really don't know. All I know is that you need to quit. Chance loves you and Joshua, but if you keep this up you're going to lose him."

"What has he been telling you?"

"Chance hasn't told me anything—he doesn't have to. I know what I see."

"I don't know what you *think* is going on, but you're wrong, Divine. I love Chance and I don't see anything wrong with me wanting to be a family. I mean, we do have a child together."

"And you're never going to let anyone forget it, are you?" I ask. "Trina, are you so selfish that you are going to try to make Chance pay with his life for getting you pregnant?"

Her eyes tear up. "I thought you were my friend, Divine."

"I thought we were friends too. I like you, Trina, but Chance is my cousin. My loyalty lies with him."

"I'm not trying to ruin his life, Divine. I just want us to be a family. Why don't y'all understand that? He's probably gonna go off to George Washington University and meet another girl. I heard they got some beautiful women up in the D.C. area." Tears glisten on her heart-shaped face. "He'll always be Joshua's father but he may not always want me."

"Last I heard, Chance wasn't sure where he's going to school, but if it is in Washington, D.C., then it's out of your control," I say. "Trina, I do get it. I know how you feel. I'd probably feel the same way. I want to be with Madison forever, but the reality is I don't know if it will happen."

She wipes away her tears with the back of her hand. "I love him so much."

"Chance loves you too. But he could stay close to home or not go to college anywhere and still meet another girl."

"I know that. That's why I wanted us to get married."

"Getting married won't keep him faithful, Trina. He has to make a conscious decision to not cheat. I should know. My dad cheated on Mom a lot. I hope now that he's married to Ava he'll be a better husband. Although being in prison, he can't do much of anything."

"Divine, I don't want to lose you as a friend. I don't like this distance between us. I know I've been real busy with the baby and all, but I really miss talking to you."

"I miss you too," I confess. "But Trina, as long as you treat Chance good we won't have a problem." Rising, I add, "We're cool as far as I'm concerned. Just don't be tripping."

"I just love him so much but I hear you."

We embrace.

"Don't forget to give Joshua a kiss for me. Hey, is he sleeping through the night yet?"

Trina laughs. "Sleep? What in the world is that? Joshua sleeps during the daytime. Mama says he's got his days and nights mixed up."

"I guess you'd better teach him to sleep at night."

Trina nods in agreement. "I'm trying."

I spot Chance walking toward us.

The bell rings.

"Hey," he greets us. "Trina, you ready to leave?"

"Yeah," she replies and rises to her feet. "Divine, I'll talk to you later."

"Okay. Don't forget to kiss Joshua for me," I tell Trina.

I walk over to where Alyssa is standing.

"Did you make her cry?" Alyssa asks as we head to our fifth-period classes.

"I told her the truth," I respond. "Trina needs to stop tripping where Chance is concerned."

She nods in agreement. "I was gonna say something to her myself. We'd better get going. I don't need to be late. I heard Mrs. Henderson is in a weird mood today."

Alyssa and I speed up our pace.

My AP World History class is okay, but I can hardly wait for school to be over. Madison's walking me home. I hope Stephen will be with him because I don't want Alyssa all up in our business. She usually tries to walk ahead of us, but I know she's nosy. But I can't say too much. Sometimes, I try to hear what she and Stephen are talking about. Looking for dirt is what Aunt Phoebe calls it.

Two hours later I give thanks to God when the bell rings.

School is over and I'm so ready to see my boo.

Alyssa and I wait for Stephen and Madison at the edge of campus.

"Girl, I thought this day would never end," I say.

"I know what you mean. I almost fell asleep in sixth period." Alyssa sets her backpack down on the ground. "I'm so tired."

Madison strolls out of the door and breaks into a run when he spots us at the edge of campus. "I have to stay here for a little while longer," he announces. "Y'all go on. I need to talk to Mrs. Tuttle about my history project."

I get this strange feeling and glance over his shoulder to find Brittany standing there watching us.

What's up with that? I ask myself.

Madison is my boo and there's nothing she can do about it, so girlfriend should just move on. Come to think of it, Brittany should stop drinking all those milk shakes and cut back on the burgers, pizza and pasta during lunch—she's putting on weight.

chapter 3

"Divine, I just hung up with your mother," Aunt Phoebe announces shortly after Alyssa and I walk into the house. "She's on her way here to the house."

I stiffen in shock. Mom has been in California working on a new movie. *When did she get back?* I wonder. My mom bought a home in Atlanta a little more than a year ago to be closer to me.

"Aunt Phoebe, do you know why she's coming?" I question, swallowing hard. I glance over at Alyssa before asking, "Did I do something? Am I in trouble?" I search my memory, trying to remember if I'd done something that had come back to bite me in the tail. It wasn't possible, right?

"I don't know," Aunt Phoebe responds, staring me down. "But by that panicked look on your face, I can't help but wonder if you're feeling guilty about something. Are you guilty of any wrongdoing?"

"No ma'am." I calm down. For a second I thought that somehow they'd found out about the virtual wedding. *The marriage isn't real,* I keep reminding myself. *So there's no reason for them to get mad over a game.*

"Is Kevin coming with her?" I inquire with a hint of disapproval. I can tell that Aunt Phoebe noticed because of the look she gives me.

"No, he's in Chicago, I believe she told me. I think he's working on a new film. But if he was coming, I'm sure you would be nice to him. Right?"

"Yes ma'am. I was just asking. That's all." I like my mom's boyfriend well enough, but there's still a part of me that worries Kevin Nash will hurt her just like Jerome. Besides, I really like the way things are between me and my mom. We've become really close since she got out of rehab and I'm not ready for that to change.

"Uh-huh," Aunt Phoebe responds. "You don't have to be jealous of Kevin. Your mom has enough room in her heart to love you both."

Whatever . . .

"I'm not jealous of Kevin Nash. I have no reason to be." Aunt Phoebe doesn't even know what she's talking about. *Jealous.* Why would I be jealous? Kara Matthews is my mom. She'll always choose me over any man.

"All right, little miss. If that's true, then stop giving your mother a hard time when it comes to him. Let Kara be happy."

"I'm not trying to keep her from being happy," I retort. "I just want—"

My cell phone rings. I look down at the caller ID. "It's Mimi."

She should still be in school because she lives on the West Coast and they're three hours behind us. Mimi wouldn't be calling right now unless it's a B.F.F. 911.

"Aunt Phoebe, I really need to take this." I head to my bedroom for privacy. I don't need Aunt Phoebe all up in my business.

"Mimi, hi. Girl, what are you doing out of class?"

"We had a half day today. Rhyann's on the phone too. I did three-way so we could talk to you together."

"What's up, girl?" Rhyann shouts over the phone.

Mimi and Rhyann are my B.F.F.s. The only bad part about being here in Temple, Georgia, is that I don't get to hang out with them except in the summer when I go back to California. Thank goodness for Instant Messenger, email and cell phones.

After closing the door and dropping my backpack on my bed, I announce, "I have something to tell you and Rhyann, but I need you to promise that you won't say a word to anybody. It has to be a secret."

"What is it?" Mimi demands. "I can't take the suspense any longer."

"Did you let that country boy get you pregnant?" Rhyann asks. "Dee, you do know about birth control, right? I remember us talking about it, so I know—"

"I'm not pregnant," I interrupt. "You know I don't get down like that."

Rhyann's relief is audible.

"Madison and I got married," I say.

Mimi gasps while Rhyann goes off on me. "*You did what?* Girl, I know you done lost your mind!"

"Rhyann's right. What were you thinking? When and how did you do this?" Mimi asks.

"We got married on the Internet. They have virtual wedding chapels."

"I've never heard of anything like that," Mimi said. "I guess we shouldn't be surprised, though. They have chat rooms for just about anything you want."

"Dee, you got me over here tripping," Rhyann mutters. "You better hope the media doesn't get wind of it—you're going to be all over the newspapers. I can't even imagine what your mom will do to you. Miss Kara is going to have a fit."

I burst into laughter.

"I don't see anything funny. This is your life you're playing with," Rhyann snaps.

"She must be lying," Mimi states. "You're lying, aren't you?"

"I'm serious. Madison and I did get married. I have a marriage certificate and everything." I decide to come clean. "Only it's not like a real marriage. It's role-playing. That's all."

Rhyann has no sense of humor. "I still think it's crazy," she tells me. "Marriage is the last thing I want to do right now. I don't even want to play at it."

"That's you," I point out.

"I'm like Rhyann," Mimi contributes. "I'm not in any hurry to get married."

"Well, it's just an expression of our love for me and Madison. We wanted to see what it felt like."

"Are you reading your cousin's romance novels?" Rhyann inquires. "If you are, then you need to quit. You tripping."

Frustrated, I let out a long sigh. "I don't know why I tell y'all anything. I wasn't asking your opinion—I was just telling you about my cyber-wedding to Madison."

"So it's not legal?" asks Rhyann.

"No," I respond, "it's not a legal marriage."

"Did you do the do?" she wants to know.

I can't believe Rhyann just asked me if Madison and I had sex. "I told you I don't get down like that."

"Well, if you did . . . girl, you're legally married."

"That's not true, Rhyann." I hear my mom's voice and say, "I have to go. My mom drove here to see me and I need to find out why. I'll give you and Mimi a call later."

We say our good-byes.

I rush out of my room toward the front of the house, following the sound of Mom's voice.

She's laughing—a really deep laugh like something's crazy funny. I haven't heard her laugh like that in a real long time. I'm glad Mom's getting back to her old self.

chapter 4

Mom greets me with a warm hug and a kiss. I hold her tight, inhaling the tropical scent of her perfume.

I love the way my mother smells. I keep a little bottle of her favorite fragrance so that when I get to missing her too much I spray some on a shirt I borrowed from her but never gave back. I keep it close to me.

"What's going on?" I ask, stepping out of her embrace. "Why did you drive all the way out here?"

Folding her arms across her chest, Mom questions, "Now is that any way to greet your mama?"

"You know that I'm happy to see you," I reply quickly with a chuckle. "But this is a surprise. I didn't even know you were back from Los Angeles. When I spoke to Stella yesterday, she didn't say anything." Stella is my mom's assistant, and she always knows where to find her.

"I flew back on the red-eye. I'm here because I just needed to see my baby girl. It's been a minute."

I admire the outfit she's wearing. "Looks like you've been shopping. Did you buy me anything?"

My hopes are dashed when she answers, "I think you have more than enough clothes, young lady. This is from Anya's latest collection. While I was in Los Angeles, she showed me your and Alyssa's prom dresses. They're absolutely stunning. She's almost done with the detailing."

Anya Jordan is one of Mom's favorite designers—she does a lot of her wardrobe when she's performing in concert and also on the movie set. Anya's designed several gowns for me as well.

I wrap my arms around her once more. "I'm so glad you're here, Mom. I missed you." She's been in L.A. for the past two weeks to discuss a new recording contract and possibly a new movie.

"That's more like it, sugar."

I relax. Apparently I'm not in any trouble. I guess she hasn't gotten her latest Bloomingdale's credit card statement yet. I went a little over my shopping budget for the month. Well, it's actually about three hundred dollars over. Hopefully, Mom's accountant will just keep quiet and pay the bill without telling her.

Alyssa strolls into the living room and gives Mom a big hug. I hear Uncle Reed's voice and am surprised to find that he's home already. He usually stays at the church until four thirty.

"I didn't expect you to be here," I say.

"I came home for lunch and decided to spend the rest of the day with my wife."

"Oh."

Aunt Phoebe whispers something to Alyssa. She glances over

in my direction and leaves the room. I notice Mom's acting kind of fidgety—like she's nervous about something.

"You okay?" I ask.

"Yeah, I'm perfectly fine," she responds.

NOT.

Uncle Reed makes himself comfortable in the wing chair while Mom and Aunt Phoebe keep passing looks. It's pretty apparent to me that Mom has something on her mind. And coming all the way out here—I can't help but wonder if Jerome's managed to get into more trouble.

My suspicion grows when they sit down together on the couch. I steal a peek over my shoulder to see if Alyssa's lurking anywhere but I suspect she's hiding out in her bedroom until it's clear whether or not I'm in trouble.

I remain standing.

Mom glances over at me. "Baby girl, why don't you sit down? I'd like to talk to you about something important."

I'm not moving an inch until I find out what's going on! "Okay, I know something's up. Mom, just tell me." I automatically assume this has something to do with my father. "What did Jerome do now? Did he get into a fight?" I wait for her answer half in anticipation, half in dread.

"Sugar, your father's fine. As far as I know, anyway."

I'm not convinced. "He's not hurt or anything?"

She's chewing on her bottom lip, so I know something is wrong despite her shaking her head no. She and Aunt Phoebe exchange looks before she turns back to me saying, "Divine, I'm sorry if I worried you. There *is* something I need to tell you but I hope you'll think its good news."

"Did you get another movie role?"

"No, that's not it."

I sit down in one of the overstuffed chairs. "Are you moving back to California?"

Mom shakes her head. "That's not it either."

"Then what is it?" I ask. "The prom dresses are really ugly, right? Are you having new ones made for us? I hope so because Alyssa and I can't go to the prom looking whack. We're way too cute for that."

She laughs. "This has nothing to do with your prom. However, I will need to take you and Alyssa to Los Angeles soon for more dresses." She pauses a moment before adding, "Bridesmaid dresses."

Frowning, I question, "Who's getting married? And why do they want me and Alyssa in the wedding?"

"I want you both in the wedding," Mom replies.

I'm still confused. "Okaay. Why?"

"Baby girl, I have wonderful news. Kevin proposed to me last night. I can barely believe it myself, but he asked me to marry him and I accepted." Mom holds up her right hand displaying a huge diamond and emerald engagement ring. She loves emeralds.

Her announcement sends my pulse spinning. "What did you say?"

"Kevin and I are engaged."

Speechless, I get up and wander restlessly around the living room, waiting for Uncle Reed or Aunt Phoebe to verbalize what needs to be said.

Mom has totally lost her mind.

Why else would she be thinking about getting married—and to Kevin Nash, of all people? There's not anything wrong with him, I guess, but I personally don't feel that he's right for her. Mom's already been through a lot—she doesn't need more drama in her life.

"Divine . . ." Mom rises to her feet.

It's a struggle for me to wrap my head around the news of my mom marrying Kevin. I try to walk around my mother but she grabs me by the arm.

"Sugar, Kevin and I really love each other and we want to share a life together."

When it's obvious that my aunt and uncle aren't planning to speak up, I sputter, "But you've only been d-dating like a couple of m-months. At least that's what you had me believing all this time." I brush past Mom and walk over to the huge picture window. She eyes me for a moment before moving to sit down beside Aunt Phoebe once more. I look over at my mom and ask, "Were the tabloids right? Have you and Kevin been dating all this time and you didn't tell me?"

She's a little taken aback by my question. I can tell by the way her mouth is clenched tight. "I haven't lied to you, Divine. Kevin and I were friends but that friendship has developed into something much more. That's the truth." She changes into Mom mode when she tells me, "Now I don't want to have this discussion with you again."

"This is not happening," I state in total denial. "Mom, I can't believe you're being so impulsive. You'd be ready to kill me if I did something like that." I stare out the window fighting back tears. I can't believe my mom.

She stands up and joins me near the window, taking me by the hand. "Sugar, I've given a lot of thought and prayer to this phase of my life. I truly feel that I've found my soul mate in Kevin."

"I'm not sure how I feel about this," I mumble. A part of me wants to shout that Madison and I got married just to send her into a coma but I'm afraid of what she might do to me once she recovered.

"I know this comes as a shock to you, but I hope that you'll see how much Kevin and I love each other. Baby, he's a good man."

"To you."

Mom's lips pucker in annoyance. "Why would you say that?" she asks. "Has Kevin ever been rude or mean to you, Divine?"

"No ma'am," I reply. "But maybe that's because he's waiting until you two get married. He'll probably change after that."

"I don't think so," Mom says. "Kevin doesn't have a hidden agenda."

"How do you know that for sure?" I ask.

"I've gotten to know him pretty well," she responds. "Divine, I love Kevin and I want to spend the rest of my life with him. It would help if you were a little bit happy for me, you know."

A wave of hurt flows through me. "Mom, it doesn't matter what I think. That's what you're telling me. You're going to marry him whether or not I'm happy about it."

"Divine, of course I care what you think," Mom argues. "But sugar, this is *my* life we're talking about. I'm not about to let you dictate how I should live it."

I don't know what to say to her. This is just so wrong.

"We're not planning to get married right away."

"Why do it at all?" I want to know.

"Kevin and I are in love."

"How come when *I* say I'm in love you don't believe me?"

Mom releases a soft sigh. She's going into Mom mode again. I can tell by the way she's looking at me. "Divine, you're much too young to know what love is—and isn't."

I fold my arms across my chest and ask, "If grown-ups knew what love was, like they say they do, why are there so many divorces and spouses hurting and killing each other? Uncle Reed says that when you get married, it's a commitment. It's a promise to God and there shouldn't be any drive-through marriages."

"I can only speak for myself, Divine. I loved your father and I married him for better or for worse—I really did."

"Then why did you get a divorce?"

Mom looks like she's about ready to shake me silly. "The marriage . . . no, we were starting to really hurt one another. It wasn't a healthy relationship. When I saw what it was doing to me and to you, I knew that Jerome and I needed to end the marriage. I did what I thought was best, but I went to God first because I needed His counsel."

I don't dare look my mom in the face when I ask, "So you're saying God gave you permission to divorce Jerome?"

"I'm saying He gave me a peace about it. It was the right thing to do, baby girl. I made the right decision."

"I hope God remembers that on Judgment Day."

Shaking her head, Mom gives a short chuckle to cover her frustration. "I don't know what I'm gonna do with you."

"I'm barely over the shock that Jerome and Ava are not only married but they're also having a baby. Now you and Kevin . . . you guys are trying to kill me."

"I'll try to make the transition easy on you, sweetie. Like I told you, Kevin and I are not rushing into anything."

I'm so tempted to blurt out, "Guess what, Mom? Madison and I got married last night." She'd lose her mind and lecture me on irresponsibility. She's got no room to talk, the way I see it. Only it's worse because she's supposed to be the grown-up.

"I need some air," I say. "I'm going outside for a while."

The weather outdoors is perfect—not too hot or too cool, but I'm too absorbed in my own issues to truly appreciate it. I sit down on the first step with my chin in my hands. I can't believe that Uncle Reed just sat there and didn't say a word. He's my mom's big brother. He's supposed to talk some sense into her.

The front door opens and closes.

"I never thought you'd respond this way," Mom says from behind me. "I thought you' be happy for me."

"I want to be."

"Why don't we take a walk?" she suggests.

"Sure." I rise up and navigate down the steps. Mom follows me.

Neither one of us says a word until we're past the house next door.

"Mom, I'd be really happy for you if I didn't think you were making a big mistake."

"Why are you so convinced I'm making a mistake?"

"I think it's too soon for you to think about getting married again."

"Did you feel this way when your dad married Ava?"

I shake my head. "I'd expect him to do something like that," I tell Mom. "But not you. You're smarter than that."

"Kevin and I have given this a lot of thought, Divine. I assure you. You're young, so I don't expect you to fully understand."

I can't believe she's playing the age card.

We stroll back to the house in silence.

I head straight to my room while Aunt Phoebe talks to Mom in her bedroom. I'm praying she'll be able to get my mom to see what she's doing to me and hopefully change her mind about getting married.

Right after I close my door, I hear a knock. I know it can't be anybody but that nosy ol' Alyssa.

"Yeah?" I call out.

"Are you okay?" Alyssa inquires, sticking her head inside.

I shake my head. She enters the room and makes herself comfortable on my bed. "Can you believe it? Mom's totally trying to ruin my life."

"Divine, do you really think that Aunt Kara marrying Kevin is gonna be a bad thing?"

"Yeah. Don't you? Kevin Nash is like one of Hollywood's sexiest guys. He's always in the top ten. I bet he has a lot of girlfriends.

You know they're always saying in the tabloids that he dates every one of his costars."

"Divine, you've said before a lot of that stuff written in the tabloids ain't true."

I grunt in response. Alyssa's getting on my nerves right now. She has no clue what I'm going through since her parents are still together. She'll never understand.

"Why are you so upset about this, Divine? I thought you liked Kevin."

"He's okay. But I don't want him for a stepdad. I don't want anybody. Mom needs to just be . . . she needs to get over Jerome."

I feel my resentment growing.

"I think she's over your dad," Alyssa responds with a chuckle. "She wouldn't be marrying Kevin if she wasn't."

"I think she's just doing it because Jerome married Ava. She doesn't want him to think she can't get somebody else."

Alyssa doesn't agree with me. "Divine, Aunt Kara's fine. She can get any man she wants. Uncle Jerome knows that."

My mouth turns downward in my exasperation. "I hope she comes to her senses soon and gives Kevin his ring back."

"You can see how much he loves your mom. I would think you'd want her to be happy."

"She doesn't need a man to be happy. At least that's what she always tells me."

Alyssa stands up to leave. "I think you need to just deal with it, Divine. Your mom's in love and she's getting married."

"Not when she sees how unhappy it makes me," I reply. "Mom doesn't want me walking around all depressed. She'll change her mind about marrying Kevin. Just watch."

MOM STAYS AND has dinner with us.

I basically give her the silent treatment. I'm too mad at her to be all chatty over a meal. I can feel her eyes on me, but I pretend I'm really interested in the food on my plate even though I don't really have much of an appetite. A wave of disappointment courses through my veins when she doesn't try to force me into a conversation.

Mom heads back to Atlanta after dessert.

I go to my room but the news of my mom's engagement is prominent in my mind. Somebody really needs to make her understand that she shouldn't rush into marriage. Before I realize it, I'm knocking on my aunt and uncle's bedroom door.

"Come on in," Aunt Phoebe urges.

I walk inside the room. My aunt's seated at her vanity rolling her shoulder-length hair with bright pink sponge rollers. Uncle Reed is sitting on the edge of their king-size bed removing his shoes.

"Uncle Reed, you and Aunt Phoebe need to talk to Mom. She's about to make a huge mistake."

"Divine . . ." Uncle Reed begins.

"Please," I say, cutting him off. "I don't think Mom should be rushing into a marriage. She hasn't been dating him that long. Don't you think she's moving way too fast?"

Aunt Phoebe gets up and walks over to me with her tall Amazon self. She gives me a hug. "Calm down, sugar. Your mother knows what she's doing."

"No she doesn't," I insist. "She's just doing this because Jerome got married."

"You don't know that to be true." Uncle Reed's gaze is riveted on me. "The fact of the matter is that it's not your decision to make."

His tone is gentle but it still makes me mad. He's mostly a big, chocolate-covered teddy bear until he gets angry, which isn't very often. My average-height uncle and his super-tall wife are devoted to each other and they agree on almost everything. I hate this about them at times.

"I know that, Uncle Reed," I respond. "But I still have feelings about it." I can't believe Uncle Reed and Aunt Phoebe are actually okay with this. "Even after everything she's been through? You want her to go through more drama? Mom had to go into rehab because of Jerome. Have you forgotten that?"

My uncle's eyes darken as he holds my gaze. "Divine, I'm not trying to hurt your feelings but I don't know any other way to say this: stay out of grown folks' business. This is not your concern."

"Uncle Reed, I don't mean to be disrespectful, but it *does* concern me," I counter. "I'm Kara Matthews' daughter." Tears form in my eyes. "She's my mother. She's been through a lot and I'm not going to let her get hurt again. *I'm not.* I don't care what you or anybody has to say about it. You didn't have to live with her when she and Jerome were constantly fighting about his cheating or his drugs or just getting in trouble all the time." I swipe at the tears rolling down my cheeks. "I don't want my life to go back to the way it was."

Aunt Phoebe comes to comfort me. "Sssh . . . it's going to be okay, sugar. Take some time to digest the news. Don't you worry your little head none. Give it over to God and trust that He's gon' work this out."

"I hope He takes care of it *before* Mom makes a big mistake," I mutter.

chapter 5

Mom's announcement leaves me in a funk for the rest of the evening.

Nobody seems to understand my feelings regarding her engagement. I know that Kevin is nothing like Jerome, but still . . . it doesn't mean he's going to treat my mom the way she deserves.

I decide to work on some of my tae kwon do techniques to ease some of my stress. I perform a series of warm-up exercises before I begin practicing my kicks. I concentrate on flexing my foot into the proper position. I'm hoping to get my brown belt on Saturday so I can't afford to make a mistake.

Jerome calls around eight. He usually tries to call me at least once a week and he writes me just as often. I guess this is his way of being an active dad. Since he's been in prison, he's trying to be a better parent. A lot of haters at school try to make comments about the fact that he's locked up for murder. Jerome didn't mean to kill anyone. He was there when Shelly died and they had an argument, but she was the one with the gun. My dad was trying to take it from her and it went off. It was an accident and I believe him. Everybody wants to think the worst because of his bad boy reputation.

"What's up, baby girl?"

"Drama," I reply with a soft groan. "Mom just told me that she's going to marry Kevin Nash. They're engaged."

My words are met with silence.

"Jerome?"

"I'm here. So Kara's getting married?" After a moment, he adds, "I'm happy for her."

I instantly regret opening my big mouth. "Jerome, I don't know if I should've told you—Mom probably wanted to tell you herself."

"It's cool. I won't say anything until she tells me. I take it that you're not exactly happy about the pending nuptials."

"Should I be? Are you?"

"Your mom and I are divorced," Jerome responds. "I'm married to Ava now, so I guess I can't say a whole lot."

"Why can't you all be normal?" I ask, frustrated. "You rushed off and got married and now Mom's doing the same thing. Nobody cares about how I feel or what I have to deal with."

"Divine, that's not true."

"Yes, it is," I counter. "Do you know how I feel when I see or hear stories about you and everything that you've done? People think you killed Shelly on purpose—nobody believes that it was an accident, Jerome."

"What do *you* believe? That's all that matters to me, baby girl."

"Jerome, I know in my heart that you're not guilty of murder. I know that, but it still makes me feel bad when I hear stuff. I don't like when the media brings up Mom's rehab either. I just want a normal life."

"Divine, I'm sorry for the pain I caused you." His voice breaks. "I'm s-so sorry."

Swallowing my despair, I respond, "I know that, Jerome."

"You were born to celebrity parents, baby girl. Unfortunately, because of it, you've had to grow up under a microscope."

"I love my life—mostly—but there are parts of it that I could return for a refund. The thing is, now you and Mom for whatever reasons can't just be divorced. You both have to run and get married. I don't get it. What's wrong with being single? I know it's too late for you but why can't Mom stay single for more than a minute?"

"I guess you'd have to ask her about that."

"I did. All she tells me is that she and Kevin are in love."

"He seems like an okay dude," Jerome says. "Pretty much keeps to himself. He's been in the press more since dating Kara. From what I've read they've been together for a while."

"That's just it. Mom says they weren't anything but friends up until a couple of months ago."

"Then you should believe her. Kara's not a liar," Jerome states. "She would never lie to you, baby girl. Your mom's not like that."

"I still think it's too soon for her to be thinking about marrying Kevin. But nobody listens to me. I may only be sixteen years old but I have a brain. I know things."

"Divine, your mother is entitled to make her own decisions. She's a very smart and intelligent woman—she knows what she's doing."

Whatever.

I can see I'm not getting anywhere with Jerome so changing the subject is probably a good decision. Not that I really care about her, but I ask, "How's Ava?"

"She's doing fine. Why don't you call her sometime?"

"Jerome, I don't know what to say to her. It's not like . . ."

"Not like what?"

I figure I might as well be honest. It's not like he can jump through the phone. "I'm not sure how I feel about her yet."

Jerome releases a small sigh. "Divine, I thought you were going to give Ava a chance."

"I am. It's just that it's kind of awkward."

"Ava told me that she called you a couple of times but you never returned her call."

"I was either busy or with Mom."

"Divine, she's trying. It won't hurt to make a phone call or two."

I bite my lip until it throbs like my pulse.

"I love Ava," Jerome tells me. "Regardless of how you feel, she's my wife and I want you to respect her."

"I haven't disrespected her," I reply, a little miffed over the way he's taking her side. He's supposed to be my dad. "I haven't done anything to her. I can't help that I'm busy with school and my life in general. Sorry, but I don't have a lot of free time, Jerome."

"I bet you have time for your friends, don't you? Especially that ol' boy Matthew or whatever his name is."

"His name is Madison." I don't bother to hide my irritation. Jerome's just mad because I'm not a fan of his new wife. "I'm not feeling this conversation, Jerome. You might love Ava, but she's not one of my favorite people and I'm not going to pretend she matters in my world because she doesn't. I'm sorry but I'm being honest."

"Divine, I'm still your father and I demand respect." His tone is firm and I can tell Jerome's not up for my attitude.

"Since when have you been a father to me?" I ask, my mood shifting quickly to anger.

My question is met with deafening silence.

"Jerome, I'm sorry. I shouldn't have said that."

"Baby girl, all I'm asking is that you get to know Ava for yourself. That's all."

"Then let me do it in my own way. I already told you that I'd consider going to visit her this summer."

"I'd appreciate it if you would," Jerome tells me. "I don't want her to be alone when the baby comes. I know you're not sure about Ava but you weren't sure about Jason either. When you first found out about your brother you didn't even want to meet him, but that's all changed. You love that boy to death."

"He's my brother and he's a little boy. He didn't really do anything. What happened was between you and his mother." I'm not real crazy that Jerome was seeing Shelly in the first place. I don't understand how he could do something like that to me and Mom. How can he claim to love us so much and have affairs? Uncle Reed's words about forgiveness come to mind. He says that when you truly forgive someone, you never bring up the past. I've forgiven Jerome.

"I know you blame Ava for my breakup with your mom but you shouldn't," Jerome states. "I'm the one who messed up. I'm the one who kept messing up. Baby girl, I'm asking you to do this one thing for me. Please."

"Doesn't she have any family?" I ask. "Why does she need me?"

"Her mother's upset with Ava for marrying me."

"Oh." I hope he isn't expecting any sympathy from me because he's not going to get any. I'm not thrilled about their marriage either.

"My time is almost up, but we're gonna finish this conversation, Divine. Ava and I are married."

I roll my eyes heavenward. *Whatever.*

Jerome and I have to say our good-byes quickly.

I call Madison, tapping my fingers impatiently on top of my desk as I wait for him to come to the phone.

"Hey baby."

I need to vent so I say, "Madison, you're not going to believe this. My mom is marrying Kevin Nash. Can you believe it?"

"Cool!"

"No, it isn't," I respond irritably. "Madison, how can you think it's cool?"

"I like the dude. He's a good actor."

"He may be a good actor but how is he going to treat my mom? That's what I care about. And how is he going to treat me?"

"Your mom's not gon' let Kevin hurt you," Madison tells me. "I think she's way too protective for something like that to happen."

He has a point. "I know . . ."

"Be happy for your moms. Your dad's remarried so it's not like your parents are gonna get back together. She's free to be with whoever she wants."

"I just wish she wasn't with Kevin Nash."

The thought of my mom and Kevin getting married just doesn't feel right to me. The way things used to be with my parents is still very vivid in my mind. If she wanted to get married—why not marry a regular guy? She could find somebody like Uncle Reed. What's wrong with that?

"Why you so quiet, Divine?"

"Huh? Sorry. I was just thinking about something."

"What?"

"I'm thinking my mom could marry a regular man—not another celebrity, you know?"

"Divine, give your mom a break. She knows what she's doing."

"Madison, I'll call you back later," I blurt. "I need some time to myself."

"You sure you okay?"

"Yeah," I respond. "Just need to think about some things. Can I call you later?"

"Sure," he tells me. "Call me back, Divine. I don't like the way you sound."

I hang up and click off my cell phone. Normally Madison and I talk for hours but right now I'm a little irritated with him. He doesn't have a clue about what I'm going through.

I log on to my computer to check my email right after I change into my pajamas. An IM pops up from Rhyann.

SexyRhyann: what's up girl?
HollywoodQT: not a whole lot. Sorry had 2 get off d phone b4
SexyRhyann: everything ok with ur mom?

Before I can type in a response Mimi comes online. She sends me an IM and an invitation to join a chat. She can see that Rhyann is available and wants us to be able to send messages to one another that we all can see.

A few minutes later, we're able to communicate back and forth.

SweetMims: how long have u 2 been online?
HollywoodQT: just got on right b4 u
SexyRhyann: IMing new boo when Dee signed on
SweetMims: I didn't get a chance 2 ask when we were on the phone earlier. When r u coming back to LA
HollywoodQT: will b there this summer
SexyRhyann: gr8t! We're gonna have a fun summer. Mimi's getting a new car 4 her bday so we're gonna b all over the place
HollywoodQT: u're getting a car? U didn't tell me
SweetMims: yes. isn't that gr8t? Forgot 2 mention it earlier but I would've told you eventually

I feel a wave of hateration washing over me. I can't believe that Mimi's getting a car before I get one. I wanted to be the first. I can't believe Mom's letting me go out like this. At least I don't have to worry about Rhyann getting a car right now. Her aunt feels the same way as mine: They don't think we need one until we're ready to go off to college.

Talk about lame.

Newsflash: We can legally drive at sixteen years old. Get a clue.

I return my attention to the computer monitor.

> **HollywoodQT:** my mom's engaged to Kevin Nash - secret 4 now
> **SexyRhyann:** that man is so fine
> **HollywoodQT:** ugh
> **SweetMims:** r u happy about it
> **HollywoodQT:** No

We chat online for the next half hour. At least my girls understand how I'm feeling about Mom's engagement.

Finally someone understands how I'm feeling.

> **SexyRhyann:** I can't believe your mom still wants to marry Kevin if u r so upset about it
> **HollywoodQT:** she's being selfish

Aunt Phoebe suddenly appears in my room, barking orders to get off the computer and finish my studies.

Muttering a string of bad words under my breath, I reluctantly sign off Instant Messenger. I can't stand Aunt Phoebe sometimes. She is such a pain with her no-kind-of fashion sense.

chapter 6

I practically fall out of bed when my alarm goes off, blasting Chris Brown's latest song on the radio. I desperately want to hide under the covers for a little longer but I know Aunt Phoebe's going to come to my room shortly to make sure I'm up and moving about. She's worse than a drill sergeant.

It's a total struggle to get up this morning after tossing and turning all night. I kept hearing that stupid wedding march over and over in my head. Some of the images were of me with Madison saying our vows, then other times it was Mom and Kevin getting married.

I wipe away the remnants of sleep from my eyes and drag myself into the bathroom, frowning at what I see in the mirror. I have a serious case of bed head going on. If Madison was to see me right now—he'd run and never come back.

A hot shower is exactly what I need to wake me up. I brush my teeth and then run a brush through my hair to eliminate the mussed-up look.

Much better, I decide.

When I emerge from my bathroom thirty minutes later, I pad barefoot straight to the walk-in closet across the room to retrieve the outfit I'm wearing today. I picked it out last night after trying on several different ones.

Before I go down to breakfast, I check my email. I have one from Madison letting me know that he's thinking about me and how much he loves me. His thoughtfulness leaves a big smile on my face. I never did get around to calling him back last night.

"Good morning, Divine," Aunt Phoebe greets me.

"Morning," I return while taking a seat at the breakfast table.

Uncle Reed and Alyssa are the next ones to join us, followed by Chance. When everyone is seated, Aunt Phoebe says the blessing over our food.

I don't say a whole lot to my aunt and uncle because I'm still angry with them for taking Mom's side. Besides, I want them to see how upset I am and report back to Mom. Hopefully, she'll feel so guilty for hurting me this way that she'll break up with Kevin. I'm sure she doesn't want him coming between us.

After breakfast, Alyssa and I grab our backpacks and head out. Chance is still finishing up and we don't feel like waiting for him.

"You're pretty quiet this morning."

"I didn't really have anything to say."

"You're mad at my parents," Alyssa responds quietly.

"Yeah," I admit. "I am. They're taking my mom's side and it's wrong. I'm mad at her too. I can't believe Mom's acting so stupid."

I see a friend of mine when we reach the end of the block and call out, "Hey, Nicholas, wait up."

Alyssa and I walk faster to catch up with him. "Where were

you last Saturday?" I inquire. Nicholas and I take tae kwon do together. "You weren't in class."

"My cousin got married in Birmingham," he responds. "We went to the wedding."

"I knew there was a good reason—you just don't miss class like that."

"Nicholas, who are you taking to the prom?" Alyssa asks him, a big grin on her face. She knows that Nicholas has only one person on the brain.

"Mia," he answers. "You know she's my girlfriend. I'm going to her prom and she's coming to ours."

Mia is a good friend of mine. She used to go to school with us until her parents moved to Atlanta a few months ago. I'm so glad she and Nicholas are together and Mia got rid of that abusive ex-boyfriend of hers. Tim was a total jerk—thank goodness he's back in Alabama.

"I can't wait for prom night," Alyssa says. "I'm so excited."

"It's going to be nice," I contribute. "But not as nice as going to the Grammys or the NAACP Image Awards or anything like that."

"I'm sure nothing can compare to stuff like that, but the prom is all we got," Alyssa states.

Nicholas nods in agreement.

"I'm going to try and hook up with Mia the next time I'm in Atlanta," I say. "She and her parents were out of town the last time I was there."

"I heard Tim was in Temple a couple of weeks ago," Nicholas tells us. "People said he was looking for me, but I never saw him."

"Be careful. I don't put nothing past that jerk."

"Divine, I'm not worried about that dude. He likes to beat up on girls. He ain't nothing but a punk."

I totally agree with him.

We arrive at Temple High School twenty minutes before the bell rings.

Madison walks across the campus to meet me. He gives a slight nod in greeting to Nicholas before saying to me, "Hey, beautiful."

"Divine, I'll see you later," Nicholas says and walks off.

"Madison, where's Stephen?" Alyssa inquires. "Did he walk to school with you this morning?"

"He went to the library to return a book."

"I'ma go see if he's still there," she announces. "See y'all later."

"You still mad at me?" Madison asks when we're alone.

"I'm not upset with you. I was just frustrated about the engagement."

"Your mom getting married must really be bothering you."

"Like *yeah*. I'd think you'd be bothered if your mom was the one getting engaged."

"It would depend on the dude."

My temper flares. "You know what? I really don't want to talk about this anymore. It's not going to change anything so I'll just have to deal with it when the time comes for them to get married. And Madison, don't you breathe a word about this—my mom will kill me if this is leaked to the media." Shaking my head, I add, "Life sucks."

"Divine, don't think that way."

I shrug. "Anyway, it doesn't matter anymore. If Mom wants to make another mistake it's on her. Not me."

"I hate seeing you so down."

"I'm okay," I say.

He wraps an arm around me. "C'mon, boo. I want to see that beautiful smile of yours."

Looking up at him, I break into a grin.

"That's better."

Madison escorts me to first period. "I'll see you later," he tells me before sprinting off to his own classroom.

The hair on the back of my neck stands up. I steal a peek over my shoulder to find Brittany and her friends, Mae and Colette, huddled together, watching me. So I stare back.

Colette sticks her tongue out.

"That's so mature," I mutter before strolling into my chemistry class, kicking the door shut behind me.

chapter 7

It's our turn to make dinner. Aunt Phoebe has a committee meeting this evening and won't make it home before six P.M.

"So, what are we cooking?" I ask my cousin.

"Something quick and easy," Alyssa responds. "I really have to finish a book report that's due tomorrow."

"Hot dogs and French fries work for me."

"I don't think Mama and Daddy want hot dogs. If we were just cooking for us it'd be okay, but we're not."

"Is Chance working tonight?" I ask, being nosy.

Alyssa shakes her head. "He doesn't go back to work until Thursday. How about pork chops?"

Taking a peek inside the refrigerator, I say, "They're in the freezer but there's some chicken in here. Did Aunt Phoebe want us to cook that?"

"Maybe," Alyssa responds. "If she left it out. I'm not in the mood to fry chicken. Too messy."

"We can make baked chicken, steamed broccoli, a salad and some rolls." Aunt Phoebe makes up batches of rolls and biscuits and stores them in the freezer.

"Okay. Well, let's get started."

I refuse to wash raw meat, so I leave that for Alyssa. I cut up the lettuce, tomatoes and cucumbers for the salad, then toss in onion slices, bacon bits and cheese. A salad has to have lots of cheddar as far as I'm concerned.

"Divine, you're going to have to touch raw meat one day."

"I've touched it," I respond. "I just don't like the way it feels in my hands—especially when it's wet." I make a face. "Ugh."

Alyssa runs the meat under running water, thoroughly soaking it. She does this a few times, rubbing her fingers along the meat. I return my attention to my salad.

"I can't wait until prom," she states without looking over at me. "We're gonna have a good time."

I nod in agreement. "You and I are going to be the best-dressed people there. Our dresses are fierce."

She turns off the water. "You know we gon' have some haters."

"That's nothing new," I say while cutting up the broccoli. "The more haters we have the more popular we are."

Alyssa places the chicken in a pan and seasons it with salt, pepper and olive oil before sticking it into the oven.

I finish the rest of the cooking, leaving Alyssa free to start her homework. She wants to be done before dinner so she can gab with Stephen the rest of the evening.

I don't have a lot of homework—mostly reading, so it won't take me long. Besides, I can talk to Madison and read at the same time anyway. We sometimes sit on the phone watching TV together or just listening to each other breathing. It's our quality time until we can officially start dating.

I really wish Aunt Phoebe and Uncle Reed would get a clue. They need to abandon all those old-fashioned rules. They don't have to be so strict—we're not little kids.

I go to my room while the chicken's baking.

Alyssa shows up at my bedroom door just as I'm logging on to my laptop. "Hey, what are you doing?"

"Nothing," I respond. "You finished with your homework?"

She nods. Alyssa sits down on the edge of my bed. "I think I'ma go call Stephen."

"No surprise there," I interject with a chuckle. "When are you *not* talking to him?"

Laughing, Alyssa leans forward and gives me a playful pinch. "I know you not trying to talk! As much as you and Madison stay on the phone."

"The chicken's almost done," I say.

"I'll check on it in a minute," Alyssa replies. "Thanks for doing the rest of the cooking. I appreciate it."

I glance over my shoulder. "Just remember that you owe me."

She laughs.

"I'm serious." Alyssa doesn't know it but she's going to have to help me clean my bathroom this weekend. I can't stand to clean the toilet. Ugh.

We have plates and silverware on the table and the food ready to be served by the time Uncle Reed and Aunt Phoebe come home.

"The chicken smells delicious," Aunt Phoebe compliments us before she and Uncle Reed change clothes and wash up.

Alyssa and I grin.

Uncle Reed blesses our meal before we dive in. Chance got called in to work so he won't be eating with the family.

"This is very tasty and the meat's tender." Aunt Phoebe slices off another piece of her chicken and brings it to her mouth.

"I wish I could take credit for it," I say. "But Alyssa baked the chicken. She did a really good job."

Uncle Reed is too busy stuffing his face to contribute to the conversation. Aunt Phoebe tells us about her prom back in the day while we finish dinner. She's in such a good mood that she even gives us a break from kitchen chores.

We run to our rooms, thrilled with the way the evening is going.

I want to talk to Madison so I reach for my cell phone, only to be interrupted by my cousin.

"Alyssa, what do you want?" I demand. "What did you come in here for?" I ask. "And no, you can't borrow any of my shoes. I can't have you stretching out my kicks with those big feet of yours."

"My feet are not big. Besides, I didn't come in here to borrow any of your stuff. I came in here to ask you to be my maid of honor. Stephen and I talked about it and we want to get married too."

"You told him?" Alyssa has such a big mouth. I point-blank told that girl not to say a word to anyone, including Stephen! "I told you that it was a secret."

"Stop tripping, Divine. Stephen already knew about it—Madison told him."

I pick up my cell phone. "You wait until I talk to him—he had the nerve to tell me that sometimes I talk too much, when he's the one."

His line is busy. I wait a few minutes and try again. "Now it's going to voice mail. His sister must be over there. Marcia has a telephone at her place but she can't even stay off the phone when she goes to her parents' house to visit."

"Why don't they get cell phones?"

"Their parents believe that you can get brain cancer."

Alyssa chuckles. "Really?"

"Uh-huh. That's why they don't want Madison and his sisters to have cell phones. That's so stupid."

"Madison might be on the phone with Stephen. He was gonna call him and ask him to be his best man," Alyssa announces. "And you know you have to be my maid of honor."

"Since I'm a married lady, it's matron of honor. Alyssa, you do know that you don't really need witnesses. You don't have to get them if you don't want any."

"I know, but this is the way I want my wedding to go."

"I can't believe y'all sitting around here planning your weddings," Aunt Phoebe says, bursting into the room all uninvited.

Alyssa looks like she's about ready to pass out because we don't know how much she's overheard. My eyes dart around the room searching for an escape route. Since Aunt Phoebe's blocking the doorway, I'm thinking the window is a good choice.

"Mama, what are you t-talking about?"

"I heard y'all talking about getting married and you wanting Divine to be in the wedding." She laughs. "Girl, y'all got a long time to think about that—focus on your studies. That's what's important now."

"We were just playing around, Aunt Phoebe," I say.

Aunt Phoebe gives us a mini lecture on the importance of education and how everything we learn now will be of some use no matter what career choices we make in the future. Like, I'm so sure I'm going to need science and history to be a supermodel.

"You've got time to meet the man who will become your husband," Aunt Phoebe is saying. "Another thing to consider—you want successful mates, right?"

Alyssa and I both nod.

"Well, what do you think a successful man wants?"

"A successful woman," Alyssa responds.

"Exactly." Aunt Phoebe smiles. "Beauty fades but your brains are with you forever." She heads to the door, stopping just outside the room. "I know you two think I'm being too strict, but it's only because I know just how special you are."

I give Aunt Phoebe a smile and a tiny wave good-bye.

Deep down, I'm relieved that she didn't hear the whole conversation. I've told Alyssa about talking so loud. She knows these walls are paper thin around here. And plus she didn't close my bedroom door all the way. That girl's begging for trouble.

I elbow her. "Why didn't you close the door all the way?" I whisper. "You know Aunt Phoebe has the hearing of a dog."

"She didn't really hear us," Alyssa protests.

"She heard more than she should've," I counter. Placing a hand to my chest, I continue. "Girl, that was close."

Alyssa nods in agreement. "Too close."

When our hearts stop racing and return to normal, I inquire, "Are you using the same place where Madison and I got married?"

"No, we can't afford it. I found a free one."

She gives me the information and I get up and walk over to my desk to check it out on the Internet. "Oh no. Alyssa, don't use them. It's a hot mess."

"I'm not giving up fifty dollars—it's not like I have it anyway, but if I did, I wouldn't want to spend it on a fake ceremony."

"Even if it's fake you should still want to do it with class. I'll pay for your ceremony. It'll be my wedding gift to you and Stephen."

"For real?"

I nod.

Alyssa breaks into a smile. "Thanks, Divine."

"They have Thursday open," I tell Alyssa. "The weekend's all booked up." I make sure to keep my voice low.

"On Thursday."

"You know that's family game night," I point out.

"Let's tell my parents that we want to play tomorrow night because we need to work on a project for Friday."

"*You* tell them that—I'm not lying unless I absolutely have to. Alyssa, you'll have to take the hit on this one. I don't know about you, but I'm keeping track of all my sins."

Alyssa laughs. "Why?"

"Because on Sunday I pray for forgiveness and I want to make sure I have them all accounted for."

"Girl, I pray for forgiveness every night—I don't need to keep a list. Besides, who keeps a better list than God? He knows all things, so I count on Him to know what I'm asking forgiveness for."

"Alyssa, you're right . . . I'm going to start doing that too."

My cousin looks surprised by my words. "Divine, you don't pray every night?"

"Yeah, I pray," I respond. "I just don't ask for forgiveness all the time. But I will from now on. I'm going to Heaven—I'm making sure of it." Then I change the subject. "How about eight o'clock on Thursday? It's open." We schedule the time for Alyssa's wedding.

Alyssa nods. "Divine, thanks so much. I'm so excited."

"Happy soon-to-be wedding day," I whisper.

"This is gonna be so much fun. I'm gonna be a married lady."

"We's married now . . ." I say with a giggle, stealing a line from *The Color Purple.*

chapter 8

Alyssa and I walk past Mae and Colette on our way into the cafeteria. I get along with pretty much everyone here at school except for these two freaks and Brittany. Mae is a bully but she doesn't scare me. Colette is a skinny little thing with a big mouth.

"Girl, I can't wait for you to see my prom dress. My aunt bought it from a boutique in Jacksonville, Florida," Colette says to Mae loud enough for us to hear.

"I can't wait to see that dress," I whisper to Alyssa. "Colette has no taste in clothes, so if she likes it that much it's *got* to be ugly."

We crack up with laughter. Glancing over my shoulder, I catch Mae and Colette staring us down.

"I hope they like what they're looking at," Alyssa utters.

"Mae, sorry, but I'm already taken," I say loudly, sparking laughter all around.

She mutters a string of curses in response.

"I'm not in the mood to be fighting so I'm just going to ignore them," Alyssa states.

I agree with her because I don't want to mess up my new pants.

The à la carte line is long as usual and I'm starving, which makes me a little irritable.

"The line is moving so slow," I complain. "I don't know why people don't know what they're going to order before they get up to the counter. And then half the time they don't have their money or their debit cards out. We don't have all day."

"It's not like the menu changes," Alyssa contributes.

A couple of students in front of us agree.

Alyssa spots Stacy near the front and says, "Let's just give her our order."

We walk up and give her money and a note with our orders, then set out to find an empty table near the windows.

A few minutes later, Stacy joins us. She places the tray of food down on the table, saying, "I picked up a sandwich for Penny. Have y'all seen her? I thought she'd be here by now."

I grab the garden salad, ham-and-cheese sandwich and bottle of green tea I ordered.

Mae strolls past our table, saying, "I can't believe that Madison's still taking that *thing* to the prom. He should be taking Brittany since she's having his baby."

I swallow hard, trying not to let my anger get the best of me, but I'm sick of Mae and the rumors she's been spreading. "If she don't shut up with that lie, I'm going over there and take her out."

"Divine, she's just trying to get to you. Ignore her," Stacy tells me. "You know that skank don't know what she's talking about."

"I'm tired of her trying to start trouble between me and Madison."

Alyssa wipes her mouth on her napkin. "Mae wouldn't have a life if she didn't go around trying to start drama. Besides, it's not true, so why worry about it?"

I really can't stand Mae. We've been getting into it since I first moved to Temple and it doesn't take much for me to want to beat her down. "I don't want her talking about me or Madison."

"It's a free country, Divine," Alyssa reminds me. "Not much you can do about people running their mouths."

Mae is still running her mouth. "Hey, Brittany . . . Girl, come over here and tell us what you're wearing to the prom. I know you gon' be looking fly. I got a feeling a certain boy is gonna be like what was I thinking."

"Ignore them, Divine." Stacy finished off her salad.

Penny comes running over. "Hey y'all. Stacy, did you get my sandwich?"

"Yeah. It's right there."

"Where have you been?" I ask as she sits down facing me.

"I was in the library trying to find this book I need for my English lit report. I'ma have to go to the bookstore." After blessing her food, Penny picks up her sandwich and bites into it.

Although I'm trying hard to ignore the three girls two tables away from us I can still hear them, so I suggest, "Let's go eat outside. It's a nice day."

We gather up our food and our backpacks.

"Awww," Mae sneers. "I think we upset the Hollywood Princess."

I glance over in her direction. "It's your breath that's so offensive, Mae. We can smell it all over the cafeteria. You really should see a doctor. I believe something's crawled into that big mouth of yours and died."

Alyssa, Stacy and Penny howl with laughter along with some of the other students.

Mae's nostrils flare and her lips thin with anger. She rushes to her feet, muttering a string of foul language.

I stop walking and set my food down on a nearby table. "C'mon . . ." Mae is totally about to get an old-fashioned beat-down.

Alyssa grabs my arm. "Divine, she's not worth it. Just ignore her."

Colette holds Mae back and says, "You don't need to be suspended again."

"Fight!" someone yells out. "It's about to go down."

I look Mae straight in the eye. "Like your little puppet said, you don't need another suspension on your record. You *need* to be in school every day."

"What you trying to say?"

"That you don't need to be so *belligerent* all the time and you need to cease *antagonizing* folk before you're the one who gets *annihilated.*"

Biting back a smile of triumph, I pick up my tray and follow Alyssa and Penny outside. Stacy follows us to a nearby picnic table. "Divine, girl, I'm glad we friends. You something else," she tells me. "Did you see that dumb look on her face? She didn't have a clue what you were talking about."

"I bet she didn't know what some of those words meant?" Penny states with a laugh.

"Knowledge is power." Alyssa continues, "Divine's even got me and Chance learning new words now. I think Mama's doing it too."

"So school us on what those words meant," Stacy asks. "They didn't sound nice."

"I'ma have to use those words on a few people I know," Penny states.

"'Belligerent' means hostile or warlike," I explain.

Nodding, Stacy says, "That's definitely Mae. Her picture should be in the dictionary under hostile."

"'Antagonizing' pretty much means the same thing and 'annihilated' means to destroy or to defeat."

As if once is not enough, I run into Mae again after school. She blocks my path to confront me about what happened earlier.

"You think you so smart," she tells me. "You ain't smart at all."

"Mae, that didn't make any sense."

Brittany walks over. "Mae, don't waste your breath. I got this. *Trust.* I got this."

Her green eyes claw at me like talons.

"You got what?" I ask.

"You'll see." Brittany glowers at me before walking away.

"What's her problem?" Alyssa questions when she walks up to me. "Why was Brittany trying to get up in your face?"

"She wasn't in my face," I reply. "I don't know why she was tripping, but if she doesn't leave me alone, I *will* punch her in the face. I'm not trying to fight over Madison—I'm just tired of her bothering me."

I fuss all the way home.

"Are you even listening to me?" I ask Alyssa, who is humming softly.

"No."

I elbow her in the side.

"Hey, that hurt!"

"That's what you get for not listening to me. I'm venting over here."

"Divine, you're saying the same thing over and over again. Brittany and Mae are nothing but troublemakers—why even listen to anything they have to say? You know the old saying: sticks and stones may break your bones but words can never harm you. Mama says you give people power over you when you react to their words."

She's right.

"Okay," I murmur. "Alyssa, you're right. I don't know why I'm letting that strumpet get to me like this."

She laughs. "You've been calling people that ever since you heard Miss Eula say it."

"I like the word. It definitely fits Brittany."

Uncle Reed is home in his office when we arrive. We check in with him to see if he has any tasks for us before going to our bedrooms.

Aunt Phoebe arrives ten minutes later. She calls for us. "Girls, come help me bring in the groceries."

We do as she asks, mostly because we want to see what all she's bought. I see the bags of shrimp, crab legs and sausage. "Aunt Phoebe's making gumbo," I tell Alyssa.

"Mama, you making gumbo?"

She nods. "On Saturday."

Alyssa and I are ecstatic. We love Aunt Phoebe's seafood gumbo.

As soon as the groceries are put away, I volunteer my assistance to prepare dinner. Tonight we're having stewed chicken, mixed vegetables and mashed potatoes. I convince Aunt Phoebe to make some of her hot water corn bread too.

She thinks I'm just doing this out of the goodness of my heart and I am, but I also have to ask for something in return. I'm still working up to it.

Alyssa elbows me after dinner. "Go ask them, Divine . . ." she whispers. "See if they'll let us have family game night tonight."

"Oh, so you want me to lie?" I plan on doing it, but I like making Alyssa beg every now and then.

"Please, Divine," she pleads. "Please do this one little favor for me."

"You owe me big-time, Alyssa. *Big-time.*"

"Only if it works," she amends with a chuckle. "They may not want to change family game night. I checked with Chance and he doesn't care. He's off tonight but might have to work tomorrow."

"All I can do is ask."

I walk out to the den where Uncle Reed and Aunt Phoebe are watching the news.

"Excuse me," I say. "Uncle Reed, if you and Aunt Phoebe don't mind, can we have our family game night tonight instead of tomorrow?"

He glances over at my aunt, who says, "Have you asked Chance?"

I nod. "Alyssa did and he's okay with doing it tonight. He said he might have to work tomorrow anyway."

"Will you set up the game for us?" Aunt Phoebe asks.

"Yes ma'am. Thanks for letting us switch it." Grinning, I add, "Can't wait to beat you one more time."

"All right," Aunt Phoebe begins. "One day all that smack talkin' gon' get you in some trouble. You don't know it, but you've inspired me. I've been brushing up on my vocabulary."

I laugh. "We'll just have to see if you'll be able to use any of those words you've learned."

Ten minutes later, I have the game out and on the table while Alyssa makes the popcorn and puts Aunt Phoebe's homemade chocolate chip cookies on a plate.

As soon as everyone is seated around the table, I say in an exaggerated Southern drawl, "Well I declare . . . y'all look right nice for the whupping I'm 'bout to lay on you."

Alyssa places her hands on her hips and responds, "Naw sistah . . . you's about to get whupped."

The game's all set up and the battle lines have been drawn.

I pick up my wooden tiles and break into a grin. I'm so gonna win this game.

"'Moil' is not a word," Chance declares when it's my turn.

"It is too," I counter.

He looks to Uncle Reed for help. "Daddy, you ever heard of this word?"

"Can't say I have. Divine, what's the definition?"

"It means to labor."

Alyssa laughs. "That's 'toil,' Divine."

"Get the dictionary," I say. "You'll see that I'm right."

Aunt Phoebe opens the thick book and looks up "moil." "Here it is . . . it means to work with painful effort; to labor; to toil; to drudge."

I clap my hands. "I told you . . . I told you . . ."

Uncle Reed is next. His word is simple: "act."

When Alyssa's turn comes, she brags, "I have a word for you, Divine."

I watch her place her tiles on the Scrabble board, the letters spelling out C-A-N-T.

"'*Can't.*' Your word is 'can't'?"

"Yeah."

"I don't think you can do that."

"It's a word," she defends. C-A-N-T is a word."

"It has an apostrophe," Chance says.

Alyssa shakes her head. "'Cant' is a word. Not 'can't.' 'Cant' means an empty or solemn speech."

I check the dictionary and Alyssa knows what she's talking about. This time anyway. "Okay, you got this one."

I concentrate on the tiles I have left, trying to come up with a word that will give me double points; instead I have to settle for something simple.

Chance isn't having any more luck than I am, which thrills me because I don't want him to catch up with me. I have fifty points more than he does. Aunt Phoebe is just ten points behind him.

Alyssa and Uncle Reed are tied for the moment but that's about to change because it's my uncle's turn.

I really enjoy playing Scrabble with them and I look forward to each family game night. I can't think of a better way to spend time with my relatives.

chapter 9

"Still feeling sore after that whupping Daddy put on you last night?" Alyssa asks with a chuckle.

"The letters just weren't falling for me like they usually do," I respond, following her down the steps and across the yard. I'm so not feeling this conversation. I don't like losing. "I'm entitled to one bad night."

"Whatever . . ."

"He beat you too," I remind her. I run my fingers through my hair, fluffing up the curls.

"I'm just glad you didn't win," Alyssa tells me. "Girl, your head was getting way too big, thinking you were the Scrabble Queen."

My gaze meets hers and I feign surprise. *"You mean I'm not?"*

We laugh.

Chance catches up with us. "Got that tail beat last night, huh," he utters as he rushes past us.

"You better hope Trina don't beat yours for being late," I say. "Oh, and putting that fart pillow in my chair this morning? Real cool, Chance. That's like so funny. Ha ha."

He dismisses my comment with a slight wave of his hand.

"Today's my wedding day," Alyssa states during our walk to school. "Divine, I feel like I'm getting married for real. I'm so nervous."

"I felt that same way," I respond. "I wanted to tell you but I was so scared. I didn't know exactly how you were going to feel about it."

"I wish you'd told me, Divine. I could've been there for you."

"Madison and I didn't really know what we were doing or how it worked. I guess we can always get divorced and then do it again with a bridal party and a reception."

"It seems like you and Madison are much closer now."

I totally agree. "I think we are. Alyssa . . . it's hard to explain but it just feels so right between us."

"That's what I want with Stephen," she admits. "We haven't been as close as we used to be since I wouldn't have sex with him. He keeps asking me if I'm ready yet. That boy won't give up."

"Is that why you're doing the cyber-marriage thingy?"

"Uh-huh. I'm hoping it'll make us closer. I want Stephen and me to be the way we used to be. I miss those times."

"That doesn't mean he's going to stop asking you for sex. You know that's all boys think about. You just better keep telling him no."

"The truth is that I'm curious about it, Divine. I hear some of the girls at school talking about how great it is and how it made them closer to their boyfriends."

"You also hear about the ones who get played too," I tell Alyssa.

"And the ones left with babies. I know you haven't forgotten how Aunt Phoebe had a hissy fit over Chance getting Trina pregnant. And look at Trina—she's already tripping about Chance going off to college next year. They're good parents to Joshua and all, but I can see how hard it is being in high school and raising a child. You should be able to see it too."

"I know it's not easy to raise a child, period, I'm not trying to go there, Divine. I am not trying to have a baby. If I decide to get down like that, I'm getting on birth control. But even if I got pregnant, Stephen's not like those other boys. He really cares about me."

"Chance cares for Trina too. I'm crazy about Madison but I'm definitely not ready for a baby either. Not sure if I ever want one after seeing Trina have Joshua." I make a face. "I'm still traumatized over that."

Alyssa laughs. "You're stupid."

"Whatever. It was gross. I don't ever want to see that much of anybody."

"Maybe that's why Uncle Jerome wants you to be with Ava," Alyssa suggests. "So you can be there when the baby comes."

"Well, he can forget that," I snap back. "I definitely don't want to see her give birth."

"You think she's really cool with Aunt Kara or just faking it?"

I shrug. "I don't know. She took Jerome from my mom. She should be happy, I guess."

As soon as Alyssa and I step on campus, I scan the grounds for Madison. We walk over to the basketball court.

"He's not here," I say.

"Maybe he's not at school yet," Alyssa responds. "Madison might be running late."

"You're right." When we see Stephen I ask about my boo.

"I haven't seen him," he replies. "I don't think he's on campus yet."

"Well, I'll see y'all later," I tell them. I don't want to feel like a third wheel so I go off by myself.

I find Chance and Trina standing near the front entrance of the school. I spend a few minutes chatting with them before moving on.

Someone runs up behind me, placing hands over my eyes. I inhale a fruity scent and know that it's Penny. She loves that raspberry body spray she wears, calling it her signature scent. Penny has a signature everything since watching *Steel Magnolias*. It's her favorite movie.

"I asked Aunt Phoebe if I could spend the weekend with y'all and she said it's fine as long as Mama don't mind." Penny sits her backpack down on the cement bench.

"Cool," I reply. "We're not watching a bunch of romantic movies, Penny. Or any tearjerkers. Girl, my eyes were nearly swollen shut after watching *Titanic*. I cry every time I see that movie."

We're soon joined by Stacy, who's wearing a fierce pantsuit.

"I like what you're wearing," I tell her. "Where did you get that outfit?"

"My aunt found it in some boutique in Dallas. She was out there last week for a conference. She actually bought it for herself but didn't try it on until she came home."

"It is nice," Penny murmurs, while we wait on the bell to ring.

I don't run into Madison until after my first-period class.

"Where were you this morning?" I demand, asserting my position as his girlfriend. He was supposed to meet me under the huge oak tree—it's our spot.

"I had to finish some schoolwork before I left home so I didn't get here until after the bell rang."

"Oh, okay. I didn't know what happened. I was worried that you were sick, Madison."

He reaches over, taking my hand in his. "No, I'm okay. Baby, you don't have to worry about me."

Lowering my voice, I whisper in his ear, "But I'm supposed to worry about you. You're my *husband*."

He gives me a big grin before kissing me. "That's right, boo. I'm your man."

The warning bell rings.

"I need to get to class," I say, pulling away from him.

"Why don't you skip with me? We could spend some quality time together."

"'Cause I really like living," I respond. "Madison, you know my aunt and uncle would kill me, and then my mother will pick up where they left off."

Madison looks a little disappointed and I can't figure out why. He knows how strict Aunt Phoebe and Uncle Reed are, so he can't be serious.

"I guess I'll see you later then," he says after a moment.

"You weren't serious about skipping class, were you? Madison, I know better."

"I just thought I'd ask," he replies with a smile. "I wanna spend some time with my girl." I turn to leave but hear Madison when he adds, "With your fine self . . ."

That's my boo.

"I see you with that big grin on your face," Trina teases. "I don't know what Madison said, but girl, he got your nose wide open."

"You're one to talk," I reply with a chuckle. "You and Chance are practically glued at the hips."

"You right about that."

I can't help but notice the dark circles under Trina's eyes. "Girl, you look tired."

She touches her face with her right hand. "I know I look a hot mess. Divine, I love my baby to death, but I can't even take a good shower these days."

"TMI . . . way too much information."

"It's the truth. Having a child is a lot of work. I'm grateful that Chance and I are together, but still . . ." Trina pauses a moment before saying, "I feel like I can't get everything done. Schoolwork, spending time with Joshua and then quality time with Chance. Some days I just feel like crying. Your aunt and uncle want to keep Joshua for the weekend—I'm gonna use that time to catch up on my sleep."

"I don't blame you," I reply.

Our next class is in the same building, so we walk together. I'm just here to listen because I sense Trina really needs to vent. I'm so grateful that I'm not in her shoes.

Alyssa and Stephen's wedding is in a couple of hours.

I rush through my math and English literature homework so that I can spend an additional thirty minutes studying for my science test. Thank goodness I finished my history homework earlier while we were in computer lab.

Alyssa comes to my room to ask, "Do you have the English lit notes? You know we're having a pop quiz tomorrow and I can't find mine—I think I left them in my locker."

I nod. "I didn't know about the test. Are you sure?"

"I heard it from Nicholas. Mrs. Simpson slipped and told their class."

"Thanks for telling me. I'm glad I went over them earlier when I was working on the assignment she gave us. Did you get yours finished or do you need that?"

"I have the assignment."

I remove my notes from my notebook. "There's a lot there, so you might want to just make a copy of them."

"I'll go to Daddy's office and use his copier."

She leaves and returns a few minutes later. "Thanks so much, Divine. I think your notes might be better than mine."

"I don't know about that. You take pretty good notes, Alyssa." I check my clock. "It's almost time for your wedding."

She grins. "I'ma go and study these notes real quick. Come to my room at five minutes 'til eight. Okay?"

"I'll be there," I tell Alyssa.

When seven fifty-five rolls around, I stroll into her room carrying my computer. "It's time."

She stuffs her notes into her backpack. "I'll finish studying these tomorrow during lunch." Alyssa closes the door to her room and is about to lock it, but I stop her.

"If you lock the door, your mom is going to really think that we're being sneaky about something."

"We can just tell her that we're studying and didn't want to be disturbed."

"Alyssa, we do that all the time but we never lock the door. Girl, think . . ."

I make myself comfortable on Alyssa's bed, positioning my laptop across my thighs.

"Ready?" I ask Alyssa, who nods. She's fidgeting and acting kind of stressed out, so I say, "Why are you looking so nervous?"

"I'm getting married," she whispers. "I can't believe I'm doing this."

"It's not real," I remind her. "We're just having some fun—we're living out our fantasies."

Alyssa sits at her desk in front of her computer and opens up the Internet, where she logs into the Champagne Cyber Wedding Chapel. I do the same from my computer.

Seconds later, we're joined by Stephen in a special chat room reserved for the ceremony.

"Where is Madison?" I ask.

"Don't worry, Divine," Alyssa answers. "He'll be here soon."

"The wedding's supposed to start in about two minutes." I'm going to have one of Aunt Phoebe's hissy fits if that boy doesn't show up soon. He'd better not mess up this evening for Stephen and Alyssa.

Totally uncool.

Madison logs on just as I'm about to send him an Instant Message.

HollywoodQT: I was just about to IM you.
BadBoyMH: I'm here
HollywoodQT: I can see that

We are soon joined by the person who will be officiating Stephen and Alyssa's wedding ceremony. He identifies himself as Preacher Bob.

Via computer, Madison and I witness their exchange of vows.

Five minutes later, Alyssa and Stephen are man and wife. As part of the wedding package, they are assigned a honeymoon suite with a private password.

While Alyssa and Stephen are in their "suite," Madison and I return to ours to chat about married life.

HollywoodQT: this is so much fun
BadBoyMH: what is?
HollywoodQT: this. Just being able to talk 2 u without someone on the other end picking up the phone
BadBoyMH: I like this but I'd like being with u even more. I wish I could c u right now
HollywoodQT: me too

BadBoyMH: we really need some time 2gether
HollywoodQT: I know, but there's nothing we can do but wait
BadBoyMH: I wish we were really married

My heart leaps with joy at reading those words. People think that we're too young to know what love is but they're wrong. When I'm with Madison, I feel like I've found a missing part of who I am. I feel so happy and, well, in love. He's so sweet and he's never lied to me. I know I can trust him with my heart.

BadBoyMH: hey did you leave the computer
HollywoodQT: no, I'm still here. I was just thinking about how happy you make me
BadBoyMH: I hope you'll always feel this way about me
HollywoodQT: I will

Madison's dad makes him get off the computer because his sister needs to use it, so we reluctantly say our good-byes and sign off. His sisters get on my nerves. They don't seem to want to get on the phone or use the computer until Madison and I get on them.

I plan on giving him a call after I take my shower and get my clothes ready for tomorrow. That way we can talk uninterrupted. That is, if Aunt Phoebe really is as tired as she says and won't be walking the halls tonight, trying to see if we're up late on the telephone or computer. She should really consider being a cop.

chapter 10

"So are you all set for tomorrow?" Nicholas inquires on the way to school, referring to our qualifying for the brown belt in tae kwon do. Sometimes Nicholas walks with us in the mornings when he doesn't have to be at school early to tutor other kids.

Alyssa and Chance walk with Nicholas and me, but are having a deep conversation about Trina and the baby. He's still trying to decide whether or not to go away to college or stay close to home.

"Hey, are you listening to me?" Nicholas asks.

"Yeah," I respond. "I've been practicing my form every day. I'm going to work on it some more when I get home tonight after choir practice. What about you?"

He nods. "I've been working a lot on my sparring and the new self-defense techniques."

"I worked some on sparring," I state. "I think I'm ready."

"Mia's doing good in her tae kwon do classes," Nicholas announces. "She told me that she really likes it."

"You know she's coming to Temple this evening, don't you?" I say. "She wants to come to our ceremony tomorrow, so she's staying with us for the weekend. We definitely have to do our best and get our belts."

"She told me last night when we were on the phone," Nicholas responds.

I look up at him. "You really like Mia, don't you?"

Smiling, he nods. "Yeah. She's a real nice girl."

"I'm so glad she's with you now and not Tim. He was so mean to her, Nicholas. I couldn't stand it but there wasn't much I could do."

"She's a different person now. Mia don't take nothing off me. I have to remind her sometimes that I'm not Tim. I don't wanna pay for the stuff he did, you know."

"I think that going through something like that would change anybody," I respond. "Tim put Mia through a lot. But now that she has you in her life—just be patient with her." Smiling, I add, "You two are so cute together."

Nicholas stares at me, trying to read my expression. "What's up with you, Divine? You been acting kind of strange lately."

I frown. "Okay, Nicholas. What do you mean I'm acting strange?"

"Look at you—you seem a little too happy. What's going on?"

"I'm just happy. *That's all.*"

"But why?"

"Nicholas, how can I not be happy? I have a great boyfriend and a great life. I just feel really good about things. Aren't you happy? You have Mia—she's the girl of your dreams. That's what you've said, anyway."

His lips turn upward. "Mia is my girl."

"See?" I murmur. "You can't resist smiling whenever we talk about her. Well, that's the same way it is with me and Madison."

Nicholas nods in understanding.

Chance takes a detour to Trina's house when we're two blocks away from the school. He likes to see Joshua before school every morning.

Alyssa eases up on the other side of Nicholas, saying, "I can't wait for prom. I'm so excited."

"I wish Aunt Phoebe would let us have a party afterward," I say.

"Aunt Shirley's having one for everybody," Alyssa announces. "She says she'd rather us come to the house instead of going to a hotel."

I glance over at Nicholas. "Where is Mia planning to stay?"

"She told me she was gonna ask if she could stay with y'all prom night."

"Good. I was hoping she'd do that." I switch my backpack from one side to the other.

"We'll probably all be staying at Aunt Shirley's house, though," Alyssa interjects. "Mama's helping to host the party. They plan on cooking breakfast and everything. We're gonna have such a good time."

We each go our separate ways once we step on campus. Thank God it's Friday. I'm a little sick of school. Mom calls it spring fever. I don't know what it is exactly but I do know I'm ready for classes to be over.

My school day is moving at a snail's pace. The best thing about today is that a group of us—Stacy, Penny, Trina, Alyssa and Mia—is going to the movies tonight.

Madison and I spend a few minutes together before first period. I don't see him again until after lunch. I find him standing on the side of the library with Brittany. He's in such a deep conversation with her that he's not even aware that I'm nearby. I fight the overwhelming urge to join them because I can't be late for my fifth-period class.

Have the clocks stopped?

That's the question I ask myself. They must have because I'm still in school waiting for the bell to ring. It feels like I should be in sixth period instead of fifth.

When is that bell going to ring?

Four looong minutes later, I send up silent praises. *Thank you, Jesus.* I thought I would die in world history. Hopefully math will go by much faster.

I don't have time to watch the clock in sixth period because Mr. Monroe keeps us busy. Some of the kids are doing oral presentations of our recent assignment on establishing how weddings are celebrated in different cultures. While listening to the various students, I complete the finishing touches on my presentation for Monday.

When the bell rings, I go home immediately after school and begin my chores. First I separate and wash my laundry to get it out of the way before we have to leave for choir practice. We're singing on Sunday and I'm doing a solo.

Alyssa and I have taken to doing our wash together. This way it gives us some free time on Saturday to do other stuff or just hang out. We gather in her room forty-five minutes later to fold the first load of warm, fresh-smelling clothing.

"I'm so glad Mia's coming. We're gonna have so much fun this weekend."

I agree with Alyssa. "Yeah. Oh, and you can't be on the phone with Stephen most of the night. It's all about us girls."

"I already told Stephen that we'd be kicking it with Mia, Trina, Stacy and Penny. He's okay with it. He plans on hanging with Madison and some of their other friends. But I have a feeling they might try and show up tonight when we go to the movies."

"Did you tell him which one we were planning to see?" I fold my T-shirts and stack them neatly.

Alyssa shakes her head. "Why would I do that?"

"Because I know you want to spend time with Stephen. You're not slick."

"Whatever. I didn't tell him anything. Okay?"

I chuckle. "You don't have to be so defensive, Alyssa."

"I'm not. You act like I can't be anywhere without him, but that's not true."

"I didn't say or imply that," I respond. "You sound like you might be feeling a little guilty about something."

Alyssa probably did tell Stephen which theater we'd be at tonight—if she did, she doesn't have to lie about it. I'm crazy about my boo, but I just want to be with my girls this weekend. If Rhyann and Mimi could be here with us, then everything really would be perfect.

Aunt Phoebe's shrill voice comes out of nowhere reminding us that we need to get ready to leave for choir rehearsal.

"C'mon out to the car," she says. "Y'all were almost late last week."

We hear the front door open and close.

In the hallway, Alyssa and I break into a run. Aunt Phoebe just might leave us, depending on her mood.

"Sorry about that," I say as we climb into the van. "We weren't paying attention to the time."

Alyssa steals a look over her shoulder. I can tell she's a little upset over our previous discussion. I lean forward and give her a playful pinch on the arm. "I was supposed to ride in the front seat this time."

She laughs. "I thought you liked the backseat since you're so used to riding around in limos."

We lapse into a conversation about our plans for the weekend. I can't wait to see Mia. We're going to have so much fun.

Mia's parents drop her off at the church shortly after six.

I smile when she enters the sanctuary. Mia takes a seat in the back row while we finish rehearsal.

The choir director gives the benediction. After an hour of singing, I'm dying to drink something. I settle for a bottle of room-temperature water I find in my Coach tote.

Aunt Phoebe is outside waiting for us, so we grab our stuff and walk out to the car. Alyssa climbs into the front passenger seat while Mia and I climb into the back of the van.

Mia greets my aunt. "Mrs. Matthews, I appreciate you letting me stay with y'all."

"We're happy to have you, sugar."

"I'm so glad you're spending the weekend with us," I tell Mia. "We're going to have so much fun."

"I've been thinking about this weekend all week long. I really miss living here in Temple. I miss my girls," Mia replies.

"Chance is going to babysit tonight so that Trina can go with us," I announce.

"For sho'?" Mia questions.

I nod.

"That's great," Mia murmurs. "I can't wait to see her. I tried to call her last night but I didn't get her. I wanna see little Joshua. I bet he's getting so big now."

"He is," I confirm.

Mia and I hang up her clothes when we get to the house, then head to the den. Alyssa's already in there talking to Aunt Phoebe, who's blinding me with her bright pink pajamas. And she has the nerve to wear a pink-and-green head scarf. Now I know what it means when people talk about a deer in headlights.

She must have felt my eyes boring into her back because Aunt Phoebe glances over her shoulder at me and says, "Don't you even say a word about my pajamas. I'll be going to bed in a couple of hours."

Alyssa and Mia burst into laughter.

"But Aunt Phoebe, as a member of the fashion police, I have a duty to tell you if you're breaking the law with your clothes. Please just let me help you pick out a few outfits. Pleeeze."

I follow Aunt Phoebe into the kitchen, where she pulls a pack of hamburger buns from the pantry. "Divine, I'm not gon' let you worry me."

"I'm just trying to help you."

"Leave my mama alone," Alyssa says to me with a chuckle as she joins us in the kitchen.

When Stacy, Trina and Penny arrive, we do some last-minute primping before piling into Aunt Phoebe's van. Uncle Reed is dropping us off at the movies. It would've been so much cooler to ride in a limo, but I already know my aunt's not having that—she loves her minivan.

Girls just want to have fun!

We intend on doing just that.

Saturday morning, I step forward into a right front stance, making sure my feet are shoulder-width apart. My hand is palm up on my hip the way I've been taught. I raise my arm, making sure that when my arm is almost straight, the hand is palm down. My other arm is bent into position to block the middle of my body. To qualify for my belt, I have to perform several self-defense techniques, break some boards, spar and pass testing on endurance and terminology.

Near the end of class, I stand in line to receive my brown belt. Nicholas stands beside me to get his as well.

Aunt Phoebe and Alyssa congratulate us afterward.

"Mama's taking us out to lunch to celebrate," Alyssa announces. "Daddy's gonna meet us at the restaurant."

"Cool . . . do you mind if Nicholas and his mom come with us?"

Aunt Phoebe nods. "Of course not. I'll go over and invite them." She returns a few minutes later, saying, "They're gonna follow us to the restaurant."

We decide to eat at Applebee's.

"I have to go order my tux when we leave here," Nicholas states after we're seated at our table. "Mia sent me a sample of the material from her gown so that I can match up my vest and bow tie."

"You haven't gone yet?" she asks.

"It's my fault, Mia," Nicholas' mom explains. "My car broke down and we had to get it fixed. We're doing it this afternoon."

"Yes ma'am," Mia responds. "I just thought maybe he was procrastinating."

"Not this time," Nicholas tells her.

It's so funny watching them. Nicholas and Mia can't seem to keep their eyes off each other but they're trying to be slick about it.

"Mia, that's a great idea about the samples," I interject. "Alyssa, we need to call Mom and have her order some samples from our gowns for Stephen and Madison. We can't be looking all whack at the prom."

Aunt Phoebe and Nicholas' mom laugh.

"We can't," I reiterate. "Aunt Phoebe, we have images to uphold. I'm a fashionista—my clothes have to be on point at all times."

"A what?" Nicholas asks.

"Fashionista. It means that I'm an avid follower of fashion. It's what I live for."

"Okay," he mutters. "Thanks for clearing that up."

"Aunt Phoebe, I'm still willing to help you out with shopping."

"I got this," she replies with a chuckle. "I have my own style, sugar. As long as your uncle isn't complaining—it's all good, as you young folk like to say."

"Mom . . . stop trying to be cool," Alyssa pleads. "It's not working."

We all laugh.

After lunch, my aunt and uncle drive us over to the mall in Carrollton to meet up with Stacy, Penny and Deonne Massey, another friend of ours.

Deonne and I have two classes together but we haven't really hung out together since she helped me sneak out of the house to meet the creep I thought was a sixteen-year-old boy named Sean. She thought maybe my aunt and uncle would have an attitude toward her, but they don't. Still, she's not real comfortable coming over to the house.

"What time should I come back to pick y'all up?" Uncle Reed asks when he drops us near the front entrance.

"We're gonna ride back with Aunt Shirley," Alyssa states. "She already said we could."

"Okay. Well, have a good time and behave."

"Uncle Reed, we're not little kids," I say. "We know how to act when we're out in public. You're raising us right." I give him a thumbs-up, adding, "You should be proud."

He smiles. "See you later."

We wave as he drives off.

Why do adults always insist on treating us like little babies?

chapter 11

"Aunt Phoebe, what . . . what are you wearing?" I ask when she comes strutting into the living room.

She glances down at her black suit. "What's wrong with it?"

I break into a grin. "Nothing! You look fabulous. I like that cream polka-dotted silk shirt." My aunt is looking pretty sharp today. "I'm rubbing off on you," I say.

She places a hand to her heart. "Lawd give me strength."

Aunt Phoebe glances over at Alyssa, who says, "Mama, you look beautiful."

"I bought some fabric that closely matched my blouse and I made a sash for my hat."

"All right, First Lady," I say. "Uncle Reed is not going to be able to concentrate on his sermon with you looking all fly."

Pleased, she lightly pats the bun styled at her nape.

"You know what, Aunt Phoebe . . . I think you shouldn't wear a hat. They're played out."

"I'm not going into the church house without my head covered."

"Why not?" I ask. "It's not like you're going to be struck down by lightning."

"It's tradition. The first lady never enters the sanctuary without a hat."

"Is it going to give you points in Heaven?" I want to know. "If so, maybe I should sport me a few hats to church."

Aunt Phoebe laughs. "Miss Smarty Pants . . ."

"Remember, you were telling us that we all had gifts—well, fashion is one of my gifts."

Aunt Phoebe laughs. "I was talking about spiritual gifts, sugar. You took the test—was fashion on it?"

I chuckle. Uncle Reed had all of us take a test to determine our spiritual gifts. "No ma'am, but mercy was and it's one of my gifts."

Aunt Phoebe embraces me. "If you don't quit, I'ma tell your uncle on you. He'll make you stand up in the front of the church and name all the books of the Bible—"

"I can do that," I reply quickly with a laugh. "I had to learn them for TeenTalk."

"Backward," Aunt Phoebe states. "He'll have you recite them backward."

"No he wouldn't."

Winking at me, Aunt Phoebe says, "He's my husband—I'm sure I can get him to see things my way . . ."

Like gross. "I don't think it's fair of you to use sex to get Uncle Reed to punish me. That's just plain wrong."

She laughs. "You finish getting ready for church. We're leaving in fifteen minutes."

"Not fair, Aunt Phoebe," I say, wanting to have the last word.

* * *

Aunt Phoebe leads the way down the aisle to the second row, looking fierce in her black suit. Now her hat is another story. She could've hung out with the Three Musketeers in that hat. That long black feather is irritating me. It's so not fashionable, but I have to admit that it looks good on her. Then she has the nerve to carry a purse with black feathers stuck all over it. Well, actually that's not too bad.

I'd carry it.

Alyssa and I have to sing this morning, so we head over to the choir room for a quick rehearsal before services start.

After the third run-through, we make small talk on our way back into the sanctuary.

This Sunday, Uncle Reed preaches on Christian courtship and marriage. I listen attentively as he discusses what it truly means to be married and the seriousness of a commitment like that.

He talks about how society has made a mockery of marriage. His words ignite a twinge of guilt in me for Internet role-playing.

"My mom should've been here to hear your dad preach this morning," I tell Alyssa as we walk down the aisle toward the exit when church service ends. "She needed to hear this sermon on marriage."

"You're still tripping off Aunt Kara's engagement? A lot of people are happy for them, Divine. Why can't you be happy for them too?"

"They don't know my mom like I do. Besides, I'm still trying to get used to Jerome and Ava being married. Way too many changes in a short time."

"Divine, how would you feel if your parents weren't happy for you if you got engaged?"

"I don't have to worry about that now," I respond with a grin. "Madison and I are already married."

Alyssa laughs. "I really don't think they'd be happy about it."

"Girl, my mom would flip out. Alyssa, I like Kevin—really, I do. It's just that I don't think Mom should marry another man in the entertainment industry. Those marriages don't really work. She doesn't need to be hurt anymore."

"Do you think a regular guy would really understand Aunt Kara's lifestyle? He might not like her having to travel so much, or he might be after her money," Alyssa points out to me. "Divine, you don't want that either."

"I hadn't really thought about that, but Mom's not stupid. She wouldn't pick someone trying to get over on her."

"She *is* smart, so you have to just trust that your mama knows what she's doing if she's ready to marry Kevin. It could be worse, you know?"

Alyssa's words weigh heavy on my mind for the rest of the afternoon.

"Why aren't you eating, Divine?" Aunt Phoebe questions when we're eating dinner. "You didn't eat any breakfast this morning and you didn't want any lunch."

"I'm just not hungry," I reply quietly.

"Divine, you been walking around this house like you've lost your best friend. For goodness sake, your mother's getting married. It's not the end of the world."

"Well, it feels that way to me," I respond. "She's making a big mistake."

"Why don't you like Kevin?" my aunt wants to know.

"It's not that I don't like him. I just don't like the way Mom is when she's married. She wasn't happy and I don't want her to be that way again."

"Your mother has changed a lot in the past couple of years," Uncle Reed interjects.

"I know that. Uncle Reed, I want my mom to be happy—really, I do—but I'm just scared that she'll get hurt again."

"Honey, I know how much you love your mother but this is her life."

"I know that, Aunt Phoebe." I release a long sigh. I don't know why I bother trying to talk to them. Nobody understands what I'm going through or how I feel about this marriage.

"Hollywood marriages don't last—I should know," I state before pushing away from the table. I pick up my plate and carry it over to the counter. "I'll eat this later," I say as I cover it with foil.

I leave them to finish their meal while I go to my room to have a pity party.

Hopefully, they'll call Mom and tell her how unhappy I am about her engagement. With any luck, she'll come to her senses and call this stupid thing off.

If not, then I'll be depressed for the rest of my life.

How can my mom do this to me?

chapter 12

As soon as I step on campus Monday morning, all eyes seem to be on me and Alyssa—not that I don't get a lot of attention anyway, but this time, it feels different. I can't really explain it any better than that. I run my fingers through my hair, making sure it's not just all over my head. I *am* looking fierce today though.

"Why is everyone staring at us?" Alyssa whispers.

I shrug. "Maybe it's this new outfit I'm wearing, or my hair. Charlene hooked me up. I like her better than Miss Mavis. She can style some hair."

Alyssa disagrees. "You do look nice, Divine, but I don't think that's it at all. I don't know what's going on, but something's up."

"No, I think it's just me. I look fierce every day but today I must really be on point."

Alyssa looks me up and down, saying, "Naw. You look the same. Tired . . ."

"Don't hate me because I'm cute," I respond.

A couple of girls walk over to us, grinning from ear to ear.

"I hear y'all been pretty busy," the one named Trish says. She lives three houses down from us. Usually, she doesn't have a whole lot to say to me and Alyssa but I guess today she's feeling chatty.

NOT.

She just wants to be up in our business for some reason.

Alyssa glances over at me, confused. I'm just as puzzled as she is, so I ask, "What are you talking about, Trish?"

"Girl, I heard that you and Madison got married. Now, what I want to know is, why weren't we invited to the wedding?"

I don't respond. My mind's working overtime trying to figure out how she knew about my cyber-wedding.

My eyes travel to meet Alyssa's nervous gaze. She shakes her head in astonishment.

Trish glances over at Alyssa. "I heard you did it too. That y'all had a double wedding."

"Can you believe this mess?" my cousin says. "People be talking all kinds of stuff."

Trish turns her attention back to me. "C'mon, Divine . . . you can tell us. Did you marry Madison? I know Brittany's gonna have a cow. She been saying that Madison was gon' leave you and get back with her. She so stupid."

After a moment of indecision, I finally say, "Trish, you can't tell anybody. *I mean it.* "

"I won't. I promise. Cashmere's not gonna say anything either. Y'all know we don't hardly talk to nobody."

I've never heard anyone say that Trish and Cashmere gossip. I guess that's why people like to confide in them—and how they know everybody's business.

“Yeah. Madison and I got married over the Internet. But it’s not like a real marriage, though.”

“Girl, it’s real,” Cashmere interjects. “Y’all said your vows, right?”

I nod.

“Then y’all married in the eyes of God.”

I laugh, but deep down, I’m thinking that it wouldn’t be so bad if that were true. I’m loving the idea of being married to my boo. “We’re not married for real,” I repeat.

“Did you get married by a preacher?” Trish asks.

I nod. “Yeah.”

Cashmere responds, “Ask anybody, Divine. Y’all married, girl. Congratulations. I can’t wait for Brittany to find out. She’ll lo—”

“You can’t tell anyone,” Alyssa reminds her.

“I’m not saying a word, but I won’t have to—it’s already going around the school. She’s gonna find out, if she don’t know already.”

“Everybody knows?” I ask.

Trish and Cashmere both nod. “We heard a couple of people talking about it,” Trish tells us.

“How did *they* find out?” Alyssa asks.

“I heard that Madison and Stephen told Tyson that y’all had a wedding and everything,” Cashmere states. “I’m mad ’cause I wasn’t invited and y’all didn’t tell us. We had to hear about it from Tyson. And y’all know he got a big mouth. That boy don’t do anything but gossip.”

“Wait until I see Madison . . .” I mumble to myself. He kept fussing about me wanting to tell Alyssa, Penny and Stacy and here he is, running his mouth. “I’ve got some words for him.” Cashmere is right about Tyson. He is one of Madison’s best friends but he loves to talk about everybody else’s business.

“Divine, you know boys talk just as much as we do. But I sho’ hope that Chance don't find out," Alyssa states. "You know he's gonna go running straight to Mama and Daddy. He's dying to see us get in trouble for something."

"That's because we kept ragging him about getting Trina pregnant," I point out.

Cashmere and Trish move on when they spot one of their friends, leaving Alyssa and me alone.

"Alyssa, do you think Cashmere's right? About us really being married?"

"Girl, noo! She don't know what she talking about. Divine, don't go listening to this mess. We can ask Daddy about it."

"No way," I quickly interject. "Then he'll be wondering why we're asking."

"You could say it has to do with your project, Divine. At least we'll know for sure."

"It tells you at the chapel that the marriage is not a legal one. But to be honest, sometimes I almost wish it were," I confess.

Alyssa gives me a strange look.

"What?" I ask. "You don't feel the same way?"

"I guess. I mean, I'm crazy about Stephen and all, but . . ."

"I love my boo, Alyssa."

"Here comes your boo now," she responds. "I need to go find mine and straighten him out about his big mouth."

"I'll be doing the same thing with Madison."

Alyssa waves to Madison before walking away.

He strolls up to me all cool and grinning from ear to ear.

I lay into him immediately. "Madison, why did you tell Tyson about the wedding? You know that boy can't keep nothing to himself. I thought we were supposed to be keeping this on the down-low."

"Divine, what's wrong? You told Alyssa. Why I can't tell nobody?"

"I told one person. You told Stephen *and* Tyson. Now that big mouth's told some people that we got married. Pretty soon, it's going to be all over the school."

Madison shrugs nonchalantly. "Well, I told him not to say anything."

I release a sigh of frustration. "Tyson can't hold water, Madison." Switching my backpack from one side to the other I ask, "What if Chance finds out? He'll go running straight to Aunt Phoebe and Uncle Reed."

"Divine, the marriage isn't real. All we have to say is that we're role-playing on the Internet. It's not a big deal, so stop tripping."

"Don't tell me to stop tripping," I retort. "You won't have to listen to my aunt's mouth—I'll be the one in lockdown until I'm thirty."

"It's just a game, Divine."

"She won't see it that way," I respond. "Aunt Phoebe would have a serious hissy fit over this—I just know it."

Nicholas comes up to me after class saying, "Hey Divine, did you know there's a rumor going around that you and Madison are secretly married?"

I laugh. "It can't be much of a secret if everybody's talking about it."

"Tyson said that Madison told him that y'all tied the knot. I flat-out told him he was lying. I was getting ready to punch him out. He don't need to be spreading rumors like that."

"He's not," I utter.

"He's not *what*?" Nicholas questions.

"Madison and I kinda got married. We did it over the Internet."

Nicholas pushed his glasses upward, then just eyes me hard.

"What?" I ask.

"Seriously? You and Madison really did it?"

"Did it as in saying 'I do'—yeah, we had a little wedding ceremony and everything." I break into laughter over Nicholas' shocked expression.

"So y'all really married?"

"Nicholas, it's a cyber-wedding."

"So what does that mean?"

"It means that Madison and I went to the chat room and got married. There's even a game where you can get extra points for being married. It's big in China."

"For real?"

I nod. "But it's not a real marriage, Nicholas."

"Are you sure?" he asks. "I've heard that those ceremonies are real."

"Not mine. The website said that it wasn't legal."

"So why did you do it?" Nicholas questions.

"I thought it would be cool. I wanted to see what it would feel like to be married to Madison." Grinning, I add, "We're practicing for the real thing."

"But why? What's the point?"

"We just wanted to do it," I say. I'm not feeling this conversation anymore, so I tell Nicholas, "We'd better get to class. I don't want to spend my lunch hour in detention."

After school, Nicholas grills me for more information on cyber-marriages while I wait for Madison to come out of the building.

I give him a sidelong glance. "Are you thinking about marrying Mia?"

He shakes his head. "When and if I do—it'll be the real thing, Divine. I don't want to play at marriage."

I don't respond.

Madison is waiting at the edge of campus. Nicholas hangs around for about a minute.

"What's wrong with you?" Madison asks when we're alone. "You look like you in a bad mood."

"I'm just tired," I respond. "I need to go home and take a nap."

He leaves when Alyssa arrives to go catch up with some of his friends.

"We have a Y Club meeting," my cousin announces. "Did you forget?"

"For real?" The Y Club is part of the YMCA and its purpose is to uplift others and serve the community. I forgot all about the meeting.

She nods. "Yeah."

I groan. "I'm so tired. I just want to go home and sleep for a couple of hours."

"It's not gonna be a long meeting. C'mon."

By the time we arrive home, Aunt Phoebe has dinner ready.

I put my backpack on my desk, wash my hands and head straight to the dinner table. Mom calls the house to talk to me just as I'm about to sit down. I excuse myself and retreat to a corner of the dining room.

"I was thinking about you so I thought I'd check on you. I tried your cell phone but it went straight to voice mail."

"I'm okay," I say, trying to sound as sad as possible.

"You don't sound okay," Mom tells me. "Divine, are you still upset over my engagement?"

"No ma'am." I hope that I'm playing my part correctly. I want her to think that I'm miserable, which really isn't that much of a stretch. My eyes travel to the huge oak china cabinet, admiring the delicate, fourteen-carat-gold-trimmed plates on display.

"Why are you so upset about this?"

"I think it's way too soon for you and Kevin to be talking about marriage," I reply. "You haven't been dating that long. It's only been, like, a couple of months."

"I have a feeling that it really wouldn't matter how long Kevin and I have been together—you'd have a problem with it either way, Divine."

"That's not true," I counter. I glance over at Aunt Phoebe, who's pretending not to be listening as she and Alyssa bring out the food.

"I thought you and Kevin were getting along."

"We are," I confirm. "Mom, Kevin is a nice person but I'm just not ready for him to be part of our family. Why can't you understand that?"

"You'd be happy if I never married again. That's the truth."

I can tell by the tone of her voice that she's frustrated. "That's not what I want, Mom. Really, I don't. If you were marrying a normal man—I'd feel differently."

"Kevin *is* normal, sweetie."

"He's in the industry. You know marriages in Hollywood don't last long."

"There are some wonderful, long-lasting marriages between actors—you don't hear about them as much, but they do exist, Divine."

It doesn't matter what I say to my mom at this point, her mind's made up. She's marrying Kevin, despite my feelings. I decide it's time to change the subject.

"Jerome is pressuring me to get to know Ava."

"Pressuring you in what way?"

"He wants me to call her and like, be her friend or something. I keep trying to tell him that I don't know her like that."

"He just wants you to have a relationship with his wife, Divine. I don't think he means to put pressure on you."

"I have to deal with so much," I complain. "I'm too young to have all this drama in my life, Mom."

She doesn't respond.

"I just want some time to adjust to all the changes. That's all I'm trying to say."

"I understand, sweetie. I really do."

"Mom, I love you and I do want you to be happy. I hope you know that."

"I do."

"But I want to be happy too."

"I want the same for you," Mom replies.

"If you really mean that, then a BMW would make me ecstatic. Mimi's getting a car for her birthday."

"You'll get a car when you graduate from high school," Mom replies. "That's the way it's always been in my family."

I say, "I keep telling Uncle Reed that you two should change that with your own kids."

Mom chuckles. "I don't think so. I like it the way it is."

"I'm making good grades in school, I don't miss curfew—can't you make an exception?"

"Divine, getting behind the wheel of a car carries a huge responsibility. I'm not buying you a car until I'm sure you're ready for something like that."

I just hate when she goes into Mom mode. So I say, "Aunt Phoebe's holding dinner, so can I call you back?"

"Sure. Give everyone my love."

"I will."

"Divine, I love you."

"I love you too."

After I hang up, I think, *If Mom really loved me like she claims she wouldn't have a problem giving up Kevin.*

I can't believe she's turned her back on me like this.

chapter 13

"*Guess* what?" Madison says as soon as he walks up to me right after first period on Tuesday morning.

We share a quick kiss.

"What?"

"My parents left this morning to go to Augusta," Madison announces. "They won't be home until tomorrow evening."

You're telling me this, why? I wonder. As far as I'm concerned, all it means is that his hateful sister is in charge and we probably won't get any phone time. I say, "See, that's why you need a cell phone, Madison. You know Marcia's going to be on the phone all night with her boyfriend."

"Leon will probably be at the house with her," he responds. "But that's not why I'm telling you this."

"Then why?"

"I been thinking about you a lot lately. All the time, actually." Madison removes his backpack from his shoulder, setting it on the ground. "I'm digging this idea of us being husband and wife, and I'm thinking . . . we need to celebrate our marriage, Divine."

I break into a grin. "So what do you want to do?"

"Skip fifth and sixth period with me. We can leave school right after lunch."

"Are you serious?"

Nodding, he responds, "Yeah. Divine, I really need to be alone with you."

I consider his suggestion. "I don't want to get into any trouble, Madison. If my aunt and uncle find out I skipped school—it's over for me. I might as well be dead."

"They won't find out," he assures me. "The school doesn't call home if you sign out early."

"Why would I be signing out early? I don't have a note—they'll check with Aunt Phoebe for sure."

"My friend Tony works in the office during fifth period," Madison announces. "He'll sign us out. Nobody will know that we're skipping classes."

"Are you sure?" I want to know.

"Mrs. Addison is always on the telephone running her mouth. She don't really pay attention to what's going on. Tony's done this before and never got caught."

The thought of being alone with my boo is so tempting. But an image of my death is at the forefront of my mind. Because that's exactly what will happen if my aunt and my mother find out.

"So what are we gon' do?" he prompts.

"You're sure we won't get caught?" I question once more. I'd die of humiliation if I got busted trying to sneak out of school to kick it with Madison. News like that would spread through school like wildfire.

"We'll leave separately. You leave out the front but stop in the office first. Make sure you act like you're talking with Tony. He's gonna tell you that your aunt is picking you up and to meet her out in front of the school."

Going against my better judgment, I say, "Okay—but if this doesn't go the way we plan, I'm not going anywhere. I'm not looking to make Aunt Phoebe crazy."

Madison nods in agreement. "I don't want that either."

"Are you sure we're not going to get caught, Madison?"

"Stop being such a scaredy-cat, Divine. It's time to grow up."

"Excuse me?"

"You know what I mean. Sometimes we have to take risks for our relationship if we want it to work out."

"I'm all for taking risks—I just don't like the life-threatening ones."

Acting as normal as possible, I go to my second-period class.

Madison's words play over and over in my mind. I know what he's asking me to do is wrong, but I want to spend some time alone with him. Uncle Reed and Aunt Phoebe will punish me for the rest of my teenage life if I skip school, but that's only if they find out.

I put my hands to my face, trying to decide if spending a couple of hours with my boo is really worth such a big risk. His plan isn't bad, I reason silently. It could work.

Madison dominates my thoughts through third and fourth periods. I'm still conflicted about skipping school, although I don't want to disappoint him.

After fourth period ends, I rush off to the cafeteria to meet up with Alyssa, Stacy and Penny. I'm tempted to confide in my cousin, but I already know what she'll tell me. It's what I've been thinking all along: I need to say no to Madison. The problem is that I *want* to skip school with him.

"What's on your mind?" Alyssa questions as we stand in line for pizza. "You look like you're trying to figure out something in your head."

"I need to make a decision about this thing," I respond, deliberately being as vague as possible.

"What thing? Are you talking about your mom's engagement?"

"Yeah," I reply.

Penny and Stacy join us as we near the counter.

"Thanks for holding a spot for us," Penny says. "I put our books and backpacks on the table. Trina's watching everything for us. She's waiting on Chance so they can leave for lunch."

"Where are they going?" I ask.

"Subway," Stacy answers. "They don't like the sandwiches here."

Alyssa sighs. "I wish I'd known before I bought this pizza. I could go for a ham-and-cheese sub right now."

"I'm in the mood for pizza," I say.

Penny and Stacy agree.

We purchase our food and stroll through the crowded lunchroom to our table. Chance arrives seconds later to get Trina.

"Chance, can you get me a six-inch ham-and-cheese with everything?" Alyssa asks. "I don't have any money with me but I'll give it to you when I get home."

He nods. "We're just picking up our food, so we'll be back in a few minutes."

I wave them off before saying the blessing. My stomach growls, a firm reminder that I'm hungry. I take a bite of my pepperoni pizza while Stacy, Penny and Alyssa are in gossip mode. Normally, I enjoy a juicy piece of gossip but today my mind is still on skipping school with Madison.

Fifth period is next and I still haven't decided if I'm really going to go through with it. *Maybe he'll change his mind or his friend can't help him out,* I tell myself.

Chance and Trina return with Alyssa's sandwich just as we're cleaning up and gathering our stuff.

The bell rings.

I see Madison for a few moments before walking into my world history class.

"I'll be outside waiting for you," he whispers.

Here's my chance to get out of skipping school, but Madison's my boo. I don't want to disappoint him, so I don't say anything.

He hugs me. "Don't be scared, baby. Everything is gonna work out perfect."

I nearly jump out of my skin when I hear my name called over the intercom, telling me to come to the office with my backpack because I'm leaving for the day.

I'm nervous when I walk into the office. I spot Tony immediately and walk over to where he's standing.

Mrs. Addison looks up from her desk. "Hi, Divine. I didn't see your aunt come in—I must have been in the copy room. Tell her I said hello."

"I will."

Guilt seeps from my pores.

A few tension-filled moments later, I walk through the doors of Temple High and down the sidewalk.

Madison is hiding behind a tree. He nearly scares me to death when I hear him say, "See, I told you we wouldn't get into any trouble."

"Boy, my nerves already frazzled. Don't be jumping out at me like that. As far as trouble goes . . . well, the day's not over yet," I state, walking as fast as my feet will carry me.

I don't want to get caught leaving campus even though it's assumed I have permission. The least amount of lying I have to do, the better I'll feel about doing something so wrong. I can't believe how easily I gave in to this temptation. I'm breaking a major rule, but being with my boo is so worth the risk I'm taking. I just want to spend time with him—parents don't understand, or at least they pretend they don't.

Parents don't want us to have any fun.

My stomach is nervous and my knees are shaking when I walk into the house with Madison. Meeting his gaze, I ask once again, "Are you positive your parents won't be coming home? I don't want to get caught here in your house. I know your mom would call Aunt Phoebe with a quickness."

"Stop worrying, baby. My parents are out of town," he responds. "They won't be back until tomorrow."

"What about your sister? When does she usually get here?" Madison's sister has her own place but she comes over like every day. I don't know why she even moved out.

"Divine," Madison tells me, "it's just me and you, baby." He pulls me into his arms, holding me close.

We stand there all hugged up for a few minutes.

"This feels so good, holding you in my arms like this," Madison whispers in my ear.

I totally agree.

"We don't have to worry about anybody seeing us or telling us we're too close. We can do whatever we want right now. Cool, huh?"

I nod.

Madison gives me a tour of his house, which isn't very big. It's still a little hard for me to grasp how people can live in such tiny houses. The rooms, though small, are very neat and nicely decorated. I'm so glad that Uncle Reed had the house remodeled but it always shrinks in size whenever I go stay a few days with Mom. I'm crazy about Madison, but if he wants to marry me for real, he's gonna have to buy me a big house.

Holding my hand, Madison takes me down the hall to a bedroom. "This is my room."

I smile. "I figured that. It looks like a boy's room." I stroll over to the poster of Ciara and say, "You need to take this down. The pictures in here should be of me."

My boo tells me exactly what I need to hear. "It ain't nothing but a piece of paper. With you—I got the real thing." Madison gestures for me to sit down on the edge of his bed. "Baby, make yourself comfortable," he tells me. "I have a present for you."

Madison's said the magic words. Nothing eases my mind like getting gifts.

Breaking into a grin, I ask, "What is it?"

He opens the top drawer of his nightstand and pulls out a little black box. His eyes meeting mine, Madison tells me, "I'm really feeling you, Divine. You don't know how much I love you. That's why when you told me about this Internet marriage stuff—I wanted to do it. I felt like I needed to show you how much I wanted to be with you."

My heart is beating so fast, I feel like it's about to jump right out of my chest.

Madison hands the box to me. "Open it."

I do and tears fill my eyes. It's a wedding band.

"I have one, too." Madison slips on his ring.

"Madison, what . . ." I'm not real sure what he's trying to tell me. "Why'd you buy me this?"

"I want to make our marriage a real one, Divine. I love you and I want to be with you forever." He takes the ring out of the box and places it on my finger. "I hope you feel the same way."

"I do," I murmur. A tiny shiver ripples through me while my heart starts hammering foolishly.

We fall back on the bed, kissing. My calm is shattered by the hunger I feel for Madison. Nothing will ever come between us.

"I love you so much, girl."

"I love you too."

Madison soon reclaims my lips, his tongue exploring my mouth. "I want you," he whispers, his words becoming smothered on my lips.

"We're married," I whisper.

"I want it to be real," he tells me. "Don't you?"

I nod.

"We can make that happen right now."

"How?" I ask, although I have a feeling where this is leading. Madison wants to have sex. In a way, I want him just as bad, but the fear of getting pregnant or my mom finding out is heavy on my mind.

"A marriage isn't valid without making love, Divine."

"It's gonna take more than that," I respond. "Like a pastor or something. That's the only way our marriage can be valid. I'm not stupid, you know."

"I didn't say you were. I did some checking myself and you don't have to be married by a preacher to have a real marriage. We've already said vows, and if we make love . . . in the eyes of God, we're married. To make it legal, *then* we need a marriage license. The only thing that really matters is how God sees it."

"For real?"

Madison nods. "Yeah. Being married legally and being married in the eyes of God are two different things."

I make a mental note to check with Uncle Reed about this, but I have to find a way to do it without making him suspicious. Maybe he'll just assume I'm referring to my mom's impending marriage.

"I thought this would make you happy, Divine. I thought you really wanted to be my wifey."

"I do," I respond. "You're my boo." I wrap my arms around him. "Madison, I'm very happy and I do want to be your wifey."

We kiss.

"I can't believe we're alone . . . finally."

I agree. My body is trembling like crazy.

"Are you scared, baby?"

I don't want Madison to think I'm a big baby, so I lie and shake my head.

"I want you so bad . . . Divine, I've dreamed about this moment for a long time."

His hands take on a life of their own.

I'm shocked by my own eager response. I finally understand what Aunt Phoebe means when she says that kissing makes babies. It's so easy to get caught up in emotions.

Madison takes off my top.

STOP.

I jump.

"What's wrong?" Madison questions.

It's then that I realize the voice I thought I heard telling us to stop had to be my own conscience.

"Divine . . ." he prompts. "You okay?"

I suddenly feel self-conscious and cross my arms to hide my black lace bra. No boy has ever seen me like this.

"Don't be scared," he tells me. "I'm not gonna hurt you, Divine."

"I'm not s-scared," I lie.

He tries to draw my arms away, but fails to break my iron grip. He pulls away from me, his eyes full of confusion. "What's up, Divine? Why you acting like you don't want to do this?"

I detect a hint of irritation in his voice.

"Madison, I can't."

"Why not? Don't you want to make love?"

"I want you like crazy, but . . . Madison, I'm just not ready for sex. I'm not on any kind of birth control and I don't want to get pregnant."

"I have condoms."

My heart is racing, beating so loud I can't help but wonder if he can hear it.

"Divine—"

"Madison, it's wrong."

He sighs. "That's your mom and your aunt talking. What does your body tell you? That's what you should be listening to—you need to think for yourself."

"I'm listening to my mind and it's telling me that this is wrong," I respond in a low voice. I'm conflicted by my mind and my emotions.

"If sex is so wrong, why would God have created it?"

"So that people could be fruitful and multiply," I state after a moment. "The Bible says that it's a sin to have sex when you're not married."

"Maybe it was back in the day, but everybody's doing it now. And if I remember, they was all doing it back then too. Women weren't waiting for marriage back then," Madison states. "They went and got pregnant all the time. What about that queen—Esther? She went and got busy with the king before they got married. God didn't punish *her.*"

"Madison, that still doesn't change the fact that I'm not feeling right about this." I pick up my shirt and slip back into it. "I'm sorry."

I could tell that he wasn't happy with the turn of events, but I didn't care. I just wanted to leave.

"We might as well go back to school then."

I get off the bed, saying, "Madison, please don't be mad."

"I'm not mad, Divine. Just disappointed."

"Well, it's not like we haven't discussed this before."

"Divine, you're ready—you just listening to your aunt and uncle. He's a preacher, what else is he supposed to say? Chance has a child. What can they tell you? Not a thing."

"Madison, I told you not to pressure me about sex. I don't know if I'll wait until marriage. That's the plan, but right now I can't afford to mess up. I'm not on birth control or nothing. I don't want any children."

"Neither do I—not right now, anyway. But you don't have to worry about that—I have some condoms."

"Madison, if you haven't had sex why do you have condoms?" I want to know.

"I got them from a friend."

I'm not entirely sure I believe him. "When?"

"Divine, why you tripping?"

My arms folded across my chest, I say, "I'm just asking a question. Don't think you're going to play me for a fool. I don't roll that way, Madison."

Madison is quiet.

"Are you going to answer my question?"

"I told you the truth, Divine. I got them from a friend of mine."

I'm not sure I believe him but since I'm not in the mood for a big fight, I just let the matter drop. For now.

I follow Madison to the front of the house. He walks to the front door, opening it wide. "Let's go. School will be letting out soon."

I feel like a cold wind just blew through me.

chapter 14

Madison walks me halfway back to Temple. I try to get him to talk but he doesn't say much. Just before he leaves, Madison gives me a reminder. "Hey, don't go back on campus, Divine. You're supposed to have gone home early. But if you do run into one of your teachers, just tell them that your aunt dropped you off to walk with Alyssa."

"That doesn't make sense, Madison," I say. "Why wouldn't she just pick her up?"

"Then just tell them whatever. I'll see you later."

I've barely set foot back on campus when the bell rings and students come rushing out of the building. I walk over to where Alyssa and I usually meet up after school.

Alyssa's clearly surprised to see me out there before her. She's usually the first one to arrive because her class is a few yards away.

"How did you get here so fast?" she asks me. "Did
out early or something?"

I shake my head. "I'll tell you later. Here comes Cha

Alyssa steals a look over her shoulder. "He looks ups
something."

"He and Trina must've gotten into a fight."

Frowning, Chance marches over to where we're standing.

"Where's Trina?" I ask.

Instead of answering my question, Chance asks one of his own. "What's going on with y'all?"

"Boy, what are you talking about?" Alyssa demands. "Just 'cause you and Trina not getting along, don't be taking it out on us."

"This don't have nothing to do with me and Trina. I've been hearing some things around school about y'all. I heard y'all got married, but that can't be true. I know better than that 'cause y'all way too smart to do something crazy like that."

Alyssa and I look at each other.

"Well?" he prompts, looking from me to Alyssa. "So, why people going around here saying you married, Alyssa? *Divine?*"

I feign innocence. "Chance, I can't believe you listening to a bunch of mess."

"Why are people saying you and Madison married?" he repeats.

A shiver of panic runs through me. I answer, "I don't know. People say stupid stuff all the time." I figure we can just play it off. Chance knows it doesn't take much for rumors to run rampant.

He surprises me by grabbing my hand. "Then why you wearing this?" Chance inquires, referring to the wedding band Madison gave me not even an hour earlier.

A wave of apprehension sweeps through me as I realize that I'm so busted.

Alyssa gasps. "Girl, when did you get that?"

I can't deal with Alyssa right now. My sole focus is making sure Chance doesn't get me in trouble. My chest feels like its about to burst.

"Chance . . ." I'm at a loss for words. I could kick myself for forgetting to take off this stupid wedding ring. "It's not what you think."

He just stands there shaking his head in disbelief. "Divine, Mama gon' have a fit when she gets this piece of news!"

"Chance, you can't say anything," I say. My stomach's churning with anxiety from skipping school and now this. I can't handle all this lying and sneaking around.

He ignores me, choosing instead to start in on his sister. "Alyssa, I know you didn't go and do the same thing following after Divine? You know Mama and Dad don't play no mess like this."

"Chance," I interject. "What do you mean by that? Alyssa has her own mind. She don't need to follow after me for nothing. Besides, these are only cyber-weddings—they're not real. *Dang* . . . people can't have a little fun sometime?"

"If this is just for fun, then tell me why you wearing a ring," he demands.

"Madison just gave it to me, but it means nothing," I say. "Chance, please don't go running your mouth to Aunt Phoebe and Uncle Reed starting mess. This is just a game."

"What kind of game?" he demands.

"Role-playing. People do it all the time on the Internet. You know how people have virtual pets?" When Chance nods, I continue, "Well, this is a virtual marriage. That's all."

"But people are thinking you and Madison married for real, Divine."

"But we're not," I counter. I stand here, clenching my hand until I can feel my nails biting into my palm. "It's not a big deal, Chance."

"Then why did he give you a ring?"

"He loves me, Chance . . . like duh . . ."

"It's just role-playing," Alyssa contributes. Her weak attempt at backing me, I guess. She's been standing there all silent and looking scared mostly. "Chance, don't say anything. *Please.*"

"If it's just a game—why you don't want Mama and Daddy to know?"

"Because they wouldn't like it," I respond. "That's why. You know how your parents trip sometimes. Promise us you won't say anything. Please . . ."

"All I can say is that y'all better hope they don't find out. But you know what Mama always says: what's done in the dark will come to light. I'm staying out of this mess. I just wanted to make sure y'all didn't do anything stupid."

Alyssa steps into my path when Chance walks off to meet Trina.

"Divine, when did Madison give you a wedding ring? You didn't have that before."

"Today. Not too long ago actually." I grab her by the arm, pulling her close so that I can whisper, "I skipped school with Madison and we went to his house. That's when he gave me the ring."

Her mouth drops open in shock. "Divine, tell me you didn't . . . *did you?* Oh my gosh! I can't believe you went out and did it—especially after all the lectures you gave me when I was thinking about having sex with Stephen. You are such a hypocrite. I can't bel—"

I interrupt her rant by saying, "Shut up, Alyssa. Let me finish . . . pleeze."

Alyssa folds her arms across her chest. "What?"

"Madison and I didn't have sex," I state. Keeping my voice low, I continue, "He wanted to and so did I but we didn't. I told him no, so you can stop fussing."

Alyssa wasn't ready to let up on me. "Then why did you go over there in the first place?"

"Because I wanted to spend time alone with him. The only time I really get to see Madison is here at school."

"I can't believe you skipped your classes like that."

"I just hope it doesn't come back to kick me in the butt. If Uncle Reed and Aunt Phoebe ever find out—I don't even want to think about it."

"Well, you better hope nobody called home and told Aunt Phoebe you didn't go to class."

"I don't think they will," I respond quietly.

"What makes you so special?"

"The office thinks that I left because I had an appointment. They think that Aunt Phoebe picked me up."

"Oooh . . . Girl, you messing with fire."

"It was Madison's idea. Not mine. I didn't set any of this stuff up."

"You still went along with it. Mama would say that makes you just as guilty."

Another knot forms in my stomach. "Alyssa, please don't say anything about this."

"I'm not."

"I need you to promise me."

"I said I wouldn't, Divine. *I mean it.* Mama will punish me for not saying anything. You don't tell her that I knew about it if she finds out."

"I won't," I vow.

We head home.

"So how did Madison act when he found out that you weren't gonna have sex with him?"

I glance over my shoulder to make sure we can't be overheard. "He wasn't too happy about it. All he said was that we might as well go back to school. You haven't seen him, have you, Alyssa?"

She shakes her head. "I didn't see him when school let out."

"He walked me back to the corner. I thought he might still be around. I guess he's mad but I don't care. I told him that I didn't want to get pregnant. He said that he had condoms."

"Why does he have condoms?" Alyssa questions.

"I asked him about it and he said he got them from a friend."

"Do you believe that?"

"I don't know," I respond.

"Divine, what if he breaks up with you again?"

"He can do what he wants to do," I reply. The reason Madison and I broke up before is because I wouldn't have sex with him. I almost didn't take him back so I don't think he'll make the same mistake twice. But I don't know . . . Deep down, I can't easily dismiss the rumors about Madison sleeping with Brittany when we were broken up.

"Are you worried about it?" Alyssa inquires.

"A little," I confess. "I don't want to lose Madison but I just couldn't do it. I kept thinking about everything I've told you and about what Aunt Phoebe, Uncle Reed and especially my mom always tell me. I'm just not ready for something like that."

"You better not be telling me one thing and doing something else. That's not cool."

"I know," I respond with a laugh. "Don't get me wrong, Alyssa. I really wanted to do it. We even went as far as getting undressed."

"Madison saw you naked?"

"He saw me in my bra. I made him stop after that."

"Did you see him in his underwear?"

I shake my head no. "Madison had his shirt off. I stopped things before they went too far."

"Stephen's still trying to get down with me. Girl, he be begging every day—all day."

"You know that's all they think about," I say. "I bet Trina and Chance still doing it. Especially since she's on birth control now."

"Eewww . . ."

I laugh. "Ugh. Don't make that face, Alyssa."

Even though we're laughing about everything, I feel really guilty for skipping school. I keep trying to convince myself that because I didn't have sex with Madison what I'd done wasn't so bad. But the truth is I'm not even buying it myself.

After dinner, Aunt Phoebe brings out my all-time favorite dessert, chocolate mousse cake.

"What's this for?" I ask.

"This is just my way of showing you how proud I am of you, sugar. You're doing so well in school and you've matured into a really sweet young lady. As you kids like to say, I'm showing some love."

Okay, *now* I feel worse.

"Thanks so much," I manage between stiff lips. "I appreciate it."

"You're so welcome, sugar."

She might as well just stab me in the heart.

I feel like I have to do something nice for her, so I say, "Aunt Phoebe, don't worry about the kitchen. I'll clean it tonight."

She looks stunned. "Have mercy . . . thanks, sugar."

In the kitchen, Alyssa asks, "What's wrong with you, Divine? You barely touched your dessert. Mama made it special for you. And then you volunteer to do the dishes, something you hate doing. Girl, what's up?"

"Alyssa, I swear she knows what I did and that's why she's being so nice. She's trying to kill me with kindness. *I can't take it.*"

Alyssa chuckles. "You're crazy."

"Really, I think she knows. That's why she's saying all that stuff, because she knows it'll make me crack."

"So, you're gonna go in there and tell Mama and Daddy that you skipped school?"

I shake my head. "Girl, I'm going to take a shower and get in my bed. I'm not talking to them anymore tonight."

"Why? You scared that you might just all of a sudden blurt it out?"

"Yeah. And I don't need that."

I clean the kitchen with Alyssa's help. We wash dishes since my aunt and uncle still refuse to buy a dishwasher like normal people. Then Alyssa sweeps the floor while I wipe down the appliances and the cabinets. We're done in no time.

I go to my room and get started on my homework.

Rhyann calls around nine for no reason in particular. I believe she's just bored; Mimi must've been either too busy or she wasn't answering her telephone.

"Hey, girl . . ." she greets me when I answer my cell.

I pull the folds of my robe together and drop down on the edge of my bed. "Aren't you supposed to be doing homework or something?"

"I'll get to it sometime tonight," she responds. "You know when I get home I need a minute to get my head together. What about you? You still studying?"

"Naw . . . I just got out the shower. So what's up?"

"Not a thing. Just calling to talk to my girl."

"Did you ever find your prom dress?" I inquire. "The last time I talked to you you were at the Beverly Center looking for one."

"I saw one I liked in Bloomingdale's but that dress cost almost three hundred dollars. I'm sorry but I don't roll like that. I can't spend that kind of money on a dress I'm never gonna wear again. Matter of fact . . . Divine, send me one of your designer dresses you wore to the Grammys or Soul Train Awards—you know you won't be wearing them again."

"Rhyann, you're crazy," I say before chuckling.

"No, I'm broke. You'll save me some money."

"Are you serious?"

"Yeah."

"But I've probably been photographed in them."

"Dee, I don't care about that. I'll wear it and still look fly."

"If you're for real—I'll send you a couple. Like you said, I won't be wearing them again, so you can have them."

"Cool. I'll have a prom dress and one for my winter formal or homecoming next year."

While still on the phone with Rhyann, I email her a couple of photos with me wearing the dresses I plan on sending her.

"Girl, I love that jade green one. I'm wearing that one to the prom."

"What size shoe do you wear now?"

"I'm still in a seven—same as you."

"I didn't know if your feet grew," I respond. "That's why I asked."

We talk for almost an hour before saying good-bye.

I hear Uncle Reed and Aunt Phoebe out in the hallway talking to Chance, who must have just gotten home from work.

I pull out my case of assorted beads and other materials to make jewelry and bring it over to my bed.

The rest of my evening is spent making bracelets. A couple of times I stop long enough to call Madison, but his younger sister, Chrystal, keeps telling me that he's not home.

I don't know why, but I have this feeling that Madison's upset with me and that's why he's not taking my calls. He already knows where I stand when it comes to sex. But if we were married for real it would be different.

chapter 15

We're up early Saturday morning to take care of our chores so we can hang out at the mall with Penny and Stacy after my tae kwon do class.

The first task I undertake is the cleaning of my closet, but only because Aunt Phoebe's been on my case about it for the past week. It's overflowing with clothes—a lot of them I haven't even worn yet. I take out the pieces I'm bored with or are no longer in style and toss them on the floor. I also pack a box of gowns and shoes to ship to Rhyann.

After I finish cleaning my closet, I decide to go through my jewelry. The first piece I lay eyes on is the ring Madison gave me. I break into a smile as I put it on my finger.

I can't let Aunt Phoebe or Uncle Reed catch this on my hand so I decide to wear it around my neck. They'll just think I'm making a fashion statement.

I find a gold chain that's perfect, slip the ring on it and put it around my neck before resuming my task.

Since I love all of my jewelry, I close the lid of my jewelry box and head out of the room.

"Benson's Boutique is having a great sale this weekend," I announce when I stroll into Alyssa's bedroom. "I'm going to get me some new clothes. I've cleaned out my closet so if you want any of that stuff—just take it. I'm going to give the rest to Aunt Phoebe for the women's shelter."

Alyssa returns her attention to making up her bed. "I'll go through the stuff in a minute. There might not be nothing left for Mama to give away—I love all of your clothes."

"Have you already gone through your stuff?" I ask. When she shakes her head, I say, "Give them what you don't want anymore. That way, we're still making donations."

Alyssa laughs. "Yeah. I take your designer hand-me-downs and give away all of my non-designer stuff. Works for me."

I steal a peek over my shoulder. "Don't let Aunt Phoebe hear you say that."

"Too late," she responds from the hallway. "I heard her."

Alyssa rushes into speech. "I'm not trying to say that you don't pick out good clothes, Mama. I just want—"

Aunt Phoebe finishes for her. "Some designer outfits like the ones Divine wears. I know. But honeychile . . . your Aunt Kara's got deep pockets. We don't."

"I don't mean to sound ungrateful."

I could tell that Alyssa's worried she's hurt Aunt Phoebe's feelings.

"I think it's nice of you to donate what you don't wear out of your closet. No need in it just sitting in there."

"Mama, are you mad?"

Aunt Phoebe shakes her head. "Not at all. In fact, you and Divine have inspired me. I'ma go and clean out my closet too."

"After you throw everything away," I interject, "we'll go shopping with you to help pick out some really nice 'first lady' suits. I'll have you looking fierce, Aunt Phoebe. You'll be the best-looking preacher's wife in Georgia."

"Sugar, I'm not trying to be no fashion plate."

That much is obvious, I think.

Aunt Phoebe narrows her eyes as if she knows exactly what I'm thinking.

I feign innocence. "What?"

"Don't think I can't read your mind."

"I didn't do nothing."

"You were thinking it, though," Aunt Phoebe responds with a laugh. "Divine, sugar, you don't even know how transparent you are sometimes."

"Aunt Phoebe, I just want you to shine. Look at the president's wife. She's always dressed nice." I quickly add, "You dress nice, but sometimes you wear the wrong colors."

"I love color—bright colors."

"You like *neon* colors," I correct her. "But they're out of style now."

"I'm not afraid to take a chance or a fashion risk," Aunt Phoebe says all proud.

I bite back my laughter. "You should be afraid. Very afraid. Some of your outfits are scary."

"Just for that, you get to mop the kitchen floor."

"Aunt Phoebe . . ." I whine. "Pleeze don't make me stick my hands on an ugly ol' mop and in dirty, stinky water. I can't stand it."

She laughs. "Aren't you getting a manicure today?"

"Yes ma'am."

"Then you don't have to worry about your hands. Go on . . . get busy."

"You know this is cruel and unusual punishment, don't you? I believe it's against the law."

Aunt Phoebe gives another short laugh. "Then sue me, sugar. But until then—get busy."

I glance over at Alyssa.

"Don't look at me," she says. "I had to do it last weekend when I talked about her hairstyle."

We meet up with Stacy and Penny outside the main entrance of the Carrollton Mall, one of our favorite hangouts on the weekends.

"Divine, I just heard that your mom is engaged to Kevin Nash with his fine self," Penny says. "It was on the radio when we were driving over here."

I don't respond.

"Did you hear what I said?"

"I heard you, Penny. I just don't want to think about my mom being married to that man."

"But I thought you liked Kevin?"

I stop walking and say, "Penny, he's okay. I just don't think he's the right person to be my stepfather."

"He's cute and sexy," she responds. "He could be my stepdaddy anytime."

Ugh. Screwing up my face, I utter, "Stop talking about him like that, Penny. You say that now, but I don't think you'd want your parents to break up."

"No, I don't," she admits. "But if they did—I'd for sure take Kevin to be my new daddy."

Alyssa chuckles. "Divine, just chill. You know if he wasn't going out with Aunt Kara you'd be going crazy over him too."

"So is it true?" Stacy questions. "Are they really engaged?"

"For now," I answer. "It probably won't last."

Frowning, Penny steals a look at Alyssa, then back at me. "Why did you say that?"

"Hollywood relationships don't last long, or haven't you heard?"

"Divine, you need to stop talking like that," Alyssa states.

"Well, it's true," I insist. "Madison and I have been together longer than Mom and Kevin. It's way too soon for them to even think about getting engaged. She'd have a fit if I came home talking about marrying some boy I've only been dating for a couple of months. You know Aunt Phoebe would be having one of her hissy fits too."

Both Penny and Alyssa agree.

I hear someone calling my name and turn around. Two girls I don't know are walking up to us. "What's up?" I say to be polite while silently wondering what these females want with me.

"Hey, y'all," one replies. "Divine, we heard about you and Madison hooking up online. Can you give us the website?"

"I'm sorry—do we know you?" Stacy asks with a bit of attitude.

"I'm Jill and this is my friend LaKisha."

"Where did you hear that Madison and I got married?" I ask.

"From some friends at school."

Great, I think. *Pretty soon it's going to be all over town.*

"Divine, your secret's safe," Jill assures me. "We're not gonna tell people where we got the information from. We promise. My boyfriend and I wanna do it too. We heard that you can get a wedding for free."

"I heard you can get a divorce online too," LaKisha says. "In case you change your mind about the marriage."

"You do know this is just for fun?" I point out.

She nods.

I pull a piece of paper from my purse and a pen. "This is the website."

"Thanks, Divine."

When they leave, I say, "I've started a trend."

"You've started something," Penny states. "I can't believe that everybody wants to go online to get married. It's not like it's for real."

"You just mad because you can't get Charlie to do it," Alyssa says.

"For your information Charlie and I are planning to wait until we finish college to get married and when we do—it'll be the real thing."

I give Penny a sidelong glance. "You guys are already talking marriage?"

She nods. "We talk a lot about our future. Charlie wants to be a doctor and I plan on being a nurse. We're going to work together."

"Good luck with that," I tell her. "A lot can happen over the years."

"Now you sound like Mama," Alyssa responds. "You know how much you hate it when she says that to you."

"Mind your own business, Alyssa," I tell her.

I can't stand it when she's right.

When we get back home, Alyssa and I have to go down to the church with Aunt Phoebe. She and some of the members of the Youth Ministry are hosting a pizza party for TeenTalk.

Alyssa and I chat with some of the other girls while the adults get the food and drinks ready.

I yawn. I'm beginning to feel tired after the day I've had. I got up practically at the crack of dawn to do chores, and then went to my tae kwon do class and the mall afterward. Now I'm here for the teen ministry—it's totally been a long day.

When the food is ready, I grab a slice of vegetarian pizza and a slice of pepperoni. "I'm getting my veggies in," I tell Aunt Phoebe, who chuckles.

While we eat, Aunt Phoebe talks to us about surviving our teenage years. As if she remembers what it feels like to be a teenager. That was like, such a long time ago. Personally, I think she's been old forever. Sure, I've seen pictures of her when she was younger. She and Mom were party girls, but even then, Aunt Phoebe always looked like she was the really mature one.

Miss Eula calls people like that old souls.

That fits Aunt Phoebe to a tee.

Tax day.

What's the big deal? I wonder. Since Sunday was the fifteenth, today is the official due date to file. Aunt Phoebe and Uncle Reed spent the last week with the accountant going over their taxes. This morning, one of our teachers was late because she was stuck at the post office trying to mail off her forms. At least that's what I overheard the substitute saying.

I remember a couple of years ago, one of Jerome's actor friends got in trouble for not paying his taxes. It was in all the tabloids and newspapers 'cause he owed, like, millions.

Big deal.

I go through the motions of being a good student, although my heart's not entirely in it right now. Madison is prominent in my thoughts.

He's still acting kind of weird around me. We used to talk for hours every single night, but now I'm lucky if I even reach him. Madison says that Chrystal has suddenly discovered the telephone but I'm not sure I really believe him. I think he's still upset that I wouldn't have sex with him.

After school, Alyssa and I meet up in our usual spot.

A tall, muscular boy walks by us. He meets my gaze and smiles.

I smile back.

When he's out of hearing range, I say, "T. J. Wellington is so cute. Not as cute as my boo though."

Alyssa agrees. "He's in my English lit class. That boy can play some basketball. I think he's probably the best on the team."

Alyssa's right: T. J. has skills. I have a strong feeling he's going to be picked up by the NBA before he graduates from college. He's just that good.

We spot Chance and Trina up ahead, so we run to catch up with them.

"I thought y'all was halfway home by now," Chance says.

"I was waiting on the diva here," Alyssa responds.

I give her a playful shove. "Whatever . . ."

Trina's back up a notch on my friend list since she's been acting better and not giving Chance a hard time.

"You and Madison okay?" she asks me.

"Yeah," I respond, puzzled by her question. "Why?"

"I haven't really seen you two together lately."

"We're fine," I lie, then change the subject by quickly asking, "How's Joshua? Is he sitting up by himself yet?"

Trina laughs. "No. Divine, he's only five weeks old."

"That's all?" I ask. "Girl, it seems like he's been around here for months. I thought you were supposed to be home for six weeks or something like that?"

"I could've stayed out but I didn't want to—I was ready to come back to school. I needed to get out of the house."

Chance walks Trina all the way home, so Alyssa and I keep straight to our house.

Both Aunt Phoebe and Uncle Reed are home.

After grabbing a snack, we take off to our bedrooms to get started on homework.

I'm halfway done with my math when Alyssa blows through

my bedroom door looking panicked. "Mama and Daddy want to talk to us. I think we're in trouble."

My heart starts to race. "For what?"

She shrugs. "I don't know. Do you think the school called about you skipping class? It's either that or Chance ran his big mouth. I can't stand him sometimes."

"I don't think Chance said anything. I just hope they don't know that I skipped school with Madison," I whisper. "We didn't do anything. We just went to his house and talked."

"It won't matter if you went over there for Bible study, Divine. Mama will have a hissy fit if she knows."

Gazing at Alyssa, I ask, "Did you slip up and say something?"

"No. Why would I do something like that?"

"To get me in trouble."

Alyssa looks hurt by my words. "Divine, I'm not like that and you know it."

"Sorry but I had to ask. I guess we better get out there," I say. "Don't go out there acting all guilty, Alyssa. Aunt Phoebe knows you like a book."

"I don't have anything to be guilty about. *I* didn't skip school."

"Why don't you say that just a little bit louder? I don't think they heard you."

Alyssa lowers her voice. "Sorry."

"They may know about the virtual marriages," I remind her. "Someone from school could've called and told them."

I'm so dead.

"We'd better go out there," Alyssa says reluctantly.

I nod, trying to swallow my panic.

My aunt and uncle are seated side by side when Alyssa and I walk into the family room.

"We've been talking." Uncle Reed begins. "About you and Divine."

Alyssa and I exchange nervous looks. We have no idea what to expect. Aunt Phoebe looks like everything is okay but sometimes she does that to throw us off. Uncle Reed's expression hardly changes so it's hard to read his mood.

Aunt Phoebe eyes me. "What's wrong, Divine? You look like a scared deer caught in the headlights."

"Nothing," I respond quietly. "Just wondering why you wanted to see us."

Her eyes travel to Alyssa. "You sure? You two look . . . I don't know . . . guilty about something."

"I don't have anything to feel guilty about," Alyssa replies quickly.

"I don't either," I say.

We sit down side by side on the love seat facing Uncle Reed and Aunt Phoebe, who isn't ready to just let this go. "You're sure there's not anything you two need to tell us?" she presses. When Aunt Phoebe asks this question, it's usually because she already knows what's going on. I prepare to confess. I open my mouth to speak but she holds up a hand.

"We want you and Alyssa to know how proud we are of y'all. You're doing well in school and you've been making curfew—being very responsible." Aunt Phoebe smiles. "I'm extremely proud of my girls."

Alyssa and I both sink down against the cushions in relief. I send up a quick prayer of thanks.

"We've been reconsidering our position where Madison and Stephen are concerned," Uncle Reed announces.

"What do you mean?" I ask.

"The boys can come over, but only on the weekends. I want to make sure you girls keep up your studies during the week."

I resist the urge to jump over the coffee table and plant a big wet kiss on Uncle Reed's cheek.

This is so cool!

"Pending your actions during this trial period," Aunt Phoebe begins, "we'll consider letting y'all double date or go out as a group." Raising a finger, she warns, "Don't mess up."

"We won't," Alyssa and I say in unison.

They lay out a few more rules, which I have to confess go in one ear and out the other. I'm hyped up because now I can kick it with my boo on the weekends. I can't wait to tell him.

Uncle Reed gets to his feet. "We have to go to the hospital to visit Deacon Daniels' wife—she had surgery yesterday. We'll be back in about an hour."

We walk them out to the car.

"Thanks so much," Alyssa tells her parents.

"We really appreciate it," I contribute.

When they pull out of the driveway, Alyssa loops her arm through mine. "We should do something special for them."

"Like what?"

"We could make dinner," Alyssa suggests.

"We'd better get started then. Uncle Reed said they'd be back in about an hour. We don't have long."

"Mama's gonna be so surprised when she gets home," Alyssa says. "Especially since we fried the chicken. She knows how much I hate frying any kind of meat. I always burn myself."

I step back when she puts the last batch of seasoned chicken into the fryer. I check on the corn on the cob and turn down the heat to keep the water from boiling over.

When Uncle Reed and Aunt Phoebe return home, Alyssa and I have dinner cooked and ready to be served.

"What's all this?" Aunt Phoebe asks, mildly surprised.

"We wanted to make dinner to show our appreciation," Alyssa announces.

"This is so sweet of y'all," Aunt Phoebe tells us. "Everything smells delicious."

"Oh, it's good," I say. "I'm not trying to brag, but we did a good job."

"Mama, you and Daddy sit down and get ready to eat. Divine, set the table—we're eating in the dining room tonight."

"You sure y'all don't need any help in the kitchen?"

"We got it, Aunt Phoebe."

In the kitchen, I whisper, "Did you see your mom's face? Alyssa, she was so happy. We really did a good job."

"Uh-huh. Mama likes when we do stuff like that. She feels appreciated and not taken for granted."

"I'm so glad that we can finally have boys over," I say, fingering the tiny gold band dangling on my chain.

"You better not let her see that ring," Alyssa warns.

I stick it back inside my shirt. "We sure don't need that to happen—it'd ruin everything. We're finally being treated like adults. It's about time."

Alyssa and I carry plates of fried chicken, corn on the cob, green beans and rolls to the table for Uncle Reed and Aunt Phoebe.

"Thank you, sweetie," Aunt Phoebe says. "This looks delicious."

We head back into the kitchen to get our plates. Uncle Reed gives the blessing as soon as we settle down in our seats.

I sample the chicken. "This is good."

Uncle Reed agrees. "You fried this chicken, Alyssa? It's almost as good as your mama's."

"I wouldn't say all that," I utter. I'm just hating because they haven't said anything about the corn or the beans.

Aunt Phoebe bites into the corn on the cob. "Divine, I like what you did with the corn. Did you add butter to the boiling water like Miss Eula does?"

"Yes ma'am," I say with a grin.

After dinner, Aunt Phoebe and Uncle Reed watch television in the den while Alyssa and I clean up the kitchen.

I call Madison as soon as I get to my room later that evening.

"You're not going to believe what happened—Uncle Reed and Aunt Phoebe said you and Stephen can come over on the weekends. Isn't that great news?"

"Sure."

His dry response shocks me. "Sure? That's all you have to say about it, Madison?"

"What do you want me to say?"

"I thought you'd be happy to spend some time with me outside of school. That's what you've been complaining about forever."

He doesn't respond.

"Madison?" I prompt.

"I'm here."

"You want to tell me what's wrong? Why are you acting so cold toward me? What did I do to you?"

"You didn't do nothing."

"Then why are you acting this way?" I want to know.

"Divine, I don't want to argue with you."

"I'm not trying to argue with you either. I called to tell you about my aunt and uncle changing their mind—you over there tripping."

"Let me call you back, Divine."

"Whatever . . ." I snipe and click off.

It's obvious to me that Madison's mad because I wouldn't have sex with him. We've already gone through this—I'm not feeling the drama.

It is too close to prom for him to start acting stupid now. I'll never forgive Madison if he ruins what should be one of the most important nights of my high school life.

That boy better get his head right.

chapter 16

Madison's been in a funky mood since that day we skipped school a week ago. I didn't see him at all this morning when I arrived at school, and I'm a little worried.

The bell rings.

On my way to second period, I see Madison near his locker. "Hey you," I say, pulling off to the side. "Are you upset with me or something?"

He doesn't look at me. Just shakes his head. "Why would I be mad with you?"

Keeping my voice low, I answer, "Because I wouldn't have sex with you that day we skipped school. I know that's what you were expecting."

He shrugs, seems more interested in the students walking all around us along the crowded hallway. "We cool."

"Why don't I believe that?"

Shrugging again, he responds, "I don't know."

"I'm not going through the same drama as before, Madison. If you don't want to be with me because I'm not doing the nasty with you—*be gone.*"

This time he meets my gaze and barks, "Why you tripping?"

No he didn't just raise his voice to me!

"First off, don't ever yell at me like that again. You know, I really don't like the way you're treating me right now. I told you when we got back together where I stood when it comes to sex. That hasn't changed." I roll my eyes at him. This boy is really acting stupid.

"Divine, tell me this: why did you come to my house with me then? What was that about? Huh?" Madison slips his backpack on.

A couple of kids nearby glance in our direction.

I stare them down until they turn away.

"Keep your voice down," I say. "I don't want everybody all in our business. To answer your question though, I went to your house because I wanted to spend time alone with you. It isn't all about sex for me, Madison."

He and I walk over to a nearby exit door for some privacy. "So you don't ever think about us in that way?"

I meet his gaze. "I didn't say that."

"*Do* you think about having sex, Divine?"

"I'm human," I reply. "I think about stuff like that, but I—"

He cuts me off, saying, "You been listening to all that church stuff. Divine, even people in the church are having sex. It can't be so wrong if everybody's doing it."

"I've never been a follower," I retort. "I have a brain of my own and I don't care what other people are doing—I do the thinking for me."

"Congratulations, Mr. and Mrs. Hartford," a girl says as she walks by.

"Tyson really has a big mouth," I complain to Madison. "He's going around telling everybody that we eloped."

Madison sighs in frustration. "I told that boy to shut up. I see now I'ma have to box him in the mouth."

"It's too late now, don't you think?" I snipe.

"Divine, I didn't think Tyson would go and tell the world about us. I was just confiding in my boys. I was happy and wanted to share our news."

"But you didn't want me telling anybody. You got some nerve."

"I don't wanna argue with you. We can talk later. I can't be late for my economics class."

Madison is gone before I can respond.

During second period, I replay our conversation over and over in my head. I can't believe he was tripping over my telling Alyssa when he told Stephen *and* Tyson! At least she's not a blabbermouth. To be honest though, I'm not that mad about it. Let those haters here at school know officially that my boo is off the market. That's right. Madison Hartford is mine.

I survive the rest of the school day. I didn't see Madison much so we haven't had a chance to talk. I guess I'll just have to wait and see what happens.

Alyssa's waiting for me in our usual spot. I wave when I see her. I hear someone call my name and turn around. It's Madison.

"Sorry about earlier, Divine."

"What's going on? And don't tell me there's no problem because I know something's wrong."

"Divine, sometimes this thing feels real to me," he confesses, bringing a big smile to my face. "That's why I wanted to make love to you. I'm sorry for trying to push you into it." Madison grins. "Girl, you just too sexy."

"Boo, I feel the same way."

We talk for a few minutes more before he says, "I can't walk home with you today. I need to take care of something."

"Okay. But call me later."

"I will."

"Well, Madison and I talked," I announce when I approach Alyssa. "I think we got everything cleared up."

She smiles. "That's good. It was looking kind of intense over there."

"I thought we were going to have a real issue," I confess. "But I'm glad he understands."

"That shows just how much he really cares for you."

"Yeah," I say. "Alyssa, I'm so happy right now. Nothing is going to ruin it."

We walk slowly, taking our time and talking about an upcoming science project we have to do.

"Hey, that looks like your mom's car in the driveway," Alyssa announces when we're a block from the house. We cross the street. "Yes . . . Aunt Kara's here."

I'm surprised. "I wonder why? I hope she and Kevin haven't done something stupid like elope."

Alyssa's eyes get bigger. "You don't think they're married already, do you?"

We rush toward the house.

I'm trying to figure out why my mom is here. I guess they must have told her just how sad I've been—hopefully, she's come to her senses and changed her mind about marrying Kevin.

Mom, Uncle Reed and Aunt Phoebe are all sitting in the living room when we enter the house. I greet them as I drop my backpack on the carpet near the sofa before dropping down beside her. I reach over to give her a hug. "What are you dong here?"

"I thought I'd better come out here to see what you've been up to," she responds.

For some reason, Mom's response makes me feel a little funny and I don't know what to make of it. I try reading her expression but I'm not successful.

"So, what have you been up to, baby girl?"

I glance over my shoulder at Alyssa, who's standing in the doorway. She looks almost afraid to move. I turn my attention back to my mom. "I've been upset about . . ."

"My engagement to Kevin," Mom finishes for me. "You don't want me to get married. You've made that clear on more than one occasion."

"Just not right now," I admit.

"You think it's too soon for me to get married?" she asks. "That's what you're saying to me, right? Because I want to make sure I'm understanding where you're coming from."

The more we talk, the more uncomfortable I feel. I sneak a peek at Aunt Phoebe. She doesn't look very happy. Okay, something's definitely up.

"It's not like I don't want you to ever get married, Mom."

"Divine, just answer the question. You think that it's too soon for Kevin and me to consider getting married. *Right?*"

Okay, why does she keep harping on that? I wonder. I figure I might as well be honest. Maybe now Mom's finally ready to see things my way. "Yes ma'am."

"Then tell me something, baby girl . . ." Mom says, pulling a piece of paper out of her oversize Chanel handbag. "Why are there a couple of charges to the Champagne Cyber Wedding Chapel on your debit card?"

I almost fall off the sofa.

"Divine . . ." Mom prompts. "What do you have to say for yourself?"

Aunt Phoebe releases something that closely resembles a moan, and then leans against Uncle Reed muttering, "Dear Lord in Heaven . . ."

Busted.

I swallow hard. "Mom . . ."

She doesn't let me get out another word. "Please tell me that you and that boy did not run off and get married. I checked and this place is in Atlanta." Placing a hand to her temple as if she's trying to ward off a bad headache, she adds, "Let me warn you first that I'm in no mood for lies. Divine, how can you be so irresponsible?"

"Mom, calm down. It's not a real chapel. If it is, I've never been there. It's a cyber-wedding chapel."

"A what?" Uncle Reed questions.

"It's a chat room. You—"

Aunt Phoebe cuts me off. "Didn't we tell you to stay out of chat rooms, after what happened the last time, Divine?"

"This was a private chat room," I explain. "Only me, Madison and Preacher David were in there. You have to have a password to get in."

Mom's mouth drops open. "Preacher who?"

"Preacher David. He married us." I pause a moment before adding, "Mom, it's just a game."

Mom rises to her feet and begins pacing back and forth across the middle of the room. "*A game?* Do you know what would happen if the media gets ahold of a morsel like this? They'd have a field day."

"The marriage is not a legal one," Uncle Reed states. "You and Madison aren't really married."

"I know that," I say. "Like I told you—it's just a game."

"Why are there two charges?" Mom asks, looking over at Alyssa. "Please tell me that they double billed you?"

Aunt Phoebe sits up. "Alyssa, did you have a hand in this foolishness too?"

I glance over at my cousin, wondering if she's going to leave me to deal with the grown-ups alone. Maybe I should just rat her out and be done with it. I might as well have some company while I spend the rest of my teenage years on punishment.

Staring down at the carpet, she confesses. "Stephen and I had a cyber-wedding too."

The room is suddenly filled with heavy silence.

Right now I'm wishing I was anywhere but here, facing not only my mom, but Aunt Phoebe and Uncle Reed as well.

My life totally sucks right now.

"Divine, tell me something. What made you decide to get married?" Mom inquires. "Especially with the way you feel about me and Kevin. Is this why you did it—to get back at me?"

"This doesn't have anything to do with you, Mom. Madison and I just thought it would be a lot of fun."

"What's fun about pretending to be a married couple?" she asks. "Tell me, because I'm not getting it."

"I love Madison and we just thought it would be fun to pretend like we're husband and wife. There's even a game where you get bonus points if you get married."

"Divine, I need to ask you something and I want the truth. Have you and Madison had sex?"

I feel my face heat up in embarrassment. *"Mom!"*

"I need to know."

"No ma'am. I'm still a member of the Big 'V' Club. A proud, card-carrying member."

Mom's relief is audible. "Thank You, Lord! Divine, I wasn't sure what to think, especially with you going around here pretending to be married to Madison."

"We can get a divorce, Mom. All we have to do is go back to the website and press a button."

"Oh, is that all?" Mom says in a sarcastic tone. "Divine, do you think marriage and divorce are that simple?"

I don't respond for a moment.

"Well?"

"It is in Hollywood."

Mom looks like she's about ready to lose it on me. She walks over to the marble fireplace and just stands there with her back to us.

I glance at Uncle Reed who looks just as unhappy. I refuse to raise my gaze toward Aunt Phoebe because I know she's shooting knives at me with those expressive eyes of hers.

This is exactly why I didn't want them to find out.

Aunt Phoebe clears her throat and says, "When I was about six or seven years old, I got married to the boy across the street. We had a ceremony, a wedding party—the whole bit. A couple of months later, the marriage ended in flames when he called me a stupid-head."

I let out a nervous chuckle.

She glares at me. "The point I'm trying to make is that at no point did we think that sex had anything to do with marriage."

"But Mama, why do you think that our getting married will lead to sex?" Alyssa says.

"Because the world has become so perverted, Alyssa. I remember when kids could play house and not be accused of sexual harassment . . . the world has changed."

"Aunt Phoebe, cyber-marriages are just an extension of what you did when you were six," I say, hoping that'll get us off the hook.

"Maybe if the world wasn't the way it is today I might agree with you, Divine," she responds in a sad voice. "However, taking things a step further seems to be the norm these days."

"But we're not taking anything further," I state.

"Baby girl, you took it a step further when you paid fifty dollars to get married by 'Preacher David' in a chat room."

I meet my mom's angry gaze. "It's just a game. It's not like I'm taking it all serious and stuff."

Mom just shakes her head.

I steal a peek over at Alyssa. Her troubled expression echoes my own.

"YOU'RE REALLY MAD at me, aren't you?" I ask Mom later. She's taking me for a walk around the tree-lined neighborhood while Alyssa stays home getting lectured by Aunt Phoebe and Uncle Reed.

Several cars drive past us, a couple of people slow down when they recognize Mom. Thankfully, they don't stop and ask for autographs.

She reaches into her pocket and pulls out a pair of sunglasses, slipping them on, then wraps an arm around me. "I'm not mad with you but I am worried about you. Divine, why do you want to grow up so fast? These are the best years of your life. Trust me."

"It doesn't feel that way. Mom, it's like we can't have a real life. There are nothing but rules, rules and more rules. Parents think teens don't know anything."

Shaking her head, Mom says, "Divine, that's not true. It's just that we've already traveled down the road you're on and we know what can happen."

My lips turn downward. "Why are parents so negative? You always think the worst."

"Well, you teens should realize that it's only because we don't want you making the same mistakes or putting yourselves in danger," Mom responds.

"How are we supposed to learn to be independent, if parents won't let us?"

"We release you little by little, Divine. As your parents, we know what you can and can't handle—or at least we should. Baby girl, we want you to enjoy life—we want you to have a healthy and happy childhood. I know you don't believe it but it's true."

I sigh in resignation.

"I'm not mad but I am very disappointed, Divine. I thought you were much more responsible than this."

She's got her *nerve,* I think.

"Mom, you and Kevin are doing the same thing. Actually, Madison and I have been together longer than you and Kevin."

"Talking on the phone every night and seeing each other at school does not qualify as a courtship."

I know all this but I can't resist pushing my mom's buttons. "I want to be honest with you, Mom. The truth is that when Madison and I said our vows—we meant them and they came from our hearts. Sometimes the marriage feels real to us."

"But it's not," Mom quickly interjects.

"That's what I keep telling you. I *know* that. You all act like we went out and just ran wild. We just did a little role-playing on the computer and we'll probably be punished for life."

"We're worried that you and Alyssa will begin to take this pretend marriage seriously, which could lead to trouble. The line between real and virtual could become blurred. Especially when you have feelings for the person."

"Mom, you don't have to worry about that. I'm not stupid."

"I know you're not stupid, but you *are* emotional, Divine."

"What do you want me to do, Mom? Do you want me to log on and divorce Madison? I will, but only if you call off your engagement to Kevin."

Mom stops in her tracks. Holding my face in her hand, she says in a hard tone, "I know you're not trying to bargain with me, Divine; that's not how it works. I am your mother and you will do as I say. I'm not worried about you divorcing Madison because that little so-called marriage you think you have ain't worth the paper it's printed on. Don't you ever try to blackmail me." The more she talks, the angrier she becomes. "I don't know who you think you are, Divine, but don't get it twisted."

She resumes our walk.

"Sorry," I mumble. "I shouldn't have said that."

"Divine, stop trying to be grown; your time will come. And one day, you're gonna wish for these days again, but they'll be long gone."

As if.

Mom continues lecturing me the rest of the way back to the house.

Life just can't get any worse as far as I'm concerned.

I FIGURE IT'S in my best interest to hide out in my room after Mom leaves for Atlanta. I'm so not ready to face my aunt and uncle. Mom's already lectured me and I'm not feeling another one, but I know Aunt Phoebe's not going to let me slide on this. I know it.

Alyssa blows into my room without knocking. "Mama just said that she's changed her mind about Stephen and Madison coming over. She says we still haven't learned anything." She wipes away a tear.

"That's so wrong!" I complain. "Aunt Phoebe's being so wishy-washy about all this and it's not like we've done anything wrong."

"Do you really believe that, Divine?" Alyssa asks me, her voice breaking. She takes a seat on the edge of my bed. "You don't think what we did was wrong?"

"It's not like we went out and got married for real, Alyssa."

"But they don't want us married either way. If it wasn't something bad we wouldn't have been so sneaky about it."

"Hmmph! I don't know about you but I don't want them all in my business."

"I know why Mama changed her mind. What we did wasn't cool. I expected it."

"Well, I think it's unfair."

"Take it up with my parents then."

"Yeah, right," I mutter. "Like I want Aunt Phoebe to lose it on me. *I don't think so.*"

Later in bed, I think back to everything my mom, Aunt Phoebe and Uncle Reed said to me. I guess I can understand them being concerned, but I think it's mostly that they're worried Alyssa and I are going to run out and have sex with our "husbands."

Although they don't know it, I almost did.

I sit up in bed.

"Are they right to be worried?" I whisper. "I'm curious about sex, but I didn't do it, God. I said no to Madison and I meant it."

I couldn't deny that if we hadn't been pretending to be married I wouldn't have risked skipping school with Madison. I went to his house with him because we wanted to celebrate our marriage.

A marriage that isn't real.

I have everything under control, I tell myself. *I said no and that's all that matters.*

Aunt Phoebe always says that what's done in the dark will come to light. Well, I'm praying that God will keep this one in darkness—I'm already in enough trouble.

chapter 17

"*Why* didn't you call me back last night?" Madison demands. "You wanted me to call you and I did."

"I had a lot going on," I respond with a soft sigh.

He eyes me hard. "You might as well tell me, Divine. Now what's the matter?"

We navigate over to our favorite bench under the oak tree. "Madison, it's the worst," I state. "Aunt Phoebe, Uncle Reed and my mom all know about the cyber-marriage."

"How'd they find out?"

"Mom got the bank statement with the charges on it. I figured I'd just lay low and not do anything. I didn't want to give my aunt and uncle any reason to go off on me."

"They were tripping that hard?" he asks.

I nod. "Yeah. I can't believe it either. I kept telling them that it was only a harmless little game."

Madison nods to a passerby in greeting before turning his attention back to me. "I thought you said your mom didn't look at stuff like that."

"She didn't use to check out the bank statements, but I guess she does now."

He takes my hand in his. "Did you get into a lot of trouble?"

"I mainly got lectured. And, of course, I can forget about dating or having company until like, the end of time." I release a long sigh. "I wish we were really married; then at least it would be worth all this drama."

"We could be," Madison says. "If we make love, Divine, the marriage will be real. That's the only thing keeping our marriage from being legal."

Shaking my head, I reply, "Madison, I don't think that's true. I haven't read that anywhere."

"Yeah, it is," he counters. "If we consummate our marriage—it's real."

"Madison, I've already told you that it's not true."

"Yes it is," he insists.

"My uncle said our marriage wasn't legal."

"The way it is now," Madison points out. "Baby, they don't want us to know the truth. Think about it, Divine . . . why would they want us knowing something like that?"

I'm still not convinced. "Madison, are you sure?"

He nods. "Why do you think people can get marriages annulled if they don't have sex? That's because the marriage isn't real until you do."

I consider his words. "I never thought about that."

"My uncle told me it's the truth. He's a lawyer. He should know.

If we make love, we'll be married for real in the eyes of God. That's what's really important, Divine."

"Married or not," I say, "I don't want a baby."

"I told you I have some condoms."

"You never did explain why you had them either."

"Divine, we got more important things to discuss right now. Like whether or not we're gonna let your family keep us apart."

"What are you talking about, Madison?"

"I want to consummate our marriage, Divine. I've been thinking about this for a while. I want our marriage to be a real one—that way nobody can tell us when we can spend time together." He places a kiss on my lips. "We'll be together forever."

I check my watch. "The bell's about to ring and we need to get to first period. Meet me after school and we'll finish talking. This is a big deal, so we really need to talk."

"I love you."

I smile. "I love you too."

He wants our marriage to be real.

I can't get the thought out of my head. Madison actually wants me to be his wifey.

Wow.

Mom would really have a fit. Aunt Phoebe would probably fall out and die right on the spot if I came home and announced that Madison and I are truly husband and wife.

Uncle Reed doesn't believe in divorce, so he wouldn't push for one. But my mom . . . she couldn't force me to get one though.

A sudden thought occurs to me. Where would we live? At his parents' house? Neither of us has a job. I have a trust fund but I don't know if Mom will allow me to have the money if Madison and I announce that our marriage is a real one.

We have so much to talk about. Madison and I have decisions to make about our lives, the first thing being the sex part.

In order for the marriage to be valid, Madison and I have to get busy. Once we do—everything is going to change between us forever.

I'm sixteen years old. Do I really want to be married right now? I mean, I love my boo and all. But do I want to be tied down to him for the rest of my life? Forever is a very long time. Am I ready for sex? I'm not taking birth control, so pregnancy is a big possibility. I know I'm not ready to be a mom. Yeah, Madison and I definitely have lots to discuss.

The school day goes by at a snail's pace. I figure it's because my boo and I have to talk.

Alyssa has a student council meeting after school so this gives Madison and me some time to talk alone. I wait for him in our favorite spot.

My eyes bounce around, looking for any sign of him. He's not usually this late. I check my watch. The last bell rang about fifteen minutes ago. *He's probably hanging around somewhere with Stephen or another of his friends.* I catch sight of Penny. "Have you seen Madison?" I ask her.

"I saw him at his locker before sixth period. That's the last time I saw him though," she replies.

"You looking for me, baby?" I hear a voice say from behind me.

I turn around to face Madison. "Where have you been?"

"I needed to talk to someone." Madison takes a seat beside me as Penny smiles at us and walks away. "Why, you looking for me? Did you miss me?"

"Yeah," I respond. "I missed you like crazy."

We kiss.

"You think about what I said?" Madison questions.

"I couldn't think about anything else."

"So what did you decide?"

I chew on my bottom lip, trying to think of the best way to say what needs to be said.

Madison looks concerned. "You okay?"

"I'm fine." I pause a moment before continuing. "Madison, you know that I love you, right?"

"That's what you keep telling me."

"You don't think I mean it?"

Madison shrugs. "I guess you do. You keep saying you do."

I'm suddenly not liking the direction this conversation is taking. "I can't believe you just said that. How can you question my feelings for you?"

"Divine, I'm not. I know you love me. Okay?"

I don't respond.

"Look, I'm sorry, I know you have feelings for me. I can tell."

I look over at him, my gaze meeting his. "But you don't think that I love you?"

"I thought we were gonna talk about making this marriage real. That's what I came to discuss."

"What's the point?" I ask. "Especially if you don't believe that I'm in love with you."

"Divine, do you want to be married to me for real? Yes or no."

"I don't need the attitude, Madison."

He rushes to his feet. "You playing games. I don't have time for this mess."

I reach for his hand. "Madison, wait . . ."

He sits back down.

"Marriage isn't something we should take lightly. It's a big deal."

Madison chuckles. "That's funny coming from you. Divine, you the one who suggested we get married online in the first place. I'd never heard about it until you told me about it."

I decide it's time to turn this back on him. "Madison, how do you know that you want to be with me forever? Are you sure you want to look at my face every single day of my life?"

"As long as we happy—yeah."

"So when we're not happy—what, Madison? What happens then?"

"We get a divorce."

"You do know that we can't just push the divorce button if we decide to do this for real?"

"I'm not stupid, Divine."

"I didn't say you were," I reply. "I'm just saying we need to really think about this before we get into trouble."

"It sounds like you don't want to be with me," Madison states.

The hurt expression on his face is heartbreaking. "I do want you. But a real marriage is a big deal, Madison. I just want to make sure we're doing the right thing. I don't ever want to get a divorce. *Ever.*"

"I want you to be my wifey." Madison leans forward, kissing me.

"Let's pray about it," I suggest. "I want to be your wife in every way, but I also want to be absolutely, positively sure. There's no going back if we do this."

Behind us, someone clears her throat loudly.

Madison and I jump up to see my cousin standing there.

"I was just seeing if you're ready to go home. I have a lot of homework to do," Alyssa says.

I gaze at Madison, who nods. "We're ready."

The three of us make small talk while walking home together. Madison leaves us a couple of blocks from the house.

"Y'all looked like you were having a serious conversation," Alyssa says when Madison turns in the direction of his house.

"We were," I confirm. "Alyssa, he wants to make our marriage a real one."

"Say what?"

"You heard me. Madison wants to be married for real."

Alyssa stops walking. "So you two are gonna elope?"

"No. We don't need to do that. All we have to do is consummate our marriage."

"Having sex will make it legal?"

I nod. "Madison says his cousin who is a lawyer told him so."

"I didn't know that," Alyssa responds. "Are you sure?"

"A lawyer ought to know, don't you think?"

"So what are you gonna do?"

I shrug. "Alyssa, I'm not ready for a real marriage. I love Madison but I'm only sixteen. I just don't think I'm ready for something like that."

Aunt Phoebe is still not really speaking to me or Alyssa. Other than the overly polite hello or good-bye, she doesn't have a whole lot to say. It's the same way she treated Chance right after she found out about Trina's pregnancy.

We usually play Scrabble on Thursdays but not tonight. It's been canceled.

Nobody can hold a grudge like Aunt Phoebe.

TRINA BRINGS THE baby over for a visit with Uncle Reed and Aunt Phoebe on Friday evening. Chance is at work and Alyssa's in her room doing who knows what. I summon up enough courage to venture out of my bedroom to say hello.

Aunt Phoebe's still acting a little frosty with me, so I try to stay out of her way. I'm not in the mood for the Arctic chill.

When I walk into the family room, Trina waves at me. I am practically blinded by the great big grin on her face.

"Why are you grinning from ear to ear like that?" I ask, taking a seat beside her.

"I heard about you and Alyssa getting married," Trina replies.

I huff. "I bet Chance couldn't wait to tell you."

"I'd already heard about it at school before he even said a word," Trina says as she searches through her diaper bag. "I didn't really listen to any of it because I figured it wasn't true. I thought y'all would tell me about it since we were girls and all."

"It was supposed to be a secret. Only Madison told Tyson, who put us on blast."

"You shoulda known that was gon' happen if he knew anything. That boy tells everything." In a low voice she asks, "So your aunt was really tripping, huh?"

I glance over my shoulder to see if Aunt Phoebe's lurking somewhere nearby. "Yeah. She's still pretty mad at me and Alyssa. I would've told you eventually, Trina. Like I said, it was supposed to be a secret for now."

She laughs. "Girl, I'm glad it's not me."

"Thanks a lot, Trina. Just what I need to hear right now." I rise to my feet. "I'll talk to you later."

"C'mon, I didn't mean anything by it," she says, grabbing my arm. "Divine, chill."

I sit back down. "I'm just stressed out." Putting my hands to my face, I utter, "I can't take all this tension in the air."

"She won't stay upset with you forever," Trina reassures me. "Miss Phoebe's talking to me."

"Trina, you have her grandson. Of course she's going to talk to you. She loves Joshua like crazy."

"But she wasn't happy when she found out I was pregnant. To be honest, I don't think any of us were thrilled. Chance and I were scared to death." Trina pulls her braids up into a ponytail, securing them with a colored elastic band.

"I wasn't happy when I found out about my little brother, but when I saw Jason that first time—I just fell in love. Babies do that to you. There's no baby in my situation. Thank you, Jesus!"

"It'll work out, Divine. Just give it time."

"That's what I'm trying to do," I reply. "I just don't like it when Aunt Phoebe gets like this."

Aunt Phoebe comes to the family room holding Joshua in her arms. Her smile disappears as soon as she spots me sitting beside Trina.

Arctic chill and I'm not dressed for it.

I tell Trina, "I'll talk to you later. Bring Joshua to my room before you leave so that I can play with him."

"Okay," she whispers. Trina's not about to get on Aunt Phoebe's bad side.

I walk straight to Alyssa's room. Walking inside without knocking, I say in a loud whisper, "Your mom is really tripping. I can't believe she's still mad over nothing. I think I'm going to spend the weekend with my mom and Miss Eula."

"At least you have somewhere to go," she tells me. "I have to stay here and be ignored all weekend long."

"Why don't you come with me?"

"Because she probably won't let me go." Alyssa releases a soft sigh. "Mama can torture me much better if I'm actually here in the house with her."

"This is so stupid," I mutter.

"Yeah," Alyssa agrees.

"Well, I might as well study for my chemistry test. It's not like there's anything else I can do. See you at the dinner table." I head back out the door.

I'm not looking forward to mealtime. The air is thick with tension and my aunt's silence. The thing is—I really miss talking to my aunt. She's smart and funny and can't dress at all, but she's my Aunt Phoebe and I love her.

Right now, I'd give anything for her to come nag me. I wouldn't even mind if she just cussed me straight out—at least she'd be talking to me.

This silent treatment is the worst.

* * *

"AUNT PHOEBE WOULDN'T even let Alyssa come with me," I complain. "Mom, she's still acting funny. You know how she was with Chance. She walked around for months without really talking to him. That's what she's doing to me and Alyssa. I bet she blames me for all this and probably wants me to move out."

"No she doesn't, Divine," Mom replies. "Phoebe's not like that and you know it. She loves you like her own daughter and right now she's disappointed in *both* you and Alyssa."

"We were only role-playing, Mom. Why is it such a big deal?"

"Phoebe and I feel the same way. We both are worried that you and Alyssa can get caught up in this role-playing to the point that you get yourselves in trouble."

"Why is Aunt Phoebe still so upset about it? That's what I don't understand. Shouldn't she be over it already?"

Mom gives me this weird look. "Baby girl, your aunt is hurt. She really trusted you and Alyssa. She feels betrayed."

"So what should I—what should we do?"

"Give her some time. Phoebe adores you and Alyssa. She's gonna get over this but she needs some space."

"I didn't think parents were supposed to hold grudges like that."

"We're human, Divine. We have feelings too."

"I don't like when Aunt Phoebe's mad at me," I confess. "It really makes me feel bad."

Mom eyes me. "You mean guilty, don't you? Divine, you know how much your aunt wants to trust you and your cousin. You know she was so proud of you two and bragged about how responsible you and Alyssa have been. Then to find out something like this—she's hurt and disappointed. I definitely understand how she feels."

"No harm was done, Mom. Why can't you and Aunt Phoebe see that? At least Uncle Reed is still talking to me."

We head out of the house and into the car. Mom's driving me over to Mia's to hang out for a little while.

"I'm still talking to you too."

"You know what I mean. You're still mad at me—I can tell."

Mom reaches over and grabs my hand, squeezing it. "I'm not mad at you, baby girl. I just want you to use your brain. You're a smart girl. I want you to make better choices."

"I am," I say. Even though I love Madison like crazy, I made the decision not to consummate our marriage.

We're silent for a while.

"What are you thinking about?" Mom inquires.

"Nothing," I respond.

"My meeting should be over by three o'clock. I'll be back to pick you up around three thirty," Mom says.

"We're still going to see Jason too, right?" I ask. I haven't seen my little brother in a couple of weeks and I miss him.

"I called Mrs. Campbell earlier and she's expecting us. I told her we would all have dinner together," Mom replies.

"Is Miss Eula going with us?"

Mom nods. "I'm picking her up right after my meeting."

Mom and I sing along with Beyoncé until we pull up in front of Mia's brick town house and park in the driveway.

"Mom, thanks so much for dropping me off," I say.

Mia rushes out of the house.

"I'm so glad you're here," she says. "Girl, come on in so we can talk."

Her mother has lunch ready for us.

Seated at the kitchen counter, I say, "I really wish you were still at Temple with us, Mia. I miss seeing you at school." I pick up my ham-and-cheese sub and bite into it.

"Me too," Mia says. She takes a sip of her soda. "I miss all of my friends there."

"Do you like your school?"

Her expression neutral, Mia responds, "It's okay. I have to deal with a couple of haters, but you know how that is."

I nod. "Girl, I understand . . . they wanna hate us for stuff we have no control over—like being fierce. Take it up with the good Lord is what I tell people. He's the one who made me. I can't help it because I'm beautiful."

Mia laughs. "Divine, you haven't changed a bit."

"And I don't intend to," I reply. "I *love* being me."

Mia munches on a potato chip. After she swallows, she says, "I wish Alyssa had come with you."

"Me too, but my aunt isn't exactly happy with us right now so she made Alyssa stay home this weekend."

"What did y'all do?"

"We got married."

"You what?"

I laugh. "Madison and I had a cyber-wedding and so did Alyssa and Stephen. It's not legal or anything."

"Girl, you 'bout gave me a heart attack. I see why your aunt was upset—especially if you went and told her that."

"Now you know I didn't go running my mouth," I state. I give Mia a quick recap of how Aunt Phoebe and Uncle Reed found out. "Any other time, my mom wouldn't even look at bank statements."

"I'm soo glad I'm not you right now," Mia says with a laugh. "I don't need all that drama."

"It's all good," I respond. "That's why I'm here in Atlanta this weekend. I'm staying out of Aunt Phoebe's way."

"I sure don't blame you."

After lunch, we head up to Mia's bedroom to watch a movie, which ends a few minutes before my mom is due to arrive.

"So what are you 'bout to do?" Mia inquires. "I bet you getting ready to hit the mall."

"Actually, I'm going to see my little brother."

"He's so cute," she murmurs. "You have any new pictures of him?"

"Not yet, but you know I have my camera in my purse. Jerome wants me to send him some and I want some for my own photo album."

"I like his little chubby cheeks and those dimples . . ."

I nod in agreement. "He's my sweetie. I don't know what it is, but Jason loves me to death. He can't stand when it's time for me to leave."

"Do you know what your stepmom's having?"

I shake my head. "They want it to be a surprise. Why, I don't know."

"Are you excited about having another little brother or sister?"

"Not really," I admit. "I'm sure I'll love whatever it is, but Ava is definitely not my favorite people after what she did to my mom, and Jerome is in prison." I fall back against the sofa cushions. "Why couldn't I have a normal family?"

Mia laughs.

We hug. "I really miss hanging out with you," I say.

"Divine, I miss you too. At least I'll see you at the prom. So is anybody at school trying to get with Nicholas?"

I shake my head. "You know how your boyfriend is—he totally keeps to himself most of the time. He's about the books."

Mia smiles in response. "He's a sweetie and he treats me nice. I really care about him."

"Nicholas is a great guy," I say. "Not as great as my, boo, though."

We laugh just as the doorbell rings.

"I guess your mom's here," Mia states. "I'm so glad I got to see you this time around."

She walks me to the front door.

I hug her. "Keep me in your prayers," I whisper. "I'm going to need all I can get."

"It's gonna be all right," she whispers back. "Parents don't stay mad forever."

I'm not so sure.

chapter 18

"Hey Uncle Reed," I say, walking into his office after Mom drops me off Sunday evening. "Did you miss me in church this morning?"

He glances up from his Bible long enough to say, "When did you get back, Divine?"

"Just a few minutes ago," I respond. "Where's everybody?"

"Your aunt took Alyssa with her to visit Sister Martha. They should be back shortly."

"Is she still mad at me?"

"Divine, sit down . . . let's have a little talk."

"I guess you're still upset with me too."

"We're not mad or upset with you, Divine. We're disappointed—yes. There's a difference."

"I know that's what everybody keeps saying, but to be honest it feels the same to me. Uncle Reed, we didn't steal anything, kill anybody or even take drugs. We didn't have sex . . ."

Uncle Reed leans back in his chair and says, "Kids today just want to grow up too fast. Life is challenging enough without rushing ahead without maturity or wisdom."

"Some of us do mature faster than others, Uncle Reed."

"I understand that, Divine. I also know that a lot of the ones who believe they're mature are not. They still have a lot to learn in this life."

"Why is it such a big deal, Uncle Reed? It was a game. A harmless game."

"Divine, to you it's a game. To some other teens it might mean more. You think it's harmless but I assure you, someone is going to get hurt."

"How?"

"What if some of these kids believe they're really married? I'm appalled at the way the world has exploited everything that's supposed to be beautiful." He removes his glasses to clean them with a soft cloth. "Marriage, sex . . . everything has been exploited and why?" he asks.

I don't have a clue so I keep quiet.

Uncle Reed slips his glasses back on. "I've been doing some research on these virtual marriages, and from what I've been reading, people are divided on whether or not this is just fun or a serious threat to real-life marriages. I recently read of a woman who is divorcing her husband for being unfaithful."

"She should if he's cheating on her," I say.

"The reason this woman is divorcing her husband, Divine, is because he is married to another woman—virtually."

My mouth drops open in my surprise. "Oh."

"This man registered to play an online marriage game. He and his cyber-wife even had a child together on the Internet."

"But it wasn't real," I interject. "It's just pretend. He probably never even met her. His wife was just being insecure."

"So it would be okay for Madison to have a virtual family then?" Uncle Reed asked.

"I didn't say all that," I muttered.

"What's the difference?"

"I wouldn't like it," I admit.

"Well, neither did the real wife. She said that after a while, her husband stopped paying attention to them and was solely focused on his virtual family."

"That's wrong," I say. "But Uncle Reed, I'm not married in real life. I'm only sixteen years old—I just wanted to see what it would be like to be married to Madison. I know it's a game. So does Alyssa. You don't have to worry about us."

He smiles at me. "I will always worry about the people I love."

I get up and walk around his desk to give him a hug.

"I love you too, Uncle Reed."

"Madison just told me that a lot of kids here at school have gotten married online," I tell Alyssa the next day during lunch. "I can't believe all these people are having cyber-weddings now. Talk about copycats." I break into a laugh. "We'd better not go jumping off a cliff or anything."

"I guess they think it's cool or something."

"Alyssa, they just want to be like me and you. Girl, we've started something! I'm not surprised though. I've always been a trendsetter."

"I hope your head can get through the classroom doors—it's so big."

"Don't hate . . . Oh, before I forget, Marla Connors wants us to make a necklace," I say, pulling a bag out of my backpack, "and a bracelet with these beads for her. She wants to wear them to prom."

"Cool . . ."

I finish off my juice. "Is Aunt Phoebe still in her mood?"

"She talked a little more yesterday," Alyssa says. "Mama's gonna be all right, Divine. You just have to let her be."

"I don't like all the tension I feel when I'm around her. I think she blames me for everything."

Shaking her head, Alyssa says, "No, she doesn't."

"You just don't see it."

Our conversation changes to the subject of Madison and me.

"Has he said anything more about you and him being married for real?" Alyssa inquires.

"Not really. Sometimes he'll throw a hint but he hasn't come right out and said anything lately."

"You still don't want to do it?"

I shake my head. "Alyssa, I'm too young."

"Oh, I agree," she replies. "You won't get an argument out of me. I'm just glad that *you* know it."

"AUNT PHOEBE, ARE you ever going to stop being mad with me?" I ask. I've had enough of her ignoring me. "I told you how sorry I am about all this."

"So you think your apologizing makes things all right with the world again?"

"No ma'am. I just thought—"

She cuts me off. "You thought what, Divine?"

"I don't want you to be mad with me, Aunt Phoebe, please give me another chance."

"It's bad enough you participated in that foolishness, but why did you have to pull Alyssa into this mess?"

Her words cut me deeply. Choking back my hurt, I say, "Alyssa has a mind of her own, Aunt Phoebe. I don't have to sway her to do anything. For all you know, it could've been the other way around."

"I know my child didn't come up with no getting married on the Internet."

"How can you be so sure? I guess you think I'm just a horrible person or something and that your precious Alyssa can do no wrong," I snap angrily. I'm treading on thin ground here, but I don't care. I don't like what Aunt Phoebe's saying to me.

"I know she isn't perfect, Divine. But I *know* my child."

"If I'm such a horrible person then . . . maybe I should move to Atlanta with my mom."

"That's probably best," Aunt Phoebe agrees, breaking my heart in a million little pieces.

I can't believe she wants me to leave just like that. Blinking rapidly to keep my tears from falling, I utter, "I'll call Mom and let her know you don't want me here anymore. I'm sure I can move out tonight."

"What is going on here?" Uncle Reed demands. He must have heard us when he walked out of his office.

"I'm going to live with Mom," I announce. I can't control my tears at this point and rush out. As soon as I get to my bedroom, I throw open the closet door and start grabbing clothes.

If she doesn't want me here—I don't want to be here.

Blinded by my tears, I can't see what I'm doing. I rip the hangers out of the closet, tossing them across the room. A few of the lucky ones end up on the bed but most of my clothing is on the floor.

"Divine, what are you doing?" Alyssa asks, wading through a sea of designer outfits.

"I'm packing. What does it look like?"

"Why?"

"Your mom doesn't want me here," I reply, wiping away my tears on my sleeve. "She thinks I get you into trouble. Aunt Phoebe thinks that *everything* is my fault."

"That's not true. Mama doesn't think that at all," Alyssa protests.

"Yes, it is—she just said so."

"Divine, please don't leave. She's just upset."

Shaking my head, I say, "I'm not staying here where I'm not wanted." I pick up my phone and call Mom but get her voice mail.

I call Miss Eula next.

"Hi, Miss Eula, it's me, Divine."

"Hey, baby . . ."

"Miss Eula, could you please tell Mom to call me right away? I really need to talk to her and she's not answering her cell phone."

"She and Kevin are meeting with the pastor, sugar. I'm sure she'll call you right after they finish. What's wrong?"

"I just really need to talk to Mom."

"I'll let her know."

"Thanks, Miss Eula."

"Please don't leave, Divine. Please don't go." Alyssa starts to cry as soon as I hang up.

"She doesn't want me here."

Before Alyssa can respond, Uncle Reed comes to my room. "Divine, come out to the family room. We'd like to talk to you."

Without a word, I follow him. It's time for the big send-off, I guess.

I sit down in one of the overstuffed chairs, my hands folded in my lap. Tears fill my eyes and roll down my cheeks but I hastily swipe them away.

"Divine," Aunt Phoebe begins, "I owe you an apology. I was out of line earlier. It's just that I have such high hopes for you, Alyssa and Chance. You kids want to grow up so fast. It's frustrating at times but I should never let it get the best of me."

I don't respond because I just don't know what to say.

"I love you like my own, but you make me so mad sometimes when you behave so irresponsibly."

"I'm sorry for upsetting you," I say quietly.

"I don't want you to leave, Divine. I really don't."

I meet her gaze. "I don't want to leave either. But Aunt Phoebe, I don't want you to blame me for everything. Alyssa has her own mind."

"You're right, sugar. And I'm sorry for doing that to you. I was wrong."

"I'm not perfect," I say. "I'm going to mess up sometimes."

"So am I," Aunt Phoebe responds. "But my love for you will never change, Divine. You own a piece of my heart and I love you to death."

"I love you too." I get up and cross the room. Aunt Phoebe stands and we hold on to each other like it's the last time we'll ever hug. Even though she gets on my last nerve, I do love her.

She's my other mother.

chapter 19

Despite the fact that Alyssa and I got in trouble for having a cyber-wedding, we still attend Stacy's ceremony on Tuesday night. She's decided to become one of the married ladies too.

While watching the exchange on-screen, I play with the thin gold band on my necklace—the wedding ring Madison gave me. I notice that the gold is wearing off. Madison bought me a cheap wedding band?! I tell myself that the cost doesn't matter. It's the thought that counts.

Whatever . . .

After the ceremony, we go into a private chat room that's designated as the reception area. Stacy's trying to make her cyber-wedding fancier than mine and Alyssa's: she paid an extra twenty-five dollars for the deluxe package. All she gets is a framed wedding certificate. Girls can be so petty at times.

I'm pretty much in lurker mode because I'm bored. I'm so over the cyber-wedding thing—it's time to move on to something new. I still can't believe so many of the kids at school are doing it. Mia told me that they are now talking about it in Atlanta at her school.

I'm going to go down in history for bringing *wanghun* to American high schools.

I'M STANDING AT my locker between fifth and sixth periods when my eyes land on Mae and Colette. I groan.

"Has your *husband* told you that he's gonna be a daddy?" Mae says, catching me off guard.

I ignore her.

With both hands on her hips, she has the nerve to try and confront me. "I know you hear me talking to you, Miss Diva. Guess you thought Madison was all yours, but he not. You gon' have to share him with Brittany and their baby. And that's only if he don't decide to drop you and get back with her."

Like that's going to happen, I think. Irritated by Mae's mocking tone, I ask, "Why don't you shut up with your lies, Mae? I'm so tired of you trying to start up mess. Just go make somebody else miserable."

I move to step around her.

Mae steps back into my path. "First of all, I'm not lying. I don't have no reason to lie. Brittany is pregnant and the daddy is Madison. If anybody's lying—it's him."

"Whatever . . ." I mutter, rolling my eyes heavenward. I can't stand Mae.

"You know what? I never thought you was a fool, but I guess I was wrong. You'll believe anything that boy tells you."

"You're just mad you don't have a man," I retort.

"You'll soon find that *you* don't have one either." Mae takes a swig of water. "C'mon, Colette . . . I'm bored with this conversation."

"Ooh, I can't stand that girl," I utter when they take off to wherever. Probably out to make somebody's life miserable.

Stacy walks over to me. "Did I hear Mae just say that Brittany's pregnant?"

"Yeah, but it's not like we haven't heard that rumor before. She's been claiming to be pregnant for a minute."

Stacy leans against one of the steel lockers, saying, "I don't know, Divine. I kinda been thinking that she might be pregnant or something. She's put on a lot of weight lately."

Personally, I thought she was just getting chubby but then again, I try not to pay much attention to Brittany since I can't stand her. "So you think she's pregnant and not just getting fat."

It's pretty clear that Stacy doesn't agree. "You need to take a good look at her, Divine. *Brittany is pregnant.*"

By who? I can't bring myself to ask the question out loud. Instead, I say, "She's nothing but a strumpet."

"A what?"

"A strumpet. That's what Miss Eula calls fast girls. Strumpet, tramp, slut . . ."

"What are y'all talking about?" Penny inquires when she and Alyssa join us in the hallway.

"Stacy thinks that Brittany is pregnant," I announce.

"She is," Penny says. "I heard her telling another girl in my class this morning. Divine, she's saying that Madison is the father."

"That's what we came over here to tell you," Alyssa contributes. "I need to get to class but we'll talk after school."

Like I'm going to be able to concentrate on my classes after this drama. I don't need to be tripping over whether or not Brittany's really pregnant. Even if she is—*which I doubt*—there's no way Madison could be the father.

He would never lie to me.

My annoyance increases when I find that my hands are shaking. *Why do I let Mae get to me?* I wonder silently. She doesn't have a clue what she's talking about.

I see Madison and Stephen on my way to my sixth-period class and pause long enough to say, "Madison, meet me after school. We need to talk."

"I can't today," he replies. "I almost forgot that I need to meet with Mr. Graham about my science project. I'll call you as soon as I get home."

Madison sounds like he's in a mood over something, but I don't have a clue why. "What's wrong?"

"Nothing," he responds.

Something isn't right. I can feel it deep down in my gut. "Madison, I know that you're upset about something."

"I'll talk to you, tonight, Divine," he snaps angrily.

"Don't take whatever is going on with you out on me," I huff in response. "Hmmph. You really don't want me to trip."

"I'll talk to you later." He walks away from me before I can say another word. Oh yeah. I got some words for Madison Hartford. Don't nobody treat me like this.

I could jump for joy when the three-twenty bell rings. I practically run out of the room and down the hallway to Madison's locker.

He isn't there.

I wait for a few minutes, but still no Madison. So I give up and decide to head home.

I see Brittany as soon as I step outside the building.

Eying her hard from head to toe, I notice the changes in her body.

"Why you all up in my grill?" she demands. "Something you wanna know?"

"Not from you." I shake my head sadly. "You know, Brittany . . . what you're trying to pull is wrong on so many levels. Madison doesn't want you and this . . . this . . . whatever it is you're trying to pull—it's not going to work. He and I are together and nothing you can do will break us up."

She chuckles. "Divine, you think you still in Hollywood, but you're not. This is the real world and in this world, Madison is gonna be a daddy. He and I are having a baby together. We're gonna be a family and it doesn't include you. *Now deal with that!*"

I feel my heart drop to the floor. It can't be true.

"I don't believe you," I say as calmly as I can manage. I'm not about to let Brittany see how her words are affecting me.

She rubs her slightly rounded belly. "I don't care what you believe, Divine. This don't have nothing to do with you. Just stay out of grown folks' business before you get your feelings hurt." Brittany swings her waist-length weave and stomps off like she's done something.

I ought to snatch that horsehair off her head. The lying strumpet.

"What took you so long?" Alyssa asks when I meet up with her and Stacy at the edge of campus. Stacy's coming over to the house with us because she's working on a project with Alyssa.

"I ran into Brittany."

"What happened, Divine?" Alyssa asks me.

"Nothing. We just had a little talk."

"So, now what do you think?" Stacy questions. "Don't she look pregnant to you?"

"Kind of," I respond. "But that doesn't mean the baby is Madison's," I add quickly. "Brittany sleeps with everybody. Besides, Madison never had sex with her."

"I'm not saying it's his baby," Stacy says. "I really believe she's pregnant though."

"I got a good look at her when she was going to fifth period," Alyssa contributes. "She definitely looks like she's having a baby."

"We've all concluded that the witch is pregnant. *So what?* It's not Madison's baby." I can't get Brittany's accusation out of my mind. Before when I thought she was lying about being pregnant, it didn't bother me, but now . . . I really don't know what to think. Madison says they never slept together.

"Divine, how can you be so sure?" Stacy inquires. "When you two broke up and he started going with her, you know it was going around that they had sex, remember?"

"Madison told me it wasn't true."

"And you really believed that?"

"Yeah. Why would he lie to me?" I'm standing by my boo. But he and I are going to have a long talk about this.

"Maybe because he doesn't want to lose you," Stacy tells me. "I don't know, Divine. Why would Brittany be telling everybody that she's pregnant by Madison if it's not true? A DNA test would prove otherwise. I don't think she'd put herself on blast like that. I know I wouldn't."

I push away the doubts ignited by Stacy's words. "Like duuh—Brittany doesn't like it that Madison and I are together. I believe that girl would do anything to break us up."

"But what if she's telling the truth?" Alyssa asks. "What are you gonna do then?"

"It's not true," I insist.

"But what if it is, Divine?" Stacy questions me this time.

"Then Madison and I are over. I don't want to deal with baby mama drama. But it's not true. Brittany's just lying. She probably doesn't know who the daddy is." My eyes travel to Alyssa. "Y'all can't really believe that Madison is the father."

"I really don't know what to believe," Alyssa admits. "He was going with her when y'all broke up and everybody said they were having sex. Why would she keep saying that it's his when it's not? That's so stupid."

"People think he and I are getting down like that but it's not true. People like to make up stuff. You know that." I can't believe Stacy and Alyssa of all people are falling for Brittany's lies. They're seriously tripping.

"It's not his baby," I state one more time.

Alyssa wisely changes the subject.

THERE'S A MESSAGE on my cell phone from Mia. I call her as soon as I get home from school.

"Divine, guess what? I just got my yellow belt in tae kwon do last night."

She sounds so excited; normally I'd be happy for her, but my mind is consumed with thoughts of Madison and Brittany. I keep telling myself over and over again that Brittany is nothing but a big liar.

"Congratulations," I murmur.

"What's going on, Divine? Why do you sound so sad?"

"Mia, you and Brittany used to be friends, right?"

"Yeah. Why?"

"Are y'all still cool?"

"We don't talk like we used to—not since you and I became friends. Brittany wanted me to not like you because she didn't. I don't roll like that."

"There's a rumor going around school that Brittany's pregnant," I state. "Do you know if it's true?"

"That rumor's been around for a long time, Divine."

"She's putting on weight."

Mia shrugs. "I don't know for sure, but the last time I talked to her Brittany kept saying she was gonna have a baby. I didn't really believe her though. She's always going around thinking she's pregnant."

"Did she say Madison's the father?" I ask, although I'm not sure I really want to know the answer.

"Yeah, that's what she said," Mia responds. "But I don't know if I believe her."

I feel a little betrayed. "Why didn't you say something to me, Mia?"

"Like I said, I didn't know if Brittany was telling me the truth." She pauses for a few seconds before saying, "Divine, do think that Madison and Brittany . . ."

"I don't know what to think," I respond honestly.

"Well, what did Madison say?"

"I haven't talked to him yet about the pregnancy. I did ask him about having sex with Brittany and he says that they never did it."

"Do you believe him?"

"Why would he lie to me?"

"I don't know," Mia says quietly. "Maybe he just didn't want to lose you, Divine."

Aunt Phoebe walks by the room but stops long enough to give me a subtle hint that I should be doing my homework and not be on the phone. I'm still walking around on eggshells with her so I tell Mia, "I have to go but I'll try and give you a call later on tonight."

"Divine, I know Brittany. She wants Madison for herself and she'll do anything to try and break y'all up. Don't let her get your man."

"I won't," I vow. "Oh, I'm coming to ATL this weekend. I'm trying to get Alyssa to come with me."

"I hope she will. Maybe we can do something together while you're here."

"Mom wants me to do some bonding with Kevin, so I'll let you know if I can get away. Hopefully I'll be able to—I can't see spending the entire weekend with Kevin Nash in my space. I see him enough on television."

"That's your mama's boo, so be nice."

Whatever . . .

We talk for a few minutes more until I hear Aunt Phoebe coming back down the hall.

Probably doing another homework check.

"I have to get off the phone," I say quickly, then hang up. Hope I didn't just cut off my girl, but Mia will understand. She has parents too.

I can't concentrate on my homework.

After an hour, I give up. My mind won't let go of those troubling seeds that Brittany planted. When Aunt Phoebe leaves the house to run an errand, I grab my cell phone and call Madison.

His sister Chrystal answers the phone.

"Can I speak to Madison, please?"

"Hold on, Divine."

I can hear someone talking in the background but can't make out what's being said—everything is muffled.

When he finally picks up the phone, I say, "Madison, I need to know the truth about you and Brittany. Did you have sex with her?"

He lets out a sigh of frustration. "I thought we already settled all this stuff before, Divine."

"I thought so too, but it just keeps coming up. I'd like nothing better than to put an end to all this drama."

"Brittany is a big liar."

"So she's not pregnant then?" I even cross my fingers.

"I don't think so."

"Well, she looks like it to me but it just might be that she's eating a lot of junk food," I say. "Every time I see her, she's got potato chips, cookies, candy or ice cream."

"I don't be looking at her," Madison snipes. "I can't stand that skank."

"Oh, now she's a skank?" I can't resist saying. "Madison, maybe you should start looking at her," I counter. "She's definitely gaining some weight, so something's up with her."

"You really think Brittany's looking pregnant? She just might be getting fat."

"I think she's pregnant, Madison. I really do."

"Well, if she is, then it's not mine."

My body sags against my chair in relief. But the feeling of uneasiness in the pit of my stomach just won't go away.

chapter 20

I sit cross-legged in the middle of my bed gabbing away with my mom. "I really want Alyssa to come to Atlanta with me. Mom, do you mind if she spends the weekend with us?"

"That's fine," she answers. "How are things going with you and Phoebe?"

"Much better," I respond. "I know she loves me, but sometimes she says stuff that's really hurtful. I guess I do the same thing."

"Well, I'm glad you two were able to sit down and talk it out. I'm actually glad you and Alyssa are coming this weekend. It'll be nice for both of you to really get to know Kevin."

My eyes travel around my bedroom, resting briefly on the framed autographed posters of Diddy, Yung Joc and Beyoncé. "So you're still planning on marrying him?" I ask.

"Yes, I am."

"Just checking . . ."

"Tell me this: are you still playing cyber-wifey?"

"No, not really," I respond. "I need to take some time and think about my relationship with Madison."

"I'm glad to hear that you're not playing that stupid game but it sounds like there's trouble between you two. What's going on?"

I lean back against the pillows. "Nothing really, Mom. I just need to take a step back to see the whole picture like Miss Eula always says."

Mom releases a short sigh. "Well, it's pretty obvious to me that you're not ready to tell me anything and that's fine. Just know that I'm here if you need me."

"Thanks, Mom." I'm not ready to hear her say, "I told you so."

"I'll be leaving the house shortly," Mom tells me. "You and Alyssa be ready to leave when I arrive. I need to get back here in time to pick up Kevin from the airport."

Great.

"We'll be ready," I say.

"See you soon," Mom says before we hang up.

I walk down the hall to Alyssa's bedroom. "Mom's going to be here in about an hour to pick us up."

"I just need to change my clothes and I'll be ready," Alyssa tells me.

Back in my bedroom, I play spider solitaire on my laptop while waiting for my cousin to get ready.

"Are we gonna be able to go to the mall?" asks Alyssa, leaning against my door.

I shrug. "I don't know. Mom has to pick up Kevin from the airport. Probably after that, I guess."

"Divine, be nice to him. I want to have a fun weekend."

"I'll be nice. I'm not going to pretend I'm happy about their engagement, though, because I'm not."

An hour and five minutes later, Mom pulls up into the driveway.

Aunt Phoebe and Uncle Reed walk us outside like we're little babies. I'm not tripping about it though—I know it's so that they can talk to Mom, who's in a hurry.

"I have to pick up Kevin, so we need to rush back to Atlanta," I hear her tell them. "I really hate to leave so quickly."

"We understand," Aunt Phoebe says. "Y'all have a good time and behave."

"We will," Alyssa and I respond in unison.

While we get settled into the shiny black Mercedes SUV, Mom and Aunt Phoebe continue gabbing. Uncle Reed gestures for Alyssa to roll down the window, which she does.

"You have any money?" he asks.

"Just ten dollars."

He pulls out a fifty-dollar bill. "I know you can't go to Atlanta without going to the mall. Pick out something nice for your mother. Mother's Day is coming up."

Uncle Reed gives me a fifty-dollar bill as well with the same instruction.

"What about us?" I ask.

He laughs. "Every day is your day."

We are soon on our way.

"Aunt Kara, can we hear your new CD?" Alyssa asks. "I love 'Being With You.' I think that's probably my favorite song."

Mom has a new gospel album out and the reviews are great. Everybody seems to love it. It's being played on both secular and gospel radio stations all over the country. Alyssa and I are especially hyped about the whole project because we did background vocals on a couple of the songs. We had so much fun doing it, but it was a lot of work.

Alyssa has dreams of being a singer like Mom, but not me. I still want to be a model.

We sing along to Mom's music during the short drive back to Atlanta.

Once we arrive, Miss Eula walks out of the kitchen to come greet us and announce that she's got a hot lunch ready. She thinks Alyssa and I are way too thin. She says we need some bragging rights. Translated, that means she wants to fatten us up.

We sit down to a meal of fried catfish, potato salad, hush puppies and lemonade. My eyes closed, I quickly bless the food.

"Miss Eula, I don't know what you're going to do about dinner—I don't think you can top this," I say.

Alyssa agrees. "This is so good."

"Eat up," Miss Eula says. "You both can use some meat on those bones."

I pick up my fork, saying, "I have to watch my figure. I'm going to be a fashion model."

Miss Eula grunts. "I don't know why in the world they got to look like sticks walking 'round here. A lil cushion never hurt anybody. Back in my day, men wanted women built like Coca-Cola bottles."

We laugh.

"When you last talk to your daddy?" Miss Eula inquires while fixing her plate.

"A couple of days ago," I respond. "He sounded really good."

Mom is awfully quiet right now, I notice. She catches me watching her and says, "I'm glad you and Jerome are communicating. It's important that you two continue to work on a relationship."

"You sound like a shrink." I reach for a piece of catfish, stabbing it with my fork and laying it on my plate. I go for the homemade potato salad and the hush puppies next. Miss Eula throws down in the kitchen.

Mom sends me a sharp look, her way of warning me that if I

don't watch my tone I may be picking my teeth up off the floor. I heed the warning because I like my teeth. They look great in my mouth.

We don't talk much during lunch because we're all busy enjoying the food. Alyssa and I both have seconds. Miss Eula insists on cleaning up by herself so that Alyssa and I can enjoy our day with Mom. She's cool like that.

Alyssa heads off to her room to brush her teeth and make sure her braces are free of any food.

"Mom, do you and Jerome still talk?" I ask her when we're in her bedroom.

"Not really." Mom eyes her reflection in the full-length mirror in her mega-size dressing room. "He writes me from time to time. We're your parents, so we have to have a civil relationship."

"Are you friends with him?"

Mom appears to be thinking about my question. After a moment, she replies, "I think we're trying to work toward friendship."

I drop down on one of two padded benches, eying the clothes, the collection of designer bags and shoes. Mom's closet looks like a boutique, complete with a huge glass case where her costume jewelry is on display. She keeps her diamonds locked away in a safe.

"How long were you and Jerome together before you got married?"

Mom holds an olive green silk blouse up to her body. She glances over her shoulder and says, "A few years. Why?"

"It didn't work."

"No, it didn't."

"How can you be so sure that your marriage to Kevin will be any better? Although I don't see what's so hard about being married."

Mom turns around to face me. "Little miss, when did you become such an expert on marriage? Cyber-marriages aren't real, so I hope you're not basing your knowledge on that."

"It might not be real, but my feelings for Madison are," I argue. "Can you say the same thing about Kevin?"

"Of course I can," Mom responds. "We wouldn't be getting married otherwise, Divine." She sits down beside me. "Look, honey, two people can get married anytime they want, but the challenge of marriage is making it work for a lifetime. And the key to that is including the Lord in the marriage."

I frown. "Why would God want to be involved in marriages? He's way too busy for that."

Mom laughs. "God wants to be a part of every aspect of our lives. Divine, He loves us so much—He just wants to be in our lives."

"That's why people get married in church, right?"

"Yeah, that's part of it, but that's not the whole of it, baby girl. A lot of times people leave God at the church—they invite Him to the wedding but not into the marriage."

"I suppose God's gonna be at your wedding?"

She smiles. "Most definitely."

Mom rises to her feet. I follow suit.

She slips on a pair of dark sunglasses, saying, "C'mon, let's go. I need to be at the airport in an hour to pick up Kevin."

We stop by the guest room for Alyssa, then head downstairs.

Mom drops me and Alyssa off at the mall. "Call me when you're ready for me to come pick y'all up. You have Kevin's number, don't you? If I don't answer my cell just call his apartment. I'll be there."

"I guess they need some *alone* time," I whisper to Alyssa.

"I can still hear you," Mom says.

Alyssa gives me a look that says shut up. She doesn't like getting on Mom's bad side. "Stop tripping, Divine. Remember, we're going to the mall because we need to buy Mother's Day presents."

"I'm not so sure she deserves a present this year," I grumble.

Alyssa gives me a playful shove. "Stop being a brat."

I laugh.

"What do we think we should get them?"

Shrugging, I respond, "I don't know."

We stroll to the jewelry section in Macy's.

Pointing to a charm bracelet, Alyssa says, "I like this. What do you think?"

Again, I give a slight shrug. "It's okay, I guess. Does Aunt Phoebe even like charm bracelets?"

"Not really," Alyssa responds after thinking it over. "Guess it's not such a good idea after all."

I release a long sigh. "I'm not going to find anything under one hundred dollars. There's nothing here for fifty."

"Let's go out into the mall," Alyssa suggests. "We'll just have to look around more."

I agree but I'm still not confident we're going to find a really nice present *under* fifty dollars. "Don't know if we're going to have any better luck though."

Alyssa sighs in frustration and places her hands on her hips. "Divine, can you not be so negative?"

"I'm just saying . . ." I roll my eyes heavenward.

We head to another store.

Alyssa and I decide not to buy jewelry for our mothers. "So what are we going to get them?"

"How about one of these?" she asks, pointing to a glass plaque with a poem engraved on it.

I read the inscription. "This is nice," I murmur. "We can have their names put on them and we can have them say something different."

We each buy one for our moms. Alyssa picks one of the poems available while I decide to write an original one. We place our order and leave the store. Now I have to get a Mother's Day gift for Aunt Phoebe and Alyssa's got to do the same for my mom.

Mom collects perfume bottles so Alyssa buys her a beautiful one made out of crystal.

I stumble across a beautiful hat—one that I know Aunt Phoebe will love to death. "This will look so good on your mom," I tell Alyssa. "It's sophisticated and elegant."

I purchase a gift for my little brother Jason's grandmother. I'm hoping to try and get by to see him before we have to go back home this weekend. Jerome wants me to take some more pictures of him. I keep praying that one day Mrs. Campbell will forgive my dad for Shelly's death and allow him to see his son.

I used to blame Shelly for what happened, although I kept this to myself. If she had just left Jerome alone, maybe things would be different. When she got pregnant, Shelly actually thought my dad would leave Mom. Jerome was wrong for having the affair and probably for the way he dogged Shelly, but she shouldn't have brought a gun to the fight.

Still, I feel so bad that she's missing out on seeing what a cute little guy she had.

"What are you thinking about?" Alyssa asks.

"Jason and his mom," I reply. "I wish that Shelly could see him."

"Does her mama still believe that Uncle Jerome murdered her daughter on purpose?"

"I don't know. We don't talk about it really. I do know she doesn't want Jerome anywhere near Jason. I do know that. I wish I could maker her understand that he's nothing like the media's made him out to be. He's not coldhearted or unfeeling. He would never *kill* anyone. It bothers Jerome that Shelly is dead. All he wants to do is be there for his son."

"I guess I can understand how Mrs. Campbell must feel. She lost her only daughter."

"It was an accident. I believe it in my heart, Alyssa. I really do."

She agrees. "So do I."

We call Mom when we have all of our shopping done. Alyssa and I spend the time on our cell phones chatting with friends. Mom calls me to say she's less than a mile away from the mall. We stop and buy a pretzel on our way out. Mom pulls up minutes later.

"So I see y'all had some luck with your shopping?" she asks when we climb into the SUV.

"Yes ma'am," Alyssa responds. "It took a while but we found some great gifts."

"Oh really?"

Mom's trying to be slick but I'm on to her. "Mom, don't even try it," I say. "You're just going to have to wait until Mother's Day."

She groans.

"Where's Kevin?" I inquire. "I thought he'd be coming with you to pick us up."

"He was tired after his flight, so I left him at home to get some rest. He's coming to the house when he wakes up. He wants to take you out to dinner."

"I'm not going unless Alyssa comes with me. I'm not leaving her like that."

"We've already discussed it and he's fine with that," Mom responds. "Kevin really wants to get to know you and vice versa. He wants to build a relationship with you."

Whatever . . .

"Divine, give him a chance," Mom pleads. "Please."

"Mom, I don't have anything against Kevin. Honest, I don't. He's all right."

She eyes me. "But you still don't want me to marry him."

"I'm over it, Mom."

"Are you?"

I nod. "I'm going to give Kevin a chance. I'm only doing it for you, though."

She smiles. "Thank you. You're not gonna regret it, Divine. He's a good man and he really loves me. You'll see."

I can't help but notice the way my mom seems to light up whenever she talks about Kevin. She really loves him.

Lord, please don't let Kevin Nash break my mom's heart, I pray silently. *She's been through enough.*

chapter 21

Kevin takes Alyssa and me to The Cheesecake Factory for dinner. I know Mom must have told him that it was one of my favorite places to eat. As soon as we walk into the restaurant, a couple of women run over to Kevin, asking for his autograph.

Alyssa stands there grinning from ear to ear. "Look at these females. They act like they haven't seen a celebrity before."

"They probably haven't," I say. "But they can at least let us enjoy our dinner. Being famous can be so hard at times."

"Divine, how would you know? It's not like you're the celebrity."

I roll my eyes at Alyssa. "Excuse me, but people *do* know who I am. When Mom was pregnant with me, the whole world was watching and waiting for my birth."

People all over the restaurant begin staring, whispering and pointing at us. I'm used to all the attention because they do stuff like this when Mom is out in public too. But my cousin is over here acting like a nut.

"Alyssa, stop waving," I whisper. "Girl, you're embarrassing me." I've got to work with her on how to behave like a celebrity. "Just do what I do."

She gives me a sidelong glance. "Divine, you not doing nothing."

"Exactly."

A man and his wife venture over and ask Kevin if he'd be willing to take a picture with them. Alyssa snaps the photo while I pose with Kevin and the couple. I'm not about to miss a photo op.

After we're seated, Kevin states, "Ladies, I really want to thank you both for having dinner with me tonight. I thought maybe we should go somewhere without your mother and aunt to talk. I'm sure you have questions."

Alyssa glances over at me.

I can feel Kevin watching me too. I guess they expect me to come out the box with a bunch of questions.

"I'm sure you'd like to ask me something, Divine," he says.

He just called me out.

I shift my position in my chair. "I guess the main thing I want to know is whether or not you really love my mom, Kevin. I need to know the truth."

He looks into my eyes. Without missing a beat, he responds, "I love her with all my heart."

"What do you love about her?"

"I love her laughter. I love her heart, Divine. I cherish our friendship and she is my best friend—I guess I love everything about her."

"How do you feel about children?" Alyssa asks him.

Real subtle, Alyssa, I think.

"I love them," Kevin replies with a smile. "I am well aware that Kara and Divine are a package deal—I don't have a problem with that." He turns his attention to me. "Divine, I want a relationship with you. I know that I will never replace your father, nor do I want to, but I would really like to be a part of your extended family."

"What if I wanted to come home to live?" I ask. "Would you have a problem with that?"

"No. Of course not. Divine, when I marry your mom, you will be a part of my family and I'd never turn my back on family."

"Why haven't you set a wedding date yet?" I inquire.

"I know you've had some reservations about my marrying your mother so I thought it best to give you some time to get used to the idea. In addition, I wanted to try and build a relationship with you first."

"Do you have any questions for me?" I ask.

He smiled. "Divine, what other reservations do you have?"

The waiter comes to the table carrying a tray with our drinks.

I wait until he leaves before I respond.

"Kevin, I think you're a nice person. Really, I do, but I have to be honest with you. I'm just scared that you and Mom are moving too fast. You haven't been dating that long. I don't want my mom to get hurt by you."

"Divine, I love your mother with all my heart. This is the way I see marriage: it's a lifelong commitment. When we marry, I want it to be until death."

We place our food orders when the waiter comes back to the table. I decide to have the jambalaya tonight while Alyssa chooses the Cajun chicken littles. Kevin orders the Jamaican black pepper shrimp.

"Did you feel that way about your ex-wife?" Alyssa asks while we're waiting for our food to be served. We're getting all up in

Kevin's business. If Mom were here with us she'd be having a fit by now.

He nods. "When I married the first time, I thought it would last forever. The thing is, I didn't consult God—I didn't have a relationship with the Lord at that time. I was a different person."

"Is that why you and Mom are going to counseling?"

"Yes. We both want to do it the right way this time."

"That makes me feel better. Kevin, I really appreciate your doing this—answering all my questions. Some guys probably wouldn't have done it."

"I appreciate your honesty as well." I smile. Our entrees arrive. I can't take my eyes off Kevin's plate. His food looks delicious.

After blessing the food, Kevin catches me staring at his plate and says, "Would you like to try some?"

"You don't mind?"

"Only if you let me try your jambalaya."

"Deal," I murmur. I have to admit it—Kevin's pretty cool.

"You can have some of my chicken too," Alyssa states. "I guess they thought I was starving or something. They gave me enough food on my plate to feed all of us."

We laugh and talk while sampling one another's food. As much as I hate to admit it, I'm actually having a wonderful time with Kevin.

A couple of people stop by the table to compliment Kevin on his latest movie and to ask for autographs. He's very polite to them and explains that he just wants to enjoy his evening with us. Kevin asks them to write down their mailing address and promises to send autographed photos.

We finish off our dinner with dessert. I have to have some of the blackout cake. I'm in a chocolate state of mind. Kevin has the German chocolate cheesecake while Alyssa chooses the lemon raspberry cheesecake. Between bites, we talk about Kevin's upcoming film.

A few more people come over to the table. Kevin is still really nice about it, but I can tell he doesn't like the interruptions. The manager comes over and apologizes.

"It's okay," Kevin assures him. "We're done here. Could you please tell our waiter that we're ready for our check?"

Mom's right. Kevin's a nice guy. But how will he be as a stepfather?

chapter 22

"*I don't* know about you, Divine, but I like Kevin," Alyssa tells me when we're alone in my room later that evening. "He's nice."

I agree. "But maybe he was just trying to win us over. Do you really think he's going to take us out to dinner once he marries Mom?" I drop down into a nearby club chair so that I can remove my shoes.

"He might," Alyssa responds, slipping out of her wedge-heel sandals. "He's very rich. This is probably like going to McDonald's for him."

"I'm telling you—Kevin probably won't be taking us down the street for a Happy Meal. He only took us to The Cheesecake Factory because Mom told him it was my favorite. He's just trying to impress us."

"You're being so negative, Divine," she tells me as she makes herself at home on my bed. "I can't believe you're being so selfish."

"Selfish," I repeat. "I know you're not saying I'm selfish, because I'm not."

"You are," Alyssa counters. "Aunt Kara is in love with Kevin and she wants to be his wife. You just want your mama all to yourself, and that's not right."

"You need to leave my room with all that," I order. "Alyssa, you don't have a clue what you're talking about."

"Divine, let Aunt Kara be happy. She deserves it."

I don't respond.

Mom knocks on the door before sticking her head inside. "Can I come in?"

"Sure," I reply.

Mom takes a seat on the edge of the bed, crossing her legs. "So what's the verdict?"

"What are you talking about?" I run my fingers over the ultrasuede fabric of my chair.

"Kevin."

I steal a peek over at Alyssa. Even though I already know she's not going to be any help. She's on Mom's side.

"Well?" Mom prompts.

"If Kevin makes you happy, then I think you should be with him."

Mom breaks into a big grin. "Thank you, baby girl."

"We had a nice time with Kevin. A few people were rude and kept interrupting us but he was nice about it. I could tell it was starting to get to him though."

Mom nods in understanding. "The price of celebrity."

"Did Kevin leave?" I ask her.

"No, he's downstairs. We're getting ready to watch a movie together. Y'all want to join us?"

Both Alyssa and I shake our heads.

"We've had Kevin to ourselves—it's your turn, Mom."

She gets up and crosses the room to where I'm sitting, and plants a kiss on my forehead. "I love you." Alyssa gets a hug and then Mom disappears from the room.

"Did you see how happy your mom looked?" Alyssa asks.

"Yeah," I murmur. "I did."

Seeing her so happy definitely gives me a lot to think about.

Trina calls so I put her on speakerphone.

"Y'all having a good time?" she wants to know.

"We always have a good time when we're here," Alyssa responds. "What are you up to?"

"Nothing. Chance is working and Joshua is sleeping. I figured I'd give my girls a call now that I have a minute to myself. I'm so tired but I can't sleep."

"Why not?" I ask Trina.

"Girl, it seems like every time I lie down, that's when Joshua wakes up. I can't rest for listening out for him. With school and trying to be a good mama . . . I'm just exhausted. Chance does what he can to help me but it's something else. I can't lie about that."

"Are you able to keep up with your schoolwork?" Alyssa questions.

"Yeah," Trina responds. "My mom or my dad will watch the baby for me long enough to do my homework or study for a test. But you know how they are. Joshua is *my* child and they won't let me forget it for a minute. Miss Phoebe and Pastor help me out when they get the baby on the weekends."

We stay on the phone with Trina for more than an hour. I know how much she loves Joshua but Trina's finding it really hard to hold it together.

"Maybe we should try and help Chance and Trina with Joshua," Alyssa suggests when we get off the phone.

"Help how?" I want to know. "I love Joshua but I'm not the changing diapers type. I did it that last time and he peed all in my face. When do they learn control?"

"Judging from my brother—never. Well, I'm gonna try and babysit him one night during the week so that she can study in peace. Trina don't need to fail."

"What about your own studies, Alyssa? You can't afford to fail either. I'm sure it's hard for Trina and I'll be there for her, but there's not a whole lot we can do. She and Chance have a child together. And that's *their* responsibility."

"Divine, you're right. I just hate hearing her sound so sad."

"She's not sad," I respond. "Trina's overwhelmed. I think she needs to talk to her parents and see if they'd help her a little more. She doesn't want to ask because they feel like this is her problem. Trina feels like she's failed them."

"Did she tell you that?"

"No, not really," I admit. "But that's the vibe I'm getting from her."

Miss Eula comes to the room bringing fresh-baked cookies and two bottles of water. "I though y'all might want a little something to snack on."

I take the plate from her and say, "Thanks so much, Miss Eula. I don't know about Alyssa, but I can't eat anything right now. I'm still full from dinner."

"Me too," Alyssa states. "You can leave the cookies up here though. We're not going to bed for a while. I'm about to beat Divine in dominoes."

"Don't y'all stay up too late. You got church in the morning."

I note that the scarf on Miss Eula's head matches her caftan. She loves long, flowing dresses and scarves. She has a thing for straw hats too. She's got a collection of them from all parts of the world.

"We won't," we respond in unison.

We try to play dominoes while I'm on the phone with Mia and Alyssa's talking to Stephen.

It doesn't go well, so we give up on the idea.

Alyssa goes to her room, seeking privacy.

"How's the game going?" Mia asks.

"Girl, that's so over." I laugh. "We can't concentrate and talk at the same time."

"So where do you and Madison stand?"

"I really don't know, Mia. Things are just really crazy between us. Prom is a few weeks away—I don't know what we're going to do."

"Divine, are you thinking about not going to the prom with Madison?"

"If we're not together, Mia, I'm sure we won't be going to the prom."

"I tried calling Brittany, but she hasn't returned my call yet."

Why did Madison have to get involved with her? My life wouldn't be messed up if it wasn't for her.

ALYSSA AND I return home Sunday evening after attending church with Mom and Kevin. After giving Uncle Reed and Aunt Phoebe a quick recap of our weekend, we take off to our rooms to call our boyfriends.

I didn't really get a chance to call Madison yesterday because of shopping and having dinner with Kevin. I miss talking to my boo.

"I tried to call you yesterday," Madison states. "Didn't you get my voice mail?"

"I told you I'd be in Atlanta with my mom this weekend," I respond. "Alyssa and I had to do some shopping for Mother's Day and then we went to dinner with Kevin. He's trying to build a relationship with me."

"So what do you think?"

"He's cool," I say.

"I missed talking to you."

His words thrill me to the core. Grinning from ear to ear, I say, "Did you really?"

"Yeah."

"That's good to hear, because things have been kind of crazy between us lately. I was getting a little worried about our relationship, Madison."

"You don't have to be," he assures me. "You and I are tight. I keep telling you that I want you to be my wifey for real. You're not hearing me though."

"I hear you, boo."

"I'm crazy about you, Divine . . . with your fine self."

Although I dread bringing up the subject of Brittany again, I feel as if I don't really have a choice. We need to put the doubts aside permanently.

"Madison, I know you're tired of me bringing up Brittany but—"

"Divine," he quickly interjects. "How many times do we have to go through this? Wait until I see Brittany tomorrow. She and I are gonna get some things straight. I'm tired of this mess."

"I am too," I confess. "The sooner we get this settled, the better. Prom is in a few weeks and I don't want any of this stuff hanging over it."

I CATCH MADISON and Brittany in deep conversation near the gym right before third period. They don't see me—they're too busy arguing over something. Probably over all the lies she's been telling. I hope Madison sets her straight once and for all. What she's doing is wrong on so many levels.

Just as I'm about to go over there, Nicholas grabs my arm. "What are you doing?" he asks.

"I think Madison's telling Brittany off. I'm going over there to give her a few words too."

"Why? This doesn't have anything to do with you."

I pull my arm out of his grasp. "Yes, it does, Nicholas. It has everything to do with me. Brittany's been doing nothing but causing trouble. She's been telling everyone that she's having Madison's baby." I steal a peek in their direction. "I'm surprised you haven't heard that rumor."

"I heard something about her being pregnant a few months back. So is it Madison's baby?"

"No. He hasn't had sex with her."

"I heard that they did," Nicholas informs me. "I heard him telling some of his friends."

"When was this?"

"When they were together." Nicholas takes one look at my face and adds, "Y'all weren't together then."

I feel a sting of betrayal. "Why are you just telling me this?"

"It wasn't my business, first of all, and second, I really thought you knew about it. It was all over school back then."

"I'm tired of all this crap," I say in anger. "I'm going over there right now to get this mess straight."

"I don't think that's a good idea," Nicholas tells me. "Just let them work it out, Divine."

I sigh in frustration. "I guess . . ." I watch them for a moment before rushing off to class.

"You mad at me or something?" Madison asks me when I run into him outside of my fifth-period class.

"No. Why would you ask me that?"

"You've been avoiding me. You ran off before I could talk to you earlier."

"I had to get to class, but I also needed some time to think about us."

"Divine, don't tell me that you still tripping over Brittany and her lies. I told that trick off too. She need to be talking to her baby daddy—not me."

"I'm not tripping at all," I respond. "Madison, I don't need this kind of drama in my life."

"Stop listening to these fools then."

"I'm not listening to anybody, Madison. I have eyes. I can see for myself that Brittany is pregnant. She keeps telling everybody that it's yours—don't be playing me for a fool."

"I'm not. I can't believe you listening to that mess."

"It's not like I want to, Madison. But I'm not sure you've been totally honest with me."

"Baby, I have been honest. I'm not lying."

"I want to believe you," I whisper. "I want to believe you more than anything on this earth."

"Then why don't you? I thought you loved me."

"This has nothing to do with love, Madison. I feel deep down in my gut that something's not right about this whole thing with you and Brittany."

He sighs in resignation. "Believe what you wanna believe, Divine. I ain't got time for this mess."

"Don't you dare try to turn this around on me! I didn't start this, Madison. You did when you started kicking it with Brittany after we broke up."

"You tripping . . ."

I walk off without another word. Madison's acting weird and I don't know why, but I definitely intend to find out what's up with him.

* * *

Okay, I've had enough!

I've been able to think of little else besides Brittany and Madison. This question hanging over my head is affecting my life in a major way, so it's time to get to the bottom of all this drama.

I seek out Brittany right after school to confront her. I find her with Mae and Colette near their lockers.

"I need to talk to Brittany alone," I state.

"We don't care what you want," Mae replies nastily. "We ain't going nowhere."

"Mae, you and Colette wait for me outside," Brittany tells her.

Grumbling, they leave.

"What do you want?" she demands when we're alone.

"The truth," I retort.

"I told you the truth but I guess you just couldn't handle it." Brittany removes her backpack from her shoulder, setting it on the tiled floor. "Madison and I made a baby. He's lying because he don't wanna lose you, but I really don't care about you or him. He's gon' take care of this baby. My daddy gon' see to that."

"Are you sure it's Madison's baby?"

Her eyes get big and her mouth drops open in surprise. "I can't believe you just asked me that."

She's a strumpet and she has the nerve to be indignant. *Whatever.*

"Is he the father?" I ask a second time. Placing my hands on my hips, I add, "That's if you can be sure of who is the daddy. I've heard all about your reputation."

"Yeah it's Madison's baby," Brittany snaps, rolling her neck back and forth. "Look, I'm not a ho, Divine. I know what all y'all be saying behind my back. You don't know anything about me. Believe whatever you want, I really don't care."

"I would've said strumpet actually. But then I'm not a ghetto chick like you are."

She steps up to me, saying, "You better be glad I'm pregnant—"

Brittany being all up in my face doesn't faze me a bit. "No, *you* better be glad," I counter. "You really don't want to go there with me 'cause I don't have no problem gittin' with you."

She sighs in frustration. "I'm tired of this mess. Let's go find Madison and get this straight right now," Brittany states. "Let him tell me that we didn't have sex to my face."

"Works for me," I say. "I'm tired of all the lies myself."

Together, we seek out Madison, and find him outside talking to one of his boys. Madison clearly looks surprised to see us together like this.

He gives Brittany a weird look before turning his attention to me. "What's up, Divine? What's this about?"

"You tell me," I say. "Brittany was just saying that you two shared more than kisses. I even heard that you bragged about having sex with her to your friends."

"Who told you that?" he demands. "Let me find out who running their—"

"I know you're not gon' try and lie your way out of this now," Brittany interjects.

His eyes full of hurt, he says, "I can't believe you doing this to me, Divine."

I fold my arms across my chest, meeting his gaze straight on. "I just need to know the truth once and for all."

Madison cuts his eyes at Brittany. "Girl, you just mad because I don't want to be with you. Why don't you get on with your life?"

"I've moved on—believe me. But this is still your baby and you know it."

Scowling, Madison shakes his head. "I don't know nothing."

I've never seen him look so angry.

"I can't believe you trying to play me like that," Brittany states. "Madison, you gon' stand here and lie in my face? We had sex and you know it."

He glances back over at me. "I can't believe you a part of this."

I don't respond. I'm still waiting to get to the bottom of this drama.

"I don't have time for this . . ." He's about to walk off but Brittany's words stop him.

"I'm willing to have a paternity test, Madison," she states. "See, I don't have nothing to hide. They can even do it before the baby is born. We can get this settled once and for all. I'm not gon' let you stress me out no more. It's time for you to own up to what you did. I know you don't want me—I don't want to be with you either—but we are having a child together."

Madison stops in his tracks.

I stare him down. "Something you need to say, Madison?"

He glances around nervously. Clearing his throat, he says, "Divine, let's go somewhere and talk. We don't need everybody in our business."

"I'm not everybody," Brittany interjects. "Besides, *I'm* the one you need to be talking to—we're the ones having the baby."

"Is it true that you slept with her?" I ask, still trying to arrive at the truth. "Did you have sex with Brittany?"

Madison doesn't say a word, just looks down at the ground.

"You did . . ." I put a hand to my mouth, swallowing hard. "Brittany's telling the truth. It's your baby."

"I told you that I wasn't lying," Brittany says with a smug expression on her face. "I don't have no reason to lie on him."

I shake my head in denial. "I don't believe this," I whisper over and over.

"Divine . . ." Madison reaches for me but I step backward, moving beyond his grasp.

"Leave me alone, Madison. Just leave me alone."

"We need to talk."

I shake my head no. Holding up my hand, I say, "I'm so done talking to you. The only person you need to be having a conversation with is Brittany. From the looks of things you two have a lot to discuss."

"We don't have nothing to talk about until she takes a paternity test."

I turn and leave them arguing back and forth. I keep walking until I get to the first restroom I come across, where I give in to my tears.

This is the second time Madison's broken my heart. There won't be a third. I'm way too fierce to go out like that.

For the rest of the evening, my cell phone rings over and over again. It's Madison and I don't want to talk to him.

"Somebody's blowing up your phone," Alyssa states. "Got to be Madison."

"It is," I confirm. I'm not ready to discuss what happened with anyone, not even with Alyssa. I feel like such a fool for giving him a second chance.

She drops down beside me on the sofa. "What's going on between you two?"

"We had a fight," I respond quietly.

"That much is obvious, Divine. You look like you've lost your best friend." Alyssa hugs me. "Don't worry . . . you two will be kissing and making up tomorrow."

Not hardly.

She scans my face. "Wow, it must've been a pretty bad fight. You've been crying. I knew something was up when you didn't wait for me after school today."

"I told Penny to tell you that I wasn't feeling well."

"She did, when she got to the student council meeting."

I hear footsteps in the kitchen and see Aunt Phoebe. She gives me a long look before asking, "Would you like some hot tea? It might make you feel better."

"Yes, thank you."

"It'll be okay," Alyssa whispers.

I nod in agreement even though I know that it'll never be okay. My whole life is over.

Aunt Phoebe returns ten minutes later carrying a cup of tea, which she hands to me. "Here you are, sugar."

"Thanks, Aunt Phoebe."

"Want to talk about it?"

"No ma'am." I take a tiny sip of the herbal tea. "I'm just tired."

Aunt Phoebe shakes her head. "Divine, I'm not stupid. This has Madison Hartford written all over it, but you don't have to tell me anything. Why don't you go lie down for a while?" she suggests. "Dinner will be ready in an hour. Alyssa, will you help me in the kitchen?"

She stands up, saying, "Yes ma'am."

I get up off the sofa and head to my bedroom.

I climb into bed and just as I close my eyes, my cell phone rings. I check the caller ID. It's Ava.

Apparently my stepmother isn't going to give up, so I answer it. "Hello."

"Divine, this is Ava."

"I know," I reply, sitting up in bed. "I saw your name on the caller ID." I'm totally not in the mood to be dealing with her right now. But if I don't talk to her, she'll tell Jerome that I'm avoiding her.

"How are you?" she asks.

"I'm okay. How are you doing? You and the baby."

She laughs. "We're getting bigger every day."

I am silent. What am I supposed to talk about with this woman?

"Did Jerome speak to you about coming to California to spend some time with me?"

"Yes ma'am."

"*Ma'am.* Sweetie, you make me sound old. Divine, you don't have to say that when you talk to me."

"Actually, I do. It's what my mom and my aunt Phoebe say I have to say."

"Oh . . . okay."

We sit in silence once more.

"Divine, I really would like for us to get to know each other. I don't know what you've been told but—"

"I haven't been told anything, Ava. It's just that I don't know you like that and I can't figure out why you want me to come to visit you."

"You're my husband's daughter, my baby's sister. I want you to be a part of our lives. Is that so wrong?"

"No ma'am."

"Are you willing to give me a chance?" she asks. "Just get to know me for yourself."

"I guess I can do that."

"How's school going?"

"Good."

"Jerome brags about you all the time," Ava says. "He's so proud of you, Divine." When I don't respond, she says, "Well, I'm sure you have some studying or something so I'll let you go. I just wanted to call and say hello."

"Thanks for calling me, Ava."

"Divine, you can call me anytime. I want us to be friends."

"I'll check in on you and the baby," I say.

"I hope you will."

We hang up.

Ava sounded a little happier, but me—I'm still as miserable as ever.

I get out of bed and fall to my knees. I pray for God to help me get over Madison.

chapter 23

Bad news travels fast.

Alyssa hunts me down after first period. "Divine, I just heard what happened between you, Brittany and Madison yesterday. Why didn't you tell me?"

"I wasn't ready to talk," I respond without emotion.

"I can't believe he lied to you like that."

"Alyssa, we really need to get to class. We'll talk during lunch."

She runs off and I head to my English lit class.

Stacy, Penny and Alyssa surround me two hours later, during lunch. While we stand in line to purchase our food, they report every tidbit they'd heard about my breakup with Madison.

"Now Mae's going around saying that Brittany and Madison are gonna get back together," Penny states.

"They should," I respond drily. "Especially since they're having a child together."

"But Madison don't want Brittany," Stacy points out. "Divine, he wants to be with you."

"It doesn't matter to me," I tell them. When we get to the counter, I say, "Can we please talk about something else? It's over between Madison and me. I don't want to even think about him."

I choose a salad with grilled chicken and a bottle of water. I'm not feeling real hungry today.

"So are you two really broken up?" Alyssa asks.

I nod, watching her get a three-wing snack plate, a bag of chips and a soda. That girl loves chicken wings.

"But the prom is eighteen days away. What are you going to do?" Penny inquires.

We spot an empty table a few yards away and rush to claim it.

"Well, all I know right now is that I'm not going with Madison," I say, sitting down on the bench. "I don't know anything else. FYI, this is not changing the subject."

"Sorry," they murmur in unison.

I manage to survive lunch.

In fifth period, instead of focusing on my class work, I count the minutes until the bell rings. I'm so mad I could . . . I can't even think straight. I can't believe Madison had fooled me all this time. I was even thinking about doing it with him too.

Alyssa doesn't know about that and I'll die before I ever tell her; especially after all my big talk about being a proud member of the "V" Club and all. If I'd been crazy enough to have sex with Madison, I'd really be looking stupid right now.

It doesn't even surprise me when I find Alyssa, Penny and Stacy waiting for me at the end of the school day. I'm sure they want to console me but all I want is to be left alone. Nothing they say will ease my pain.

"You okay?" Stacy asks.

"Yeah," I mumble. "Why wouldn't I be? Madison only made a big fool out of me." I shake my head in disbelief. "I truly thought he was telling me the truth all this time. I bet Stephen knew the truth though."

"He didn't," Alyssa says. "I already asked."

"He might be lying to cover up so you won't be mad at him."

She continues defending him. "I don't think he knew anything, Divine."

"Madison tells him everything, Alyssa," I snap. I feel myself getting angrier and angrier. "He told Stephen about our cyber-wedding. You can't tell me they don't talk about sex. I don't care what you say. Stephen knew about Brittany. I'd bet money on it." Then I shrug. "That's okay though—Stephen and Madison are best friends. He's going to look out for his boy."

Alyssa opens her mouth to speak but thinks better of it. She knows me well enough to know that she can't convince me otherwise.

The four of us walk down the street in silence. Penny lives a block away from Temple High, so she's the first to leave us. Stacy sees her boyfriend and runs off to catch up with him.

Alyssa wraps an arm around me. "I'm really sorry, Divine."

"Me too."

We don't see Aunt Phoebe's van in the driveway.

"Mama's not home."

Deep down I'm relieved. She'd take one look at me and know something's terribly wrong with me.

Chance arrives a few minutes behind us. As soon as he walks into the house, he comes straight to my room asking, "How you doing? I heard about everything."

"I've had better days."

"What Brittany's doing—that's dogged out . . ."

"Yeah, it is," I respond. "But if Madison really is her baby's father, then he's wrong. He keeps denying that he ever had sex with her but it doesn't matter to me anymore. It's not my issue."

"Have you and Madison sat down and really talked about this?"

"No reason to," I reply.

"So you broke up with him?"

"Like yeah," I respond. "Why would I stay with him after all this drama? I'm not ugly or anything—I can get a man."

Chance sits down on the edge of my bed. "It's not like he cheated on you, Divine. You and Madison weren't together when he was messing around with Brittany."

"Regardless, he lied to me, Chance. I asked him if they'd ever had sex and he told me no. Besides, whose side are you on?"

"Madison was wrong for lying, but you know he really cares about you."

"I guess he cried on your shoulder."

"We talked some after school," Chance confesses.

"Y'all can keep talking because I don't have anything to say to him."

"Divine, I know you're upset. You have every right to be, but you should give Madison a chance to explain himself. You don't have to take him back."

"Why? So he can lie to me some more? I don't have nothing to say to Madison. He had a chance to be honest with me and tell me everything. Maybe we could've worked through it, but now . . . he can forget it."

"Madison doesn't think that it's his child."

"Not my problem." I sit down at my desk and power up my laptop.

"What if the paternity test proves that he's telling the truth?" Chance asks. "What then?"

I glance over my shoulder, meeting Chance's gaze. "He still lied to me."

"Madison was going with Brittany at the time, Divine. He didn't have to tell you his business like that."

"We've been back together for a couple of months now," I respond. "He could've told me the truth anytime. I really don't want to deal with baby mama drama."

"But he might not be the father," Chance says.

"I don't care. I don't like everybody going around talking behind my back about me and Madison. He made me look like a fool."

Chance gives up when he finally figures out that he's not going to change my mind and leaves me in solitude.

I get up long enough to close my door and lock it. I want to have a conversation with God without any interruption.

"I don't really understand it, God. I don't know why this is happening to me. I really loved Madison—I even married him in a virtual way. How could he hurt me like this? Why didn't he tell me the truth?" My hands up to my face, I wipe away hot tears. "The prom is just eighteen days away. What am I supposed to do, Lord?"

My life totally sucks big-time.

I pass on dinner because I'm too upset to eat. I blame it on a tummy ache. Aunt Phoebe isn't really buying my story but she lets it go this time.

"What are you doing?" Alyssa asks when she enters my bedroom and finds me on my laptop.

"I thought you were eating dinner."

"I'm done," Alyssa states. "Mama set aside a plate of food for you. So what are you up to?"

Alyssa can be so nosy at times.

"Not that it's any of your business, but I'm divorcing Madison. I'm not about to stay married to a lying, cheating dog." I lean back in my chair, running my fingers through my curls. I can tell by the way I'm feeling now that tomorrow is going to be a ponytail day.

I'm depressed.

I'm heartbroken.

I just want to die.

Alyssa bends over, wrapping her arms around me. "I'm really sorry, Divine."

I shrug. "You didn't do anything to be sorry about. It was all that lying, cheating dog."

My cell phone rings and it's Madison. This is the fourth or fifth time he's called since I've been home. I continue to let it roll over to voice mail.

"Chance thinks you're being unfair about all this. He thinks you and Madison need to try and work this out."

"Like I care what he thinks," I retort. "He doesn't see anything wrong with what Madison did."

Alyssa questions, "But how are you gonna feel if it turns out that he isn't the daddy? Are you gonna give Madison another chance then?"

"No," I say, but deep down my heart knows I'm lying through my teeth. I really *do* hope it comes out that Brittany is lying about Madison being the father. I think I might be able to eventually forgive his lie, but not if he turns out to be the daddy. I refuse to be a part of the drama.

"To be honest, Alyssa . . . I hope it's not his child. Maybe we can talk about getting back together but who knows. We'll just have to wait and see what happens."

"Brittany sleeps around. You know she has a bad reputation. Why are you so willing to believe that Madison is the father? You know that you can't trust a word Brittany says. She wants him for herself."

"Why lie about something like this? It's not like people won't find out the truth."

She leans against my dresser with her arms folded. "People do it all the time, Divine."

"Well, once Madison gets the paternity test done and he can prove he's not the father—then maybe we can talk. And that's a big maybe."

We hear Aunt Phoebe's shrill voice, calling out for Alyssa.

She sighs. "I guess I better go see what she wants."

Alyssa leaves and when she doesn't return, I decide to call Rhyann and tell her everything that's gone down between me and Madison.

"I knew that boy weren't right," Rhyann states.

Like I really need to hear that right now.

"Dee, you need to just punch him and that tramp in the face. I told you that he was lying about doing it. I had a feeling he was getting down with that chick; especially since he broke up with you because you wouldn't have sex with him."

I love Rhyann but right now she's getting on my last nerve. When she's right about something, she never lets anyone forget it.

"Can you stop with all the 'I told you so's,' Rhyann?"

"Sorry about that."

"Hold on," I say. "Mimi's calling on the other line. I'll call her back on three-way."

A few minutes later, the three of us are on the call.

Before I can get a word out, Rhyann tells Mimi about my ending things with Madison.

"Dee, I'm so sorry. How horrible for you?"

"I'm okay," I lie. "There are other cute boys in school. I'll have a new man in no time."

"What are you going to do about prom?" Rhyann asks. "Dee, you can't step up in there by yourself."

"I'm not going."

"I think you should go," Mimi quickly interjects. "If you don't, then Madison's going to think that you're home depressed over him. Don't give that baby daddy that kind of satisfaction."

My head's starting to hurt.

"I don't know what I'm going to do—I'm still in shock over everything that's happened."

"Mother took me to the doctor yesterday for birth control pills," Mimi announces.

When the shock wears off, I ask, "Why? Are you doing it, Mimi?"

"No. But just in case I do—she doesn't want me to get pregnant. She doesn't believe in abortion, so she figures it'll be best if I use protection."

"Aunt Phoebe says that putting kids on birth control is giving them permission to go out there and have sex."

"I'm sure she'd rather you be on the Pill instead of being pregnant," Rhyann states. "You said she almost died when Chance's girlfriend got pregnant."

"She's not putting Alyssa on birth control. Mom's not going to put me on it either."

"You can go get it yourself, Dee," Rhyann interjects. "You don't need their permission and the doctor can't even tell them a thing."

"I don't need any birth control. I don't have a man, remember?"

"It won't be that way forever."

I'm not feeling very optimistic. "I don't care," I lie. "I don't need a man."

"I don't need one either," Rhyann says. "But I like to have one around. It's like a vitamin—only it's for the ego."

Her words spark a chuckle from me and Mimi. Rhyann is stupid. However, the more we talk, the more depressed I feel. I sit quietly just listening to Mimi and Rhyann gab about everything from makeup to clothes. Not even a discussion on fashion is able to bring me out of my funk.

When I can't bear it anymore, I say, "I need to get off this phone." I hang up and allow my tears to run free.

How could Madison hurt me like this?

chapter 24

It's still hard for me to believe that Madison and I are really over. I'm so down that I don't even want to go to my tae kwon do class this morning. All I feel like doing is staying in bed. Just thinking about Madison brings tears to my eyes.

Uncle Reed comes to my room when I don't join them for breakfast.

"We tried holding breakfast for you, but we were hungry so we ate already."

"That's okay. I'm not hungry."

"I'm surprised you're not dressed already. Aren't you going to class?"

"No sir," I respond. "I'm not feeling well."

He surveys my face. "What's wrong?"

"I just don't feel good," I reply. "I think I just need to lie down for a little while longer."

Thankfully, Uncle Reed leaves without giving me the third degree.

Aunt Phoebe issues an invitation to go to the mall with her and Alyssa a couple of hours later. I turn down her offer. Okay, I'm really depressed because I never turn down trips to the mall. She's clearly shocked and so is Alyssa.

Aunt Phoebe confronts me when I don't join them for dinner after they return from shopping. "Divine, you've been moping around the house since yesterday. I have a strong feeling that this is all boy-related. Did something happen between you and Madison?"

"We broke up."

Aunt Phoebe's surprisingly very sympathetic, which totally shocks me. "Oooh sugar, I'm sorry to hear that. I know how much you liked Madison."

"I'll be all right," I respond.

She agrees with me.

Deep down, she's probably jumping up and down over the news that Madison and I are over. Aunt Phoebe's never really been crazy about him. I guess she could see things in him that I couldn't.

I really didn't want her to be right about him.

Aunt Phoebe comes over, her arms open. "C'mere, sugar." She holds me close to her. "Divine, you're a very beautiful and intelligent girl. There are gonna be so many other boys interested in you. More than I'd like knocking on my door, but it's gonna happen."

"Because I'm fierce," I say.

She laughs. "Because you are a beautiful gift from God."

I look up at her. "Aunt Phoebe, do you really mean that?"

Her eyes narrow. "Have you ever known me to lie?"

"No ma'am."

"Don't you waste another tear on that boy—you hear me?"

"Yes ma'am."

She hugs me again. "It might hurt real bad right now, but sugar, it won't feel like this always."

"I hope you're right, Aunt Phoebe. I feel like I can hardly breathe sometimes. My pain is choking me."

"I know," she responds. "I've had days like that myself. But I can promise you. It might look real dark right now but the sun will shine again."

Aunt Phoebe is masquerading as a grape today but I really don't have the energy or motivation to give her some much-needed fashion advice this Sunday. I tried to get out of going to church, but she wasn't having none of that.

I pull my hair back into a simple ponytail and dress in a black skirt and pink top. I'm not looking as fly as I usually do when I go to church, but I have a good excuse.

I'm in mourning.

Uncle Reed preaches on joy coming in the morning or something like that. I don't think I'll ever feel happy again. My heart hurts too much.

He says that the Lord is our strength and in Him we can find joy. Raising my eyes heavenward, I send up a silent prayer. *Please help me, Lord. Fill me with this joy that You're talking about. I'm heartbroken and I don't want to be like this for the rest of my life. I really need Your help, if You have the time. Amen.*

Service can't end quickly enough for me. I rush out of church right after the benediction. When Chance and Alyssa finally exit the building, they find me waiting by Aunt Phoebe's van.

"You ran out of there like something was after you," Chance states with a chuckle. "I thought maybe you had to go to the bathroom."

"I just needed some air," I say.

We climb into the van. I watch as Chance places a sleeping Joshua gently into his car seat. "You're so good with him."

He smiles. "Thanks."

Chance gets into the driver's seat.

"I bet Trina loves the weekends you have Joshua," I say. "She's not looking as tired as she did in the beginning."

"Joshua's starting to sleep longer. He only wakes up once a night now. Plus her parents are helping her out more."

"That's good," I reply. "Did she ask them?"

Chance nods. "Yeah. She finally went to them for help. Her grades were going down and she fell asleep in class a couple of times. I told her she came back to school too soon after having the baby."

"I'm glad she's getting some rest."

"She's feeling better about a lot of stuff," Chance states. "She's not trying to pressure me anymore about marriage."

"I'm glad to hear that," Alyssa states.

"Chance, have you decided what you're going to do about college?" I ask. "Are you going off to George Washington University or do you plan to go to Morehouse or somewhere else close by?"

"You know I really want to go to George Washington, but I got accepted into University of West Georgia so I'm gonna go there. Carrollton's right down the road. I don't want to be too far away from Joshua."

"Are you sure about this?" Alyssa inquires.

Chance replies, "I'm positive. I'm staying close to home."

"I know Trina's happy," I state.

"She is," he confirms. "Trina found out yesterday she got accepted there too, so we'll be at the same school."

"I'm glad that worked out for you both," I manage.

"Divine, me and Trina are going to the movies later," Chance says. "Alyssa and Penny are going too. Why don't you come with us?"

"Not this time," I respond. "I'm not feeling that well."

Alyssa gives me a gentle nudge in the arm. "Divine, you need to cheer up. Don't let Madison get you down like this."

"I'm not," I say. "I just don't feel like hanging out. I'm not ready yet."

The door to the van's passenger side swings open and Aunt Phoebe steps inside. "Y'all must be ready to go home," she says. "I usually have to run y'all down."

Chance turns the ignition, starting the van.

A few minutes later, we're rolling out of the parking lot.

Chance and Alyssa make small talk with Aunt Phoebe while I stare out the window.

I head straight to my room as soon as we get home. Alyssa follows me, totally irritating the heck out of me.

"I told you that I'm fine," I say.

"I know that's what you're saying, but I'm not buying it."

"Alyssa, just go on and have fun. Leave me alone."

"Divine, come on. Go to the movies with us, please. You need to get out of this house."

Maybe she's right, I silently consider.

I make the decision right before they leave for the theater.

Alyssa breaks into a grin when she sees me. "You look great."

"I do, don't I? I figured I might as well come out of my funk, so I set my hair with steam rollers and put on some makeup. My hair is fierce, my face flawless and I look good in this outfit," I say, referring to the black jeans and the polka-dotted top I'm wearing.

Trina arrives and checks on Joshua first thing.

"I missed my little man," she coos. "Hello, sweetie pie."

He gives her a lopsided grin.

Penny finally shows up. She was supposed to be here fifteen minutes ago. Chance fusses her out before we pile into the minivan. "Girl, you gon' mess around and be late to your own funeral."

Penny dismisses his comment by saying, "Shut up, Chance. I hope you know you sound like an old woman."

We laugh.

Just when I decide coming out was a good decision, I run straight into Madison. Apparently he decided to come to the movies too.

"Hey," he says.

"Hello, Madison."

I notice that he keeps looking around the lobby area all nervous like.

"You must be with someone," I say.

Before he can respond, some girl I've never seen walks up to him. "Here you are, boo. I wondered where you went off to." She looks over at me and smirks.

I guess it didn't take him long to get over me. Hurt, I walk off as fast as I can.

"Divine, I'm so sorry," Chance says. "We can leave if you want to."

"No," I say. "I'm not going to let Madison Hartford ruin my life." Swallowing my pain, I utter, "We're here to have a good time. Let's do it."

Madison confronts me just minutes after I step on school grounds. Why he keeps insisting on talking to me I don't have a clue. There's nothing left to discuss as far as I'm concerned. "Get away from me, Madison. Just leave me alone."

"Divine, I really think we should talk."

I feel my face flush warm with anger. "Well, I don't. You're a liar and I don't have time for any more of your lies."

I try to move around him, but Madison blocks my exit.

"Please don't be this way. I want to say I'm sorry for lying to you. And what happened last night—it wasn't what it looked like. She was just a friend."

I don't respond.

He gives me this pitiful, sad-looking expression. "I'm crazy about you—you know that. I just don't know why you'd let Brittany come between us like this. I keep telling you that baby isn't mine."

"So, did you use protection?" I ask.

"Brittany told me she was on the Pill."

I look at him like he's lost his mind. *"And you actually believed her?"*

"She out there having sex—I thought she was taking birth control."

"Madison, I know you don't want to consider it, but there's a big chance that Brittany is carrying your child. I'm sorry but I don't want to be a part of that."

"What about the prom?"

"What about it? Take your *friend* from last night."

"So you've changed your mind about going with me?"

"I'm not going to the prom." A few people are lurking nearby, trying to overhear our conversation. I look over at them, eyeballing them until they catch the hint and leave.

"Divine, you're not being fair."

"How am I not being fair to you, Madison?" I make a conscious effort to keep my voice low. We move to a nearby bench and sit down.

"I'm sorry that I didn't tell you I had sex with that girl, but that's not my baby she's carrying."

"Then prove it to me. *Have the paternity test.*"

Madison doesn't respond.

I meet his gaze. "But you don't need one, do you?"

"Divine . . ."

Standing up, I say, "I feel so stupid for ever believing in you. As soon as you broke up with me, you ran to Brittany the last time.

This time I see you out with another girl. It takes you no time to move on—I'll say that for you."

"You know that's not true, Divine. I told you Daphne is just a friend of mine. She goes to school in Bremen and we were just kicking it last night. I can't believe you acting like this. I wanted you to be my wifey."

"No, you just wanted to have sex with me. Madison, I'm not stupid."

He opens his mouth to say something but I stop him. "You know what? I really don't want to hear it. We're so over, Madison."

I see Alyssa and walk toward her.

"How did it go with Madison?"

My eyes fill with tears. "It's over, Alyssa. It's really over. He knows that Brittany is pregnant with his baby. Madison is a big liar—I see that now and I can't deal with it."

"Did he tell you that?"

"Not in so many words."

She hugs me. "It's his loss, you know?"

I reach into my backpack and locate my packet of tissues and my compact mirror. I wipe away my tears and touch up my makeup.

"So what about prom?"

"I'm not going."

"Divine, it's the *prom.* You can't just stay home. Come with me and Stephen."

My lips turn downward. "No way, Alyssa. That's like, totally whack."

"There are a lot of boys who'd want to take you, Divine. Just wait until the news is out that you and Madison aren't together anymore."

"Alyssa, I feel so hurt and betrayed. I don't know if I'll ever be able to trust another boy." My eyes fill with tears. "Right now, I just don't want to be bothered. My heart can't take another hit."

chapter 25

Uncle Reed comes to my room shortly after he arrives home. I'm pretty sure Aunt Phoebe sent him to find out how I'm doing.

How am I doing? Let's see, my heart has been ripped out my chest and I've been totally humiliated. I feel like the biggest idiot on earth.

"I just wanted to check on you," he tells me.

"I'm okay," I respond. "You can tell Aunt Phoebe that she doesn't have to worry about me."

He smiles. "We'll always worry about the people we love." He gestures toward the chair at my desk. "Mind if I sit down?"

"No sir. Go ahead."

"You feel like talking about what happened?"

I rearrange the pillows behind me. "Do you already know?" I ask. "Did Alyssa or Chance tell you?"

Shaking his head no, Uncle Reed answers, "Nobody's talking apparently."

"Madison's going to have a baby with Brittany Wilkes," I say bluntly.

Uncle Reed's eyes grow large in his surprise. "Excuse me?"

"When Madison and I broke up that time, he started going with Brittany. Well, she's pregnant now."

He takes off his glasses and wipes them with a handkerchief. "Divine, I'm sorry."

"I'll be okay."

"Yes, you will," Uncle Reed says.

"I really thought I knew Madison. He . . . I thought he cared about me."

"I'm sure he did, Divine. He will not be the only boy you'll ever meet or care for."

"I don't like the way I'm hurting right now. Uncle Reed, I don't ever want to go through this again. I can't take it. I've been praying and asking God to take the pain away."

"He'll do just that."

"I know He's real busy and all, but I feel like He's the only one who can make me feel better."

"God loves it when we come to Him with our hurts. He wants to be there for us for everything. God wants to be a part of every decision made."

"Even the unimportant stuff?"

"God's never too busy for one of His children. You remember that."

I smile. "You think God can help me find another boyfriend—a good one?"

"Seek Him first, Divine," Uncle Reed rewards me with a big

smile. "But yes, He can guide you when it comes to boys. Like we've been telling y'all—focus on your spiritual life and on your studies. There's time for the other stuff."

"Thanks, Uncle Reed, I feel better now."

He rises to his feet and heads to the door. Looking back over his shoulder, Uncle Reed tells me, "You're a beautiful girl, Divine. Not just on the outside, but on the inside too. One day, some boy is going to recognize the jewel that you are."

I grin. "I am fierce, aren't I?"

He laughs. "And humble."

After Uncle Reed's little visit, I begin to feel a little more like myself. I guess I have a lot of people worried because even Nicholas calls to check on me.

"I told Mia I'd call her back because I wanted to check on you. I know how much you liked Madison."

I assure him that I'm in better spirits. "You need to get off this phone and call Mia back. You're not getting me in trouble."

He laughs. "You know she's not like that. Mia knows that we're friends."

Our conversation turns to our tae kwon do class. We talk for the next fifteen minutes.

Mom calls me an hour later.

"Hey you."

"It's about time you called me back," I say. "I called you two days ago."

"I'm sorry, baby girl. I've been in the studio working on that new album. What's going on?"

I don't want to ruin her day with depressing news so I just say, "Ava called me."

"Really?"

"Yes ma'am. She says that she wants to be friends with me."

"I think that's a good idea," Mom responds.

"None of this bothers you?" I ask, trying to hide my surprise.

"What?" Mom asks. "That she's calling you, wanting to be a part of your life? No, it doesn't bother me."

"Wow, Mom . . . you're being so mature about this. I wanna be like you when I grow up."

"There's no point in blocking my blessings by holding grudges. How would we like it if God did that?"

"I see your point. I guess I'll try and be nice to her. Maybe I'll even send her a card for Mother's Day. I saw some the other day for moms-to-be."

"I think Ava would really appreciate that, Divine. That's so sweet of you."

"Are you really sure that none of this bothers you, Mom?"

"Not at all."

My conversation with Mom leaves me in a much better mood. I love talking to her except when she's in Mom mode.

Kevin hosts a big dinner in honor of Mother's Day.

After church on Sunday, we all drive to Atlanta following Mom's direction to his town house.

"This place is so nice," Alyssa whispers when we arrive.

"It's pretty," I say. I don't know why but I pictured something totally different in my mind. I think I expected it to look more like a bachelor's pad. The town house is beautifully decorated—I know Kevin didn't do this. "Who was your interior decorator?" I ask.

"Your mom. She did a great job, don't you think?" Kevin replies.

"She's got good taste," I say.

He wraps an arm around her. I nearly gag when they start making goo-goo eyes at each other. I'm hatin' and I know it.

We sit down to a delicious dinner that Kevin keeps saying he cooked but I don't believe it.

"Did you go to cooking school or something?" I ask.

"Mm-hmm. If acting hadn't panned out for me, I'd planned to be a chef and one day own a restaurant."

I'm impressed.

After we're stuffed from all the eating we did, we waddle over to the family room to distribute the Mother's Day presents.

Kevin gives Mom a gift.

"Hey, I object," I say. "She's not your mother so technically you should give that present to me."

Everyone laughs.

He also hands one to Miss Eula.

"Miss Eula, my mother died last year. She was a good person but she had me when she was fourteen years old. We lived with my grandmother—she's the one who raised me. You remind me of her a lot. You are an important part of Kara's family and I want you to know that you are also a part of mine. If you'll have me."

Kevin's words bring tears to my eyes.

"Now, son, you done filled me up with all that good food and now you filling me up with emotion." Miss Eula puts a chubby hand to her chest. "You make my Kara happy. I can look in your eyes and see you a good man. You ain't hard on the eyes neither. Thank you, son."

"Are you done yet, Kevin?" I ask. "I knew I should've gone first."

He laughs. "I have one more." Kevin presents Aunt Phoebe with a nicely wrapped present.

She hugs him. "Thank you, Kevin. You didn't have to get me anything."

I pass out my gifts next.

Mom cries when she reads my poem on the plaque I gave her and Aunt Phoebe loves her hat.

Miss Eula loves *Star Trek,* so Mom and I bought her the entire series on DVD, and we bought her a gold necklace and matching bracelet with all of our birthstones on it.

After Alyssa, Chance and Uncle Reed hand out their gifts, we head back into the dining room for dessert.

I pull Kevin to the side and say, "You're such a show-off."

He laughs.

I give him a hug. "Seriously, thank you for all this. We're having a great time."

"I'm glad."

My eyes bounce around the room. "You know, if you don't have any idea what to do with this town house after you and Mom get married—just save it for me."

"I'll keep that in mind."

We leave around eight o'clock to head back home.

Not once did Madison cross my mind.

Until now.

chapter 26

The prom is next weekend.

Everywhere I go, people are talking about it—I can't seem to escape the subject of prom.

Life truly sucks right now.

"Can you find something else to talk about?" I ask the girl sitting across from me.

"What's wrong with you?"

"Nothing," I say. The rest of my day is just as awful. Everybody chattering about what they're doing before and after the prom. *It's just a stupid dance, people.*

When the three-twenty bell rings, I'm ready to run out of the building.

Alyssa wisely keeps her mouth shut about the prom.

However, as soon as we get home, there's package waiting on us.

Our prom dresses have arrived.

"Great."

"Divine, they're beautiful." She looks over at me. "Please come to the prom."

"I can't," I say. "Alyssa, I'm not stepping up to the prom alone and looking like a loser."

"You don't have to go alone. You already turned down a couple of boys."

"One was a total loser and the other just wants to have sex." I shake my head. "I'm not desperate, Alyssa."

"All I'm saying is that you can get a date, if you really want one."

"I don't want one."

My cell phone rings. "It's my mom," I tell Alyssa, shooing her out of my room. "I need to talk to her."

"Hey, sweetie. I got your message earlier. Kevin and I had a premarital counseling session. I just got home a few minutes ago."

"You're still going to those?"

"Yes," Mom responds. "We're learning a lot about marriage and commitment from a Christian standpoint."

"You're really serious about this—getting married."

"I want this marriage to last forever, Divine. Kevin and I'll be standing before God vowing to spend the rest of our lives together. I don't want to make it a big lie. If I'm getting married again, I want it to work. You know, Kevin wants to include you in the ceremony."

"I'm already in the wedding. Or did you forget that you asked me to be a bridesmaid?"

"I'm not talking about the bridal party—I'm talking about the wedding ceremony. Kevin plans to speak vows to you. He wants to make sure you know how much you mean to us both."

"Am I getting a wedding ring too?"

Mom laughs. "I think so."

"I want at least a couple of carats."

"Don't be so greedy."

I fall back against a stack of pillows. "Yours is what, Mom? Five or six? And you're calling me greedy."

She laughs.

"Oh, the dresses came. They look nice."

"Phoebe told me that you were thinking about staying home on prom night. Is that true? I know how much you've been looking forward to this."

"Madison and I broke up and I don't feel like going by myself or as a third wheel. Talk about being a loser."

"You can go with some of the other girls then," Mom suggests. "I'm sure there will be some going together as a group."

"Mom, I'd rather stay home."

"None of the other boys have asked you to be their date?"

"Not anybody I'd want to go with."

"Well, I really hope you change your mind, baby girl."

"Mom, can I give you a call later?" I ask. "I need to get started on homework before Aunt Phoebe jumps down my throat. I've been home for a while now but haven't even started studying."

"Sure, baby. Call me back."

We hang up. Picking up the framed photo on my desk, I remove Madison's picture and rip it to shreds.

"I hate you for doing this to me," I whisper. "Uncle Reed says I have to forgive those who hurt me—hmmph. I won't be forgiving you anytime soon."

"So WHY ARE you and Stephen getting a divorce?" I ask Alyssa. She's on the website getting ready to press the button when I walk into her bedroom. "You guys don't have to do it because of me and Madison."

"We're not ready for marriage—even if it is a cyber-wedding."

I'm not fooled at all by Alyssa's ploy. "You're doing this because you don't want me to feel bad. Admit it."

"Okay, that's part of it, but that's not all," she confesses. "I was thinking about what Daddy said about marriage a few weeks back. I don't want to mock the seriousness of it, so I think it's best me and Stephen divorce too."

"Don't do it because of me."

"We're not," she assures me. "It's the right thing to do."

Alyssa gets her cyber-divorce from Stephen. "It's done."

"Since when is divorce ever the right thing to do?" I ask with a chuckle.

"When the marriage is a fake one." Alyssa moves from her desk chair to the edge of her bed. "When you were on the phone with your mom earlier, Madison called me."

My eyebrows rise in surprise. "He called *you*?"

She nods. "You know all he wanted to do was talk about you. He wants me to try and get you to talk to him. Girl, Madison loves you."

"I can't deal with him, Alyssa."

"But Brittany could still be lying."

I give a slight shrug. "I don't think she is—not about Madison being the father of her baby, anyway."

"Divine, he doesn't want to be with Brittany. He says he'll take care of the child if it's his, but he still wants you."

"Then I guess he'll have to work through his feelings. Just like I do." I navigate to the door.

"Divine, I know you're angry right now."

Her words halt my walking out. "Alyssa, how would you feel if Stephen got some girl pregnant? Would you take him back?"

"I don't know," she answers honestly. "I guess it's hard to say when you're not in that situation."

"I can't stand the thought of Madison touching Brittany, much less having a baby with her. It makes me sick to my stomach."

I STRUGGLE TO pick up the pieces of my heart while trying to focus on my studies. Everyone at school is buzzing about Brittany, Madison and me. One rumor has it that Madison dumped me to be with Brittany and their baby. Another story is that they've gotten married online and will be going to the prom together.

I just know that I've never been as embarrassed and totally humiliated as I feel right now.

It doesn't help when I run into Mae and Colette, who can't resist taunting me. "Hey, Divine. How's your husband doing? Oh, that's right . . . he's not your husband anymore." They crack up laughing.

A group of students form around us, egging us on and hoping to see a catfight.

"You know, Mae, you might want to make a little visit to the girls' restroom."

Her smile disappears. "And why do I need to do that?"

"I'm sure anyone standing near you can answer that question." Wrinkling my nose, I fan my hand back and forth. "I know I can smell you all the way over here. Especially your breath—what the heck did you eat for lunch?"

Everyone laughs.

Mae lunges for me, but is held back by Colette. "Girl, you don't need another suspension. You just got back to school."

I say, "I wondered why it's been so pleasant the last few days here on campus. That's because you weren't here."

"One day . . ." Mae warns.

How typical. Laughing, I walk away from the two idiots. They aren't worth the effort or the suspension.

"I heard that Mae was trying to fight you," Alyssa says when we meet. "I had to finish my research paper in the library during lunch—she wouldn't have done that if I'd been there."

"Mae's not crazy. She didn't do anything but talk—that's her usual MO."

"She's so stupid."

I totally agree. "She doesn't have a life, Alyssa. All she can do is hate on me." I shrug. "That's too bad."

"Mae is such a joke. I can't stand that girl."

Switching my backpack from one side to the other, I say, "Let's not dwell on that chick. I don't want to think about her anymore."

"Fine by me," Alyssa says. "Oh, there's this boy in my class who wants to meet you."

I shake my head. "I'm not ready."

"He's real nice, Divine. And he's cute."

"Then you talk to him," I say. "Seriously, I'm not interested. I'm still trying to get over Madison."

"Maybe T. J. will help you do that."

I stop in my tracks. "T. J.," I repeat. "You mean T. J. Wellington?"

Alyssa nods. "Yeah."

"The star basketball player . . . that T. J. Wellington? Six foot one, black wavy hair, cute and fine . . . that T. J.?"

Laughing, Alyssa says, "That's the boy. Divine, I think he wants to ask you to the prom. You should talk to him."

"I don't know if I can do it."

"Why not? I've never known you to be at a loss for words." Alyssa pulls out a piece of paper from her jeans pocket. "He gave me his phone number. He wants you to call him."

"I'm not going to make the first move," I say. "No way. Dude need to call me if he wants to talk—I don't go chasing after no boys."

"Then is it all right for me to give him your cell number?"

After a moment, I say, "Sure. I guess it won't hurt to talk to him." I get Alyssa to tell me everything she knows about T. J. on our way to the house. He sounds almost too good to be true.

We're not home a good hour before Alyssa comes into my room, saying, "Divine, T. J.'s on the phone."

"You just had to get involved, didn't you?"

She smiles. "I'm tired of seeing you walking around here all depressed. It's time for you to move on with your life." She holds out the phone to me, whispering, "Talk to him . . ."

"I don't know what to say," I whisper back.

"Girl, take this phone."

I roll my eyes at Alyssa, then take the receiver. "This is Divine," I say.

"Hey, this is T. J. Wellington. Your cousin and I are in the same math class."

I climb onto my bed and make myself comfortable. "She told me that you wanted to talk to me."

Alyssa's about to plop down on the edge of the bed until I gesture for her to leave. I don't want her all in my business.

"Yeah. I know that you and Madison are not going together anymore. I'm sure you're probably not ready for another relationship, but I thought maybe we could get to know each other as friends."

"That sounds good to me," I say.

"I'm glad to hear it."

We talk for an hour before making plans to have lunch together tomorrow at school. After getting off the telephone, I run down to Alyssa's room.

"Well?" Alyssa questions. "What do you think?"

Leaning in the doorway, I reply, "T. J. seems nice, but then again, all boys are nice when they're trying to talk to you."

"T. J. is real nice. I think you'll like him, Divine." She turns back to her mirror and picks up a brush. "I'm trying to decide if I'm going to wash my hair or wait until tomorrow night."

"You might as well do it tonight," I say. "What else do you have to do?" While she's taking down her ponytail, I announce, "T. J. and I are having lunch together tomorrow. So you, Penny and Stacy are on your own, and do me a favor—don't be all up in my space."

"I really think you're going to like him."

"I know one thing," I say. "I won't be marrying him."

We laugh.

"T. J. is a good guy. I've never heard anything about him jerking girls around. You don't even see him with a whole lot of girls—he focuses on sports and on his schoolwork."

"We'll see what T. J. is like after a few months," I respond. "That's when he'll show his true colors."

chapter 27

I *meet* T. J. in the cafeteria as planned.

Oh my goodness . . . he's so fine. I have to tear my eyes away from his toned, muscular body. T. J. must work out every day. He carries my tray for me, proving that he's a gentleman as well.

Out of the corner of my eye, I spot Alyssa sitting across the cafeteria along with Penny and Stacy. I glance over at them and wave.

I hide my laughter when Mae nearly drops her food, she's watching me and T. J. so hard.

"Alyssa told me that you're thinking about not going to the prom," T. J. begins. "Please don't be mad at her for mentioning it to me. I asked her if you were still going with Madison."

"I'm not mad." I bite into my turkey sandwich.

"I don't have a date either."

"Why is that?" I ask. The boy is cute so finding a date shouldn't be a problem for him.

"My girlfriend and I broke up a few months ago. She goes to Villa Rica High and she met this boy over there—they're together now."

"It's her loss," I state. "You seem like a really nice guy, T. J." I take another bite of my sandwich.

"I try to be," he responds. "Divine, I was thinking that maybe we could go to the prom together. That way we won't look pathetic and dateless by staying home." He drinks from his bottle of water.

I smile. "Image is everything."

We talk and laugh our way through lunch. T. J. and I have a lot in common. We both love action-adventure movies and mysteries. We enjoy games like Scrabble, dominoes and Monopoly. His father is a pastor so he's very involved with church.

When I see Alyssa after school, I give her a hug. "You were right. T. J. is a sweetie. I'm going to the prom with him."

"Uh-oh . . ."

I follow Alyssa's gaze. Madison is standing a few feet away. Judging from the unhappy expression on his face I'm pretty sure he overheard me. I have to admit that it gives me some pleasure to see him look as miserable as I've felt.

"You going with T. J. now?" he asks when he joins us.

"I don't think that's any of your business, Madison." My tone has a little frost to it, but I really don't care.

"He's a cool dude."

"I don't need your permission." I reach into my pocket and pull out the tarnished wedding band he gave me. "You can have this back. I certainly don't need it."

Alyssa and I leave him standing there.

I resist the urge to look back.

* * *

THE ONE DAY that every teen lives for outside of getting a driver's license is here. Aunt Phoebe and Mom have us up with the chickens. We're at the hair salon by seven to have our hair washed and styled for prom.

Next, we head to the nail salon for manicures and pedicures.

By the time two o'clock rolls around, I'm ready for a nap, but I'm way too excited to sleep.

We shower and get dressed in the dresses Mom had Anya design for us. Thankfully, Alyssa and I won't have to worry about anyone else wearing the same gowns we have on.

The haterade will be flowing tonight!

Kevin arrives around four with jewelry for Alyssa and me to wear. He's so sweet and he really wants to be a part of this. I don't mind—I really like the necklace and matching earrings.

"I feel like I'm on the red carpet," Alyssa says when we pose for pictures before our dates arrive.

"You look beautiful," I tell her. Her hair falls prettily around her face in shiny curls, and her black and white gown looks great on her.

"You look beautiful too."

I know I'm fierce in the gold gown that I'm wearing. T. J. was able to find a black-and-gold striped vest and bow tie at the very last minute. I thought we were going to have to settle for a solid black vest and bow tie.

Stephen is the first to arrive; T. J. arrives five minutes later.

I initially worried that Stephen was going to act weird to T. J. out of loyalty to Madison, but that doesn't happen at all. In fact, they're pretty cool with each other.

We take more pictures. Mom and Aunt Phoebe act like they're doing a documentary or something.

The limo arrives and we prepare to leave.

"You look really beautiful," T. J. tells me.

"Thank you. You look pretty good yourself."

"I couldn't stop thanking God for allowing us to go to prom together."

"Excuse me?" Did I hear him correctly? Naaw, I couldn't have.

His smile is dazzling. "I'm a Christian, Divine. I love the Lord and I'm not ashamed of it."

"I'm a Christian too," I say. Deep down, I'm thinking, *Wow.* I know his dad is a preacher and that he's active in church but now I understand his dedication. I have to admit, I like this quality about him. I glance over at Alyssa and wink.

She gives me a thumbs-up.

After stopping long enough to eat dinner at a nearby restaurant, the limo pulls up in front of the gym and we get out. It's time to make our grand entrance.

T. J. and I pose for our official prom picture. I'm grinning from ear to ear because I know I'm looking fierce, and so is T. J. We really do make a cute couple.

When we stroll by Mae and her frogman of a date, I can't resist saying, "Don't hate . . ."

I totally ignore Madison when I see him. I can hardly believe what I'm seeing. He's here all alone. Maybe Madison should've asked Brittany to be his date.

T. J. and I have a wonderful time talking, laughing and dancing.

I'm thoroughly enjoying the look of misery on Madison's face. I almost feel sorry for him, but then I think about how he tried to trick me into having sex with him and all the lies about Brittany—no better for him. Still, I can't believe he actually came to prom alone. I feel a twinge of jealousy when I spot Madison all up in some girl's face. I knew he wouldn't be alone too long.

Alyssa and I excuse ourselves to go to the ladies' room.

"You look like you're having a good time," she tells me.

"I am," I confirm. "Seeing Madison looking so miserable is the best."

"I kinda feel bad for him." Alyssa runs her fingers through her curls.

I reapply my lipstick. "I don't. He's already grinning and laying on the charm with his next whatever."

The bathroom door opens and in drag the gruesome threesome—Brittany, Mae and Colette.

"I see it didn't take you long to find a replacement for Madison," Brittany says. "I guess it wasn't true love after all."

I ignore her.

Mia enters the restroom behind them. "What's going on in here?" she asks.

"Nothing," I respond. "Outside of the roaches in here—everything is cool."

"Oh no she didn't . . ." Colette utters. "I know she not calling us roaches."

I walk up to her, forcing her to take a step backward. "Make no mistake, Colette. I did call you a roach."

To Brittany, I say, "You've succeeded in breaking up me and Madison, so you should be happy. *Now just leave me alone.*"

Alyssa puts away her lip gloss. Smiling sweetly, she says, "I hope y'all enjoy the rest of the prom. I know we will."

THE PROM IS all Chance, Alyssa and I can talk about the next morning. I'm still a little sleepy since we were up so late at Penny's house. We wanted to spend the night but Aunt Phoebe made us come home with her. She said we weren't missing church for nothing.

"We had such a great time," Alyssa says during breakfast. "I had a feeling Trina was going to be prom queen but when they called Chance up there too—I was shocked. Prom king . . . wow."

"I don't know why you'd be so surprised," Chance says. "I'm not."

"Whatever."

"I think Chance deserved it," I contribute. "Even though your sister obviously has no faith in you—I'm happy you won."

Alyssa leans over and pinches me on my arm. "Stop trying to start mess."

"Ouch! That hurts."

"No better for you," she replies.

Aunt Phoebe strolls out of her bedroom wearing the hat I gave her for Mother's Day and a simple turquoise dress with pearls.

I give her a standing ovation. "You look beautiful, Aunt Phoebe. Just beautiful. You been showing out lately."

"Girl, sit down," she says with a chuckle. "Thank you, though."

We finish eating our cereal and prepare to leave for church.

In the car, all I can talk about is T. J.

"So T. J. is pretty nice then?" Aunt Phoebe asks. "That's Pastor Wellington's son?"

"Yes ma'am. He is really nice. But this is still all so new. I'll let you know what he's really like in a couple of months."

"Giving him a probationary period," she says. "Good for you."

"I have to do something. I don't want to get hurt again. *Ever,*" I say firmly.

chapter 28

Trina and I spend most of our lunch hour talking about T. J. and Chance. Alyssa, Penny and Stacy are in the cafeteria eating; we opted to eat outside.

"He's nothing like Madison," I say. "Which is totally a good thing."

"Y'all looked like you were having a good time together at the prom. I'm so glad you changed your mind about coming."

"Me too."

"Chance and I had a great time. It was nice just being out and doing high school stuff, you know? I love Joshua and I don't regret having him, but sometimes I wish I'd held off. Does that make me sound like a bad person?"

Shooing away a fly trying to land on my food, I shake my head. "I think what you're feeling is normal. It's like marriage, I guess.

The thought of being married to Madison sounded so great to me. But the reality of it is that marriage is spiritual, emotional and physical. The truth is that I'm not ready for all of that."

Trina agrees. "I feel that same way. I really wanted to marry Chance. We both love Joshua and we love each other, but we're not ready for that type of commitment. The truth is we still have a lot of growing up to do."

"I'm so happy things worked out so that you two can attend the same college. I think that's great."

Trina grins. "So do I. We're going to try and work our schedules so that we can make time for Joshua and still do what we have to do in college. My parents said they're going to help out a lot more. My mom is retiring in July so she's going to watch Joshua for us."

"That's great, Trina." I'm genuinely happy for her. I'm also glad she's not tripping like she was before.

THE WEEK FLIES by in a blur. On Saturday, after a delicious breakfast of pancakes, bacon and scrambled eggs, we pile into Aunt Phoebe's van and head off to Atlanta.

We're spending the day with Mom and Kevin to help plan their wedding and engagement party. Alyssa and I are going to be junior bridesmaids.

"I bet they're gonna get married at Christmas," Alyssa says.

Aunt Phoebe turns around in her seat. "I told Kara I thought they should do it on New Year's Eve."

"I don't care when they do it as long as it's sometime next year," I respond.

"I don't think they want to wait that long," Aunt Phoebe tells me. "It's gonna be sooner than that. They want to hold the engagement party in June."

"Is it gonna be in Los Angeles?" Chance asks.

Aunt Phoebe and I both answer, "Yeah."

I put in my earbuds and listen to my iPod during the rest of the drive into Atlanta, closing my eyes and allowing the music to take over. I don't open my eyes again until we're turning in to the exclusive Tuxedo Park neighborhood where Mom lives.

I'm the first one out of the car, and I run up the steps to the porch. Kevin opens the door when we arrive before I can pull my key out of my purse, taking me by surprise.

I give him a hug anyway.

Alyssa and Chance enter the house behind me with Uncle Reed and Aunt Phoebe following.

Mom comes out into the foyer looking like a million dollars. I rush into her waiting arms, hugging her tight.

I spot Miss Eula coming out of the bathroom and rush to her side. We embrace and tease back and forth until Mom gestures for everyone to join her in the huge family room off the kitchen.

"Kevin and I have set a wedding date," Mom announces when we settle down. "Now please keep this quiet. The media's already trying to get a lead on it and we don't want our wedding ceremony to become a circus. *You can't tell anyone, Divine.* Not even Mimi and Rhyann."

"I'm not telling a soul," I assure Mom. "So when is the wedding?"

"We're getting married the Saturday after Thanksgiving."

"But Mom, that's a big shopping day," I complain. "We're going to miss all the great sales."

"Since when do you care about a sale?" she questions with a short chuckle.

"I told your mom the same thing," Kevin says. "That's when I usually try to do all of my Christmas shopping."

I laugh. "I guess we'll have to spend all day Friday shopping then."

Mom shakes her head no. "I don't think so. The rehearsal and dinner are on Friday. We're going to be way too busy to shop, I'm afraid."

"Why don't you and Kevin get married the following weekend?" I suggest. "We're not doing anything then."

"We've already decided when we're having the ceremony, baby girl. It was hard enough to decide on that date. We're not changing it."

I glance over at Kevin. "C'mom . . . if you really want to get on my good side, change the date."

He laughs. "I tried already, but your mother's not having it."

"Don't you hate when she goes into Mom mode?"

Kevin nods.

"You two stop ganging up on me. Is this what I have to look forward to?"

Kevin and I both nod before bursting into laughter.

"You wanted us to be close," I say. I rise to my feet and walk over to the breakfast bar. Mom's Day-Timer is lying on the granite countertop, so I pick it up and start thumbing through it.

She breaks into a grin. "I don't know what I'm gonna do with you two."

"Sure you can't get married the following weekend?" I ask. "It's open on your calendar."

"Divine, get back over here," Mom demands. "Young miss, you need to learn to mind your own business. For your information, Kevin is busy that weekend. He's speaking at a charity function."

I'm not giving up. "What about New Year's Eve?"

"I suggested that," Aunt Phoebe says.

"We really want to get married right after Thanksgiving," Mom says. "I have much to be thankful for and I'd like to start my life with Kevin along that vein."

"Okaay," I utter. Like whatever. It's her life. "I guess I can shop some other time."

Mom gives me a smile. "Thank you for being so unselfish."

"I want you to know that I'm expecting some really nice Christmas presents this year."

She laughs. "Like that's something different."

I can't deny it—she really looks happy. Happier than I've seen her in a long time. She looks like . . . like she's in love.

I sneak a peek over at Kevin.

He looks just as happy and in love. Kevin can barely take his eyes off my mom. He catches me watching him and smiles.

"Aunt Kara, where are you having the wedding?" Alyssa inquires. "Is that gonna be in Los Angeles too?"

Mom shakes her head. "Kevin and I want to do it in Antigua. That's where he's from."

She jumps up dancing. "We're going to Antigua . . . we're going to Antigua . . ."

"Girl, sit down," Chance tells his sister. "You act like you ain't never been nowhere."

"I've never been to Antigua," Alyssa argues. "This is so cool."

"Shut up," I say.

Mom pops me on the arm. "Don't say that to her."

"Well, Alyssa's driving me crazy."

"Like you don't get on my nerves."

We banter back and forth until Mom threatens to run us out of the house.

I watch my family for a moment laughing and talking. Everyone seems to be having a pretty good time.

Mom and Kevin are sitting side by side holding hands. I'm happy for them but I'm also a little sad.

I miss Madison.

I still think about him constantly even though I won't admit it to anyone. I don't want people thinking I can't get past him. He's so not worth my time and energy. And now that I've met T. J., I'm hoping he'll help to erase all traces of what I felt for Madison. I'm not looking for him to be my boyfriend or anything—just a good friend.

I ease away, intent on going up to my room for a while, but Miss Eula catches me in the hallway.

"Talk to me, chile," she says.

I follow her to her first-floor bedroom.

"I know you say you fine, but c'mon over here with me and tell me the truth. How are you really doing?" Miss Eula asks me.

I sit down beside her. "I'm okay."

"Stop lying. I can see it plain as day. Now don't you come in here trying to cook my last grit. Tell Miss Eula the truth."

I pretend I don't know what she's talking about. "The truth about what?"

"What happened between you and that boy? The way you walking around here with your face hanging down to your knees—I know it has something to do with that boy."

"Madison and I broke up," I respond. "This time it's for good."

"Why? Is it because you wouldn't do the do?"

I laugh. "Do the do . . . Miss Eula, where you come up with all this stuff?"

"Never you mind about me and my sayings. What happened between you and Mr. Hot Stuff? You was liking him pretty hard for a time."

"You don't want to hear my problems."

"I wouldn't be asking if I didn't," she counters. "I'm not being nosy for the sake of nothing else to do. Divine, you own a piece of my heart and when you hurt, I hurt. I love you like my own chile."

"Miss Eula, he got another girl pregnant."

"Say what?"

"He's going to be a daddy soon."

"For shame . . ." Miss Eula mutters. "Oh, sugar . . . I know that 'bout to broke your lil heart. You liked him hard. It weren't no puppy love you had for him. You had that big dog love."

"It hurt," I admit. "It hurt bad."

Miss Eula takes my chin in her hand, forcing me to gaze into her eyes. "You didn't give up any goodies—did you? Tell me the truth, Divine."

"No ma'am. I'm still a member of the Big 'V' Club. I'm waiting."

"Thank the Lawd . . ." Miss Eula covers my hand with her own. "I'm so proud of you, sugar. Just hold on and God will send just the right person for you."

"I know," I say. "I've actually met another boy. Miss Eula, he's so cute and nice. Of course, I'm just getting to know him so he's on his best behavior. We'll see in a few months."

"You know I heard something strange from your mama. I heard that you and Madison got hitched over the Internet."

"It was just role-playing, Miss Eula. It was stupid now that I think back on it. Especially since Madison lied to me. He told me that he and Brittany never had sex."

"Brittany . . . that's the girl with the bun in the oven?"

"Yes ma'am. They got together when he and I broke up the first time. Madison keeps saying that he wants me, but I can't deal with the baby mama drama. I can't."

"I can understand your side of things. You should be enjoying your young life."

"I'm trying," I say.

"You really liked this boy."

"I did. It's over now though. I need to just move on. It's not like there aren't other cute boys after me. The boy I went to the prom with—T. J. Wellington—he was really nice and we had a lot of fun. This other guy is interested in me too, but I wasn't feeling him, Miss Eula."

Screwing her round face into a frown, she asks, "Why do you have to feel them? I don't understand that."

I laugh. "That means I'm not interested in him. I know what he's all about. He's just trying to score—you know, to get me to have sex with him."

Miss Eula shakes her head. "Somebody needs to take a bat to them—old fast tail, wet-behind-the-ears, good-for-nothings. Some of 'em can't half read, write or count, and they trying to get in some girl's pants . . . for shame."

She makes me laugh when she talks this way. Miss Eula is really funny.

"Divine, you a smart girl. Keep your mind on your books. Get your learning while you can."

"I am, Miss Eula."

"I married young," she says. "I had my first young'un by the time I was your age. Life wasn't too easy for me. I couldn't read that well because I dropped out of school to help my mother when Papa died. That's why I married Mr. Noble."

"How old were you when you got married?"

"Fifteen."

I gasp in surprise. "I didn't know you had gotten married so young. How old was he?"

"About twenty-five or twenty-six," she tells me. "He was a good man and he treated me well. His wife had died and he had a small baby."

I frown and shake my head. "That's nasty, Miss Eula. You were a kid."

"Back then, times were different, chile."

"When did you learn to read?" I ask.

"When Mr. Noble died. I had two children to take care of. Jerome's mother was my friend and she taught me. Bless her kind soul. Your grandmother sho' was a good woman."

"You miss her, don't you?"

Miss Eula nods. "I sho' do. I miss your daddy too."

"Ava called me not too long ago. She wants to get to know me . . . wants me to visit her this summer. She's going to be by herself when she has the baby. Miss Eula, what do you really think of her? Honestly?"

Shrugging, Miss Eula answers, "She all right, I guess. I haven't had many words with her though. Just seen her a few times when she was at the prison. She loves herself some Jerome. I can tell you that."

"You didn't know her when she and Jerome first got together?" I inquire.

"Naw. I didn't see him much back then. What's with all the questions? Something troubling you about Ava?"

"Jerome wants me to get to know her better. He wants us to have a *relationship*."

"What's wrong with that?"

"She messed with my mom. I'm sorry, but I have a problem with that. Nobody messes with Mom."

chapter 29

T. J. and I take a few minutes to talk before we have to be in first period. Out of the corner of my eye, I spot Madison lurking nearby.

"You look beautiful as usual," T. J. compliments me.

"You're so sweet," I say loud enough for Madison to hear.

T. J. smiles that dazzling smile of his. "I give credit where credit is due."

He's an old soul, I think. My eyes travel from his head to his feet. *He wears it well, though.*

Our classes are right next to each other so we begin walking in that direction. The bell is due to ring in about five minutes.

"Do you think your aunt and uncle would mind if I take you to the movies on Saturday? A group of us are going—Stephen and Alyssa can come too."

"I'll ask. Hopefully they won't have a problem with it."

As soon as the bell rings, we enter the building.

The hair on the back of my neck sticks up and I get this weird sensation of being watched. I glance over my shoulder.

Madison's staring holes through me.

T. J. stops walking. "You okay?"

"Yeah." I break into a smile. "I'm great."

He leaves me safe and sound in my AP Chemistry class. I peek out, looking for Madison, but I don't see him anywhere. He probably rushed off to his class since it's located on the other end of the school.

Alyssa meets me at my locker after class ends. She seems upset about something. "You okay?" I ask.

"Divine, did you hear about Trey Barton?"

Putting away my chemistry book, I shake my head. "No. What happened? Did he get hurt or something?"

"No, nothing like that. Trey's in big trouble at home—he was stealing money from his parents to send to his *wife*."

My eyes widen in surprise. "He was giving Shanice the money?"

Alyssa shakes her head and says, "No . . . Trey met some girl on the Internet and married her too. She told him that he needed to send her money because she was his wife and he needed to take care of his family."

"And he did it?" I can't believe what I'm hearing. I thought Trey was much smarter than that.

Alyssa nods. "Trey ain't never seen that girl and he sending her money like that. Now you know Shanice is all fired up. They been together for six months—he ain't giving *her* no money."

"I can't believe this!"

"It's true," she assures me. "Trey's brother told me about it. Shanice broke up with Trey for cheating on her. I think she mostly mad about the money part. I know I would be."

"This is crazy," I say. "Why is that boy sending some stranger money like that? Trey is tripping. It's just a game."

"A lot of people don't see it that way, Divine," Alyssa tells me. "You know Sandra Horne, don't you?"

"She cheers on varsity, right?"

Alyssa nods. "She and her boyfriend made their marriage real."

I fall back against my locker, my heart pounding loudly. "They did *what*?"

"It's a real marriage. They did it."

"Nooo . . ."

"But after that, he divorced her, saying he didn't want to be married no more. Plus, he supposed to be married to another girl—she goes to Villa Rica High." Alyssa pauses a moment before adding, "But you know what was up: he just wants to get her into bed."

I feel like I've been kicked in the gut. "I can't believe this," I mutter. "Madison was trying to tell me that we had to have sex to make our marriage real. I'm so glad I didn't listen to him."

"A lot of the boys are telling girls that—they're tricking them into having sex and then divorcing them," Alyssa reveals to me.

I shake my head in disgust. "It's really getting crazy . . . Alyssa, this is all my fault."

"Why do you say that?"

"If I hadn't mentioned cyber-marriages, nobody would be doing it. I never wanted anybody to get hurt."

"Divine, this isn't your fault."

"Yes, it is, Alyssa. Aunt Phoebe was right. You never would've done it if I hadn't."

"I made my own decision. So did everyone else. You can't take the blame for all this," she protests.

"Well, I do. Sandra's just been dogged by John Daniels. That's so not cool. And look at Trey. He's stealing from his parents. *It's crazy.*"

Guilt seeps through my pores. This is all my fault!

I don't see T. J. again until lunch. We pay for our food and then go outside to an empty picnic table.

"Something's bothering you," he observes.

"T. J., did you hear about the online marriages?" I want to know.

He nods. "I'd heard that you and Madison had a virtual wedding. Is it true?"

"Yeah. I don't know what I was thinking about when I did it. It was so stupid." I take a bite of my sub sandwich.

"I think all girls dream of having weddings."

"It wasn't just the girls doing it, T. J.," I say. "There were a lot of boys here at school wanting to get married online too."

"But their reasons weren't the same." He finishes off one carton of milk and opens another.

"Then why did they do it?"

"It was just another way to get girls to have sex with them."

I suddenly don't feel hungry anymore. "You're kidding me?"

T. J. shakes his head. "I heard them all talking about it." He finishes off his hamburger.

"If I hadn't found out about virtual weddings, none of this would've happened. T. J., this is all my fault. I started this."

"Divine, you're not responsible for the choices others make."

"But . . ." I blink rapidly to keep my tears from falling. I don't want T. J. seeing me blubbering like a baby. "People at this school are getting hurt because of a silly game I started."

He wraps an arm around me. "That's not true, Divine."

I excuse myself to go to the bathroom to regain my composure. Shanice is in there and I can tell she's been crying.

"You okay?" I ask, handing her a tissue.

She nods. "I guess you heard what happened."

"Yeah, I did. Shanice, I'm really sorry."

She shrugs. "It's my fault for believing that lying dog. I should've known better." Her tears start falling again. "I just l-loved him s-so much."

"I know you did."

"How could he do th-this t-to me?"

I try to comfort her as best I can.

I'm mildly surprised that T. J. is still at the picnic table waiting for me when I come back from the girls' bathroom.

He rises when I approach the table. "I was getting worried about you. I thought I was going to have to come in there after you."

"Shanice was in there and she was crying," I say. I sit down beside him. "I couldn't leave her in there by herself upset like that."

T. J. takes my hand in his own. "You have a good heart, Divine."

"I feel really bad about everything that's happened." I check my watch, then say, "The bell's about to ring. I need to go to my locker before class. Feel like walking with me?"

"Ready when you are," T. J. responds.

T. J. and I make a quick stop by my locker before moving on to our classes. When I enter my classroom, one of the kids asks, "Are you and T. J. going together?"

I break into a smile but don't respond. I'm not about to go running my mouth after what Madison did to me. My relationship with T. J. is my business.

When school ends, Alyssa and I walk home.

I can tell that Aunt Phoebe's making spaghetti for dinner as soon as I walk through the front door. Alyssa yells out a greeting before rushing off to her room. I head straight to the kitchen.

"The spaghetti sauce smells so good, Aunt Phoebe."

Aunt Phoebe stirs the sauce, then places the lid on the pot. Turning to me, she says, "Thank you, sugar."

I take a seat at the breakfast table and reach for an apple. "I think you were right when you said I was leading Alyssa astray."

She joins me at the table. "Divine . . . I never shoulda said that."

"You were right though."

Aunt Phoebe gets this worried expression on her face. "What happened today?"

"There's a boy at school—his name is Trey and he's been stealing money from his parents to send to his Internet wife. And then there's this girl at school who had sex with her boyfriend only because she thought doing it made them legally married. Well, he 'divorced' her. A lot of boys are doing that now. They lie and tell these girls that they'll really be married—then they dump them. Aunt Phoebe, I never intended for all this to happen. I was just trying to have some fun."

"So you're blaming yourself?"

I nod. "It's my fault because I started it. Nobody had ever heard of cyber-marriages before Madison and I did it. Now people are using it to get over on each other."

"It's become distorted."

My eyes water. "Aunt Phoebe, I didn't mean for this to happen."

"I know that, sugar. Divine, I've told you before that you are a role model to these kids. They're fascinated by you. You're a celebrity to them. Whatever you're doing may attract others to follow. Now I'm not blaming you for what happened. I just want you to remember that our lives should lead others to Christ and not astray."

"It's a huge responsibility, Aunt Phoebe. I don't think I can do it."

"It's not your mission alone, sugar. It's the mission for each of us, but only a few are brave enough to carry it out. If you want to know what I think—I think you're a very brave girl. So, what are you going to do about it?"

"What can I do?"

"Those kids at Temple High look up to you, Divine. They watch you and they imitate you. I think they'd listen to whatever you had to say."

"You really think so?"

Aunt Phoebe nods. "I do."

"What should I tell them?"

"Educate them, sugar. Tell them more about this Internet marriage—what it was meant for and how it's been distorted."

"You might as well go on and say you were right about me, Aunt Phoebe. I already know that this is my fault. If I'd never said anything about it to Alyssa or Madison, none of this would be happening."

"I don't need to say a word. You're doing a bang-up job of blaming yourself for all this." Aunt Phoebe gets up to check on her sauce and put the water on to boil for the pasta. "You don't need me adding to it."

"I feel so bad, Aunt Phoebe."

She comes over to where I'm sitting and places an arm around me. "Don't take it to heart. Just learn from it and educate others."

"I love you, Aunt Phoebe."

"I love you too, sugar. Now go on and get your homework done. Dinner will be ready soon."

"Did you and Mama have a good talk?" Alyssa asks when I run into her in the hallway.

I nod.

She loops her arm through mine as we walk toward her bedroom. "Divine, I hate seeing you so down. This is not your fault."

"Then why do I keep feeling this way?" I ask. I take a seat on the edge of her bed. "I felt so guilty when I ran into Shanice earlier. Alyssa, she was crying her eyes out."

"It's still not your fault though. I'm sorry Shanice got hurt, but she chose to have sex with Trey. You didn't force her or tell her that the marriage was a real one."

"I just never should've mentioned it in the first place."

"We all would've found out about it sooner or later. Things like that get around, Divine. You know that."

I nod in agreement.

Chance arrives home a few minutes later. He looks flustered, like he and Trina have been arguing. I make sure to stay out his way because I don't need him taking his issues out on me.

I don't need the drama.

I go to my room to take a short nap before dinner. But instead of sleeping, I make a phone call.

"Hello."

"Ava, it's me . . . Divine." Deep down, I am trying to figure out why in the world I'm calling this woman. It's not like we're friends or anything. But she is Jerome's wife and she's carrying his child. I guess I should be mature about all this.

"How are you?"

I can't get over how happy she sounds to hear from me. It's only a phone call and I don't plan on being long.

"I called to see how you're doing," I respond.

"Baby and I are great. I just sent off a care package to your father. He asked for a new Bible. He wanted a different translation."

"Jerome wanted a Bible?" I ask in surprise. "He's reading the Bible?"

"Yes," Ava responds with a chuckle. "Believe it or not, your father is actively participating in the Bible study program at the prison. He never told you about it?"

I search my memory. "No ma'am. Jerome had me thinking that he reads it every now and then, but he never told me he was like, really studying it."

"Maybe he's waiting to surprise you."

"Why would he do that?"

"Jerome's getting a certificate in biblical studies, Divine."

I gasp in shock. "Jerome Hardison?"

She laughs. "He's really seeking the Lord."

I'm totally in shock.

"That's wonderful," I say after I find my voice. "Wow. I can't believe it."

"He's changed a lot since he's been locked up."

I agree. "I guess you're very good for him."

"It's not me, Divine," Ava says. "Your father loves you so much; he wants to earn your respect. He wants to redeem himself in your eyes. It's very important to him."

Ava and I talk longer than I planned, but it was a good conversation. I hang up after promising to call her again.

Madison calls me around eight thirty.

At first I decide I'm not answering his call, but then I change my mind—mostly out of curiosity. "What do you want?" I say in icy tones.

"I miss you, Divine."

I drop down on the edge of my bed and slip off my tennis shoes. "I told you not to call me anymore."

"I want you to give me another chance. Please, Divine . . . we belong together. I can't stand seeing you with T. J. I know you still love me."

"How do you figure?" I climb off my bed and walk over to the window, peeking outside.

"We love each other. Brittany don't mean a thing to me."

"What about the baby?"

"What about it?" he demands.

"Madison, what are you planning to do?"

"I'll do what I can for it, but that's it."

This boy has me pacing back and forth in my bedroom. I really need to get him out of my system. "It's over between us, Madison. Like I told you before—I'm not interested in any baby mama drama."

"I don't want a relationship with Brittany. I wanna be with you."

I shake my head. "I can't do it, Madison. The truth is that our breakup isn't just about Brittany and your baby. You tried to play me."

"What are you talking about?"

"Remember when you were telling me that we needed to consummate our marriage to make it real?—well, that's a big lie."

"No, it isn't."

"Madison, I'm not stupid. A lot of boys at school were saying that so they could get girls to have sex with them." My tone turns angry. "You really tried to run a game on me. I don't know why you even bothered to get back with me. All you've ever wanted from me is sex. I see that now."

"I don't know what T. J.'s been telling you but—"

"How do you know he said anything to me? See . . . you must be trying to lie. This was supposed to be a game—something fun to do. How could you all try to use it to get over on girls? That's like, so wrong, Madison."

"Divine, I wasn't trying to run a game on you. I really thought it was true. Look, we belong together. Just give us another chance. I know you still care for me."

I switch my phone from one ear to the other. "It really doesn't matter how I feel, Madison. It's over between us."

"Can we at least be friends then?"

"I don't know about that. Maybe one day, but not anytime soon."

"Divine, I was miserable at the prom, watching you with T. J."

"I'm sorry but I have to move on with my life."

"Divine—"

I quickly interrupt him by saying, "I need to go. I have to finish studying."

"Divine, I just want you to know that I love you and I miss you."

" 'Bye, Madison," I whisper before hanging up.

I regret talking to him because now I'm depressed and can't fully concentrate on my studies. I give up after fifteen minutes and decide to just call it a night.

In the shower, my tears run down my cheeks merging with the steady hot blast of water. I miss my boo. Only he's not my boo anymore.

My heart breaks all over again.

chapter 30

The next day at school, I hear about another girl who'd been suckered into making her marriage real.

"This has got to stop," I say to Alyssa. "I started this, so I'm going to put an end to it."

"Divine, what are you gonna do?"

"I don't know but I'll figure something out."

It doesn't come to me until the middle of my chemistry class. I go up to my teacher and ask if I can go see the principal.

After a short wait in the reception area, I'm ushered into Mr. McPhearson's office. He gestures for me to sit down.

I close the door behind me before dropping down in one of the visitor chairs facing his desk.

"What can I do for you, Divine?"

I swallow my uneasiness. "There's something you need to know,

Mr. McPhearson. I don't know if you've heard about the marriage game—have you?"

"The marriage game?" He shakes his head. "No, I haven't heard about it. However, I have heard rumors of some of the students being married. I didn't think much of it."

"It's my fault," I blurt out. "Mr. McPhearson, I was on the Internet doing some research on marriage and I found out about cyber-marriages. There's even a fantasy game in China where you get married for bonus points. I thought it would be fun, so my boyfriend and I had a virtual wedding."

Mr. McPhearson's eyes are glued to my face as he settles back in his chair.

"Word got around about what I had done and before I knew it, everybody was doing it. I didn't think it was a bad thing because I am trendsetter, after all, but then the rules of the game changed—boys started using it to get girls into bed and one boy started stealing money to give to his 'wife.' That's not the way it was supposed to be."

"I appreciate your coming in here to discuss this, Divine. I can certainly understand why you're concerned."

"Since I started this mess, I thought maybe I should be the one to try and clean it up."

"Do you have something in mind?"

"As a matter of face, I do."

I go over my idea with him.

When I leave Mr. McPhearson's office, I'm in much better spirits.

Everyone is called to the auditorium for an assembly shortly after the bell rings the next day.

Mr. McPhearson briefly addresses the student body before he calls me up to the podium. My eyes scan the audience, searching for friendly faces. I smile when I spot Alyssa, Penny and Stacy. A few rows back, I find Aunt Phoebe and Uncle Reed. I'm touched that they were able to come. Their being here gives me strength. On the other side of the auditorium, Nicholas and T. J. are seated side by side.

T. J. rewards me with a smile and waves at me.

I wave back. Then I clear my throat, summon up my courage and begin. "Virtual marriages have become a new fashion among students in China and now here in this school. I found out about virtual marriages when I was doing some research for a project." I pause for a moment when my eyes meet Madison's gaze. "I thought the idea of getting married online would be something fun to do. It was harmless."

I take a deep breath and then exhale slowly. "But then, I think, people started getting the wrong impression. Boys started using virtual marriages to get girls to have sex with them. Everyone, I need you to understand that these types of marriages are not legal. Don't listen to anyone who tells you that consummating the marriage will make it valid."

My eyes travel back to Madison. "It's not true. I am so sorry for ever bringing this game to Temple High School. I never dreamed that people would take it so far. My fear is that if you don't stop now, more and more people will get into serious trouble by getting involved with the wrong person. I know about that firsthand. Please stop playing this game now. Marriage is sacred, not a game. Marriage is a commitment. It's a spiritual, emotional and physical commitment. At our ages, we're not ready for something so permanent, so please listen to me and don't risk your heart for a fake one. That's all I want to say, I guess."

The room is so quiet; you can hear a pin drop.

T. J. suddenly stands up and starts clapping. Alyssa joins him a few seconds later, followed by my aunt and uncle. Soon, the entire school is on their feet, cheering and clapping.

I glance over at Mr. McPhearson, who gives me one of his rare smiles.

After the assembly is over, I look for Uncle Reed and Aunt Phoebe. I find them standing at the back of the auditorium near the exit.

"You did a wonderful job," Uncle Reed tells me when I join them.

Aunt Phoebe agrees. "We're very proud of you, Divine."

"I just hope the kids will listen to me," I respond.

"We have to leave because I need to get back to the church for a meeting, but we wanted to show our support by being here with you. We'll talk when you get home," Uncle Reed states.

Alyssa comes over to greet her parents. I excuse myself and seek out T. J. He walks up to me and gives me a hug. "Divine, you did great up there."

"Thank you."

He's such a sweetie.

Shanice is standing outside the auditorium when I walk out.

"I really appreciate what you said up there, Divine. I just wish I'd known about this earlier. Maybe I wouldn't have . . ."

"If I could change things for you, I would, Shanice. I feel horrible over what happened to you. I'm so sorry and I hope that one day you'll be able to forgive me."

"Divine, it's not your fault."

My friend Deonne stops me on my way to class. "You did a good job up there, Divine. I'm so glad you said something. I was planning on skipping school tomorrow with my boyfriend. We . . . well, I thought we would be making the marriage valid." She hugs me. "Thanks so much. You saved me from making a huge mistake."

"See?" Alyssa says. "Some good did come out of all this."

* * *

I SEEK OUT my aunt and uncle as soon as I walk through the front door. I find them in the kitchen. I grab an apple and take a bite out of it. I hug Uncle Reed and then my aunt. "Thanks so much for coming. It really meant a lot to me to have you there."

"We're very proud of you, Divine," Aunt Phoebe says. "What you did took a lot of courage."

"Being a role model is pretty cool but I had no clue what a huge responsibility it can become," I state. "I never wanted to hurt anyone or cause them to be hurt in any way." I take another bite of my apple.

Uncle Reed retrieves an apple from the fruit basket. "Sometimes people get caught up in their role-playing."

"I know I almost did. I almost—" I stop abruptly. I don't want to give Aunt Phoebe a heart attack by blurting out how close I was to having sex with Madison. I nearly fell for the hype too, but finding out about Brittany stopped me before I could. I guess that's one of those *outs* that Uncle Reed says God gives you. I don't like this one much because I lost Madison in the process, but there's nothing I can do about it now.

Except just go on with my life.

Thankfully, I'm cute; I'll find another boyfriend easily. Who knows, if things keep going well with T. J.—he might be my new boo.

Aunt Phoebe's words cut into my thoughts. "What were you going to say?"

"Oh. Just that I'm glad I found out about Madison and his lies."

"I spoke with T. J. earlier," Uncle Reed announces. "He asked for permission to take you to the movies. He assures me that it's a group of teens going out."

"I guess you told him no."

"Actually, we gave our permission."

My eyes widen in my surprise. "You did?"

"You have earned it, sugar. Alyssa and Stephen will be going with y'all, too," Aunt Phoebe says.

I jump up and down. "I can't believe it. Thank you, Jesus!"

Alyssa comes running into the kitchen. "What happened?"

"We're going out with T. J. and Stephen and a group of other people on Saturday to the movies."

Alyssa is just as surprised but she recovers quickly. "Cool . . ."

"Thank you," we say in unison.

As soon as we get to Alyssa's room, she starts squealing with delight. "We're going on a date! We're going on a date!"

"With a group of other people," I state. "It's not like a real date."

"But we're going out with our boyfriends, Divine."

"*You* are, Alyssa. I don't have a boyfriend. T. J. and I are just friends."

She drops onto her bed. "I thought you liked him."

I sit down beside her. "I do, but we're taking things really slow."

"Girl, I bet before school ends you and T. J. gon' be more than friends. Just watch."

"I don't know about that," I respond. "He might turn out to be a bigger jerk than Madison. You can never tell."

Jerome calls me right before I get into the shower. I grab my robe and slip it on while talking to him.

"Hey, baby girl . . . how you doing?"

I take a seat on the edge of my bed. "I'm fine. How about you? Everything going okay?"

"As well as can be, I suppose. My lawyer came by today. Hopefully, I'll be able to get out of here real soon."

"I hope so," I respond. "You need to be home with your new baby."

"How's my little man doing?"

"Jason's getting so big, Jerome, and he's such a sweetie. He loves to talk. Mrs. Campbell is thinking about putting him in preschool for half a day twice a week."

"I sho' hope I get to see my son one day."

I don't respond.

"It's my prayer," Jerome tells me. "I want to be in my lil boy's life. I owe him that much."

"Ava told me you were taking a class in biblical studies. Why didn't you tell me?"

"I wanted to surprise you, baby girl. I want to make you proud of me."

"I am," I tell him. "Jerome, I'm very proud of you. You've changed so much since you went to prison. You're more of a dad to me now."

"You don't know how much that means to me to hear you say that. It's a shame I had to get locked up in here to learn how to be a father to you. Better late than never, I guess."

"My conversation with Ava was a good one. She seems pretty nice."

"Baby girl, she was so happy to get that phone call from you. You really lifted her spirits that day."

I smile. "I'm glad to hear that. I really didn't know what to say to her, but then it felt like we'd been talking to each other forever."

"What's up with that boy? I haven't heard you talk about him lately. I also noticed you didn't go to the prom with him."

"Mom told you?"

"She sent me some pictures that she took before y'all left. You looked so beautiful in that gold dress. So what happened to the other dude?"

"His name is Madison and we broke up."

"The boy in the picture—he your new boyfriend?"

"No sir. T. J. and I are just friends."

"T. J., huh?"

I laugh. "His name is Thomas James Wellington, Jr. His father is a preacher. He's a really nice boy."

"You looked real happy."

"I had a great time, Jerome. At first I wasn't going to go, but then T. J. asked me. I'm glad I went with him. I would've regretted staying home."

"I want nothing but happiness for you, baby girl. Don't ever forget that."

"I won't."

Jerome's time is up and we have to end our call.

"I'll write and tell you all about the prom," I say quickly. "I love you, Jerome."

He gets all choked up and sounds like he's about to cry, but we get cut off. His twenty minutes are up and the prison doesn't play when it comes to telephone privileges.

T. J. calls me ten minutes later.

"Were you busy?" he asks.

"I just got off the phone with Jerome."

"Jerome?"

"That's my dad," I explain. "He didn't want me calling him Daddy, so I've always called him Jerome."

"Are you two very close?"

"We weren't in the beginning, but since he's been away—he's doing so much better in the dad department."

"That's good."

I smile. "I think so."

"I guess Temple is a lot slower than what you're used to, huh?"

"It's very different from California," I respond. "But I really like it here. I didn't at first. Since I've been here, though, I'm really enjoying Temple. I really like school and I've made some good friends."

"So you don't miss being in all those magazines and on television?"

"Not really. I mean, when I go with Mom to the Grammys or Soul Train Awards the media's going to photograph me. That's just a part of my life—I'm used to it."

We talked for hours about everything. What's it like to have celebrity parents? What's it like to have a preacher for a dad? Favorite books, movies, music.

"You actually recorded with your mom?"

"Alyssa and I both did background vocals on her latest album. It was fun but a whole lot of work. We were in there for about six hours trying to get them right."

"You lead an interesting life, Divine," T. J. says.

"I heard you play saxophone?"

"I do. I love music. I play for my dad's church."

"I'll have to come hear you sometime."

"I'd like that," he says. "Divine, can I ask you a question?"

"Sure. What is it?"

"Are you over Madison?"

"I'm getting there," I tell T. J. honestly.

I steal a peek at the clock, we've been on the phone for two hours. At ten o'clock, I tell him, "I'd better get off the phone now. I don't want to do anything to mess up my going to the movies with you guys on Saturday. I'm really looking forward to it."

We say our good-byes.

Singing softly, I pad across the room to my bathroom and turn on the shower. Aunt Phoebe was right—the pain of losing Madison lessens with each new day.

THE NEXT DAY, I'm surprised to run into Madison just as I'm leaving the girls' locker room. I debate whether or not to pretend I don't see him.

"Hey," he greets me.

"Madison, hello," I respond drily. I try to step around him, but he moves to block my exit.

"You looking good as always."

I give him a tiny smile. "Thanks."

"You and T. J. seem like you getting real close."

"It's not your business, Madison."

"I'm not ready to be a dad," he blurts.

I meet his gaze. "Then maybe you should've kept your pants zipped up. I'm sorry for you but you should've learned from Chance and Trina's situation."

"I hate that I don't have you in my life, Divine. I really miss talking to you."

"Why don't you actually try being nice to Brittany? Who knows, maybe you two can work things out before the baby comes. Every child should have two loving parents."

"I don't love her, Divine."

I shrug. "You must have liked something about her, Madison. You had sex with her."

"She can be cool sometimes."

I hold up a hand. "I don't think I want to hear this." Switching my backpack to the other side, I say, "It's time for you to grow up and accept your responsibility."

Madison shakes his head. "I messed up real bad, Divine. Real bad. Look, if you don't believe nothing else I say, believe this: I'm sorry for lying to you. I just didn't want to lose what we had. We'd just gotten back together—"

"I understand all that, Madison. I really do. But we can't be together—especially now that Brittany's having your baby. You're going to be a father soon. It's just over for us."

"But I don't want to be with Brittany," he says. "I'm not gonna be with her just because of a baby. I don't have feelings like that for her."

"We're talking in circles, Madison," I reply. "This is not my problem."

"Divine, can we at least be friends?"

"Not right now. I need some time, Madison." I brush past him, pausing long enough to say, "I wish the best for you and I pray God will guide you to do the right thing by Brittany. Remember, she didn't do this all by herself."

Without looking back, I head off to the cafeteria for lunch.

Although I'm saddened by my breakup with Madison, I know that one day I'll meet someone who's worthy of me. With God's help, of course. Aunt Phoebe always tells us that some people are only in our lives for a season.

I spot T. J. waiting for me outside the cafeteria. Who knows—maybe T. J. is supposed to be a part of my life in this season.

I smile and wave.

But in the meantime, I think I'll just focus my energies on my studies, keeping up with the latest fashions and my relationship with God. School's out in a couple of weeks and then I'll be off to California.

I'm looking forward to seeing Mimi and Rhyann, and even visiting Jerome on the weekends. I also plan to spend some time with Ava because I promised my dad that I would. I've got a lot to look forward to, including my mom's wedding.

I'm still not quite convinced that God wants to know about all the relationship drama in my life, but I'm willing to give it a try.

author's note

I hope you have enjoyed *Divine Match-Up*, the fourth book in the series featuring Divine Matthews-Hardison. Although many of you may not believe that cyber- or virtual marriages actually exist—they do. As of 2005, more than 120,000 cyber-marriages have been registered online according to *Chinese Women* (Zhen, 2001), *News Weekly* (J. Li, 2004), and *Youth Reference* (Feng, 2004).

The whole idea of online marriages is based on the premise that it's a harmless little game, but according to an Internet article on sify.com, cyber-marriages are emerging as a serious health hazard in China, the world's second largest Internet market. It has become a new fashion among students, with them marrying several times and even "giving birth" to virtual babies online.

It was important for me to write this story because of my concern that virtual marriages could lead teens into misunderstanding the reality of marriage. The rules of the game allow you to marry and divorce easily and casually, which leaves you with a wrong impression of marriage. Many teens have been duped into believing that their marriage is a real one if they have sex with their spouses.

THIS IS NOT TRUE.

This type of marriage ceremony is not legally binding. In order for a marriage to be legal, a couple has to have a marriage license, which is granted by legal entities such as the local county courthouse, city hall, provincial or magistrate offices or a department such as a Registrar of Marriages.

The Bible begins with a marriage and it ends with a marriage, which should give you an idea of how sacred such a union is to the Lord.

REMEMBER . . . a cyber-marriage in a cyber chapel is *NOT* a legal marriage. While this type of fantasy game has not yet reached popularity here in the United States or other countries—it's coming.

Knowledge is power.

Reading Group Guide for *divine* **match-up**

Summary

Smitten with her boyfriend, Madison, sixteen-year-old Divine does what any twenty-first-century girl in love would do—she secretly "marries" him in an online virtual marriage ceremony! Her fake-wedded bliss only lasts for a moment, though: fresh on the heels of their pseudo-union, Divine's celebrity mother comes to visit and informs everyone that she is engaged to her boyfriend, Kevin. Divine wants to be happy for her mother, and she likes Kevin, but everything about this situation just feels wrong. She's afraid her mother will get hurt again, and she's wary of another man—especially another celebrity—coming into their lives. Her thoughts are troubled further when news of her "marriage" leaks and ugly gossip about Madison starts spreading through the school. Soon Divine has to figure out how to mend a broken heart, be a responsible role model, and improve her relationship with God, all while balancing the demands of high school life.

Questions for Discussion

1. Divine tells Alyssa, "You can find anything on the Internet." (page 4). Do you think that the easy accessibility of things in today's high-tech world affects their value? Are there different standards for what happens online vs. the real world, especially when it comes to friendships and relationships?

2. *Wanghun* is, as Divine constantly explains, just a role-playing game in which people pretend to be married and even have families online. What concerns do the adults in the novel express about this kind of role-playing? How might this or other types of role-playing games also be useful? After reading the author's note and considering this story, what will you say if someone at school tells you about virtual marriages?

3. Several teens in this novel remark that they are proud virgins, or as Divine says, "card-carrying members of the Big V Club." What reasons do these characters give for waiting to have sex? Explain whether you agree or disagree with these reasons, and why.

4. On page 30, Kara tells Divine that she's too young to really understand what love is. Has anyone ever said this to you? How does it make you feel? Given what happens in the novel, or what may have happened in your life, why do you think adults say this so often? What do you think about Divine's comeback: that if grown-ups know so much about love, why are there so many divorces and incidents of violence between spouses?

5. As the daughter of wealthy celebrities, Divine lives a lush lifestyle of designer clothes, fancy award shows, and photo ops. If you suddenly became rich and famous, what changes would you make in your lifestyle? Do you think you'd enjoy the attention, like Divine, or would it be an interruption, as it is when Kevin tries to take the girls out to dinner?

6. Whenever someone disagrees with Divine about her mother's engagement, she says they just don't know what she's going through. Do you think this is true, or is it something else? What do you think Divine is really upset about?

7. While Divine insists that the cyber-marriages are no big deal and that she and Madison didn't do anything wrong, Alyssa points out that if that were true, they would not have been so sneaky about it. Do you agree more with Divine or Alyssa? Why? What other reasons might there be for keeping a secret?

8. Divine complains repeatedly that she wishes her family could just be normal. What is normal, really? Do you think her family is as strange as she seems to think it is? Why or why not?

9. Madison tells Divine that because they said vows before a clergyman, all they need to do to make their marriage valid in the eyes of God is to consummate it by having sex. But Divine knows that isn't enough to make a marriage legal in the United States. What is the difference between God's law and the law of the land? Are there situations in which one might take precedence over the other? What does Divine's uncle say about this subject when he finds out about Divine and Madison's "wedding?"

10. When Divine and her uncle have a private heart-to-heart, she argues that some kids mature faster than others, but he reminds her that some kids who think they are mature, aren't. In what ways do the teens in this novel show their maturity, or lack thereof? What do you think you would do in their shoes?

11. Divine desires Madison, but she feels in her heart that she isn't ready to have a sexual relationship with him or any boy. Have you ever wanted something you knew wasn't good for you? How did you handle the situation?

12. Aunt Phoebe, Uncle Reed, and Divine's mother, Kara, are all extremely concerned about the effect of make-believe marriages

on their teenage daughters. On page 141, Divine wonders, "Are they right to be worried?" Given what happens in this novel, what do you think? Have you ever witnessed a similar situation in your own life?

13. In this novel, Trina and Madison both struggle with an unexpected pregnancy that disrupts their lives and causes them pain. Do you sympathize with Trina? Do you feel sorry for Madison? What do you think about Madison's insistence that he doesn't love Brittany and doesn't want to be with her, even though she is having his child? Do you agree with Divine's assessment that Trina needs to "stop tripping?" Why or why not?

14. When Divine learns that boys are using the cyber-marriages to trick girls into having sex, she feels responsible. But Alyssa tells her that it isn't her fault, and that everyone has his or her own mind to make choices with. What do you think? Describe a time when you were positively inspired or negatively influenced by the behavior of someone else. How do you try to live by example?

15. If you've read previous novels in this series, how do you think Divine has been changed by her experiences? In what ways do you see her responding differently to situations?

Activities to Enhance your Book Club Experience

1. As the daughter of popular celebrity parents, Divine gets to enjoy the "high life," even though she's now far from the everyday glitz of Los Angeles. Get a taste of the celebrity experience by asking your parents to take your book club to the swankiest restaurant or teen-friendly nightclub in town. Try searching on www.citysearch.com or www.zagats.com for the right place, make a reservation, don your nicest outfit, and don't forget the sunglasses!

2. Many characters in this novel find the solution to their problems by letting God into their lives and involving Him in all their decisions, even the little ones. At your next book club meeting, go around the circle and share your own stories about the moments when you've felt God's presence in your life.

3. Take some time to browse the author's websites at www.jacquelinthomas.com, simplydivinebooks.com, and www.myspace.com/simplydivinebooks.

A Conversation with Jacquelin Thomas

Q. Many first-time authors write semi-autobiographical novels. Now that you've written several, how much of your own life still ends up in your stories?

A. *I believe I bring some of my life experiences to each of my novels, including the teen stories. I still remember being a teen and feeling as if my parents just didn't understand, but I bring my experiences as a mother to those books as well. I hope to show that parents were teens once and yes, we do understand what you're going through—just trust us and allow us to help you make wise choices.*

Q. You have written books for both adults and young readers. How is it different to write for each audience? Do you have a preference?

A. *I actually enjoy writing for both audiences, the only difference is that for teens the Divine series really speaks to their issues. I had a large teen readership before I began writing the series—they are the reason I created Divine and her friends.*

Q. You began your writing career as an author of romance novels. What prompted you to change genres? Do you think you'll ever write romances again?

A. *My mother was an avid romance reader, and when I was in my teens I would sneak into her room and read her novels when I ran out of my own. I developed a love for both historical and contemporary romances so writing romance was my first choice. But as my faith matured, I felt a desire to write books that not only entertained but would also minister to the readers. I've written a few inspirational romances recently—so yes, if inspired, I'll write more.*

Q. This novel is set is Temple, Georgia, but you live in North Carolina. Have you ever lived in Georgia? How did you choose Temple as the setting for your Divine stories?

A. *I grew up in Georgia and used to visit relatives in Villa Rica during the summer months. One of my cousins actually lives in Temple now and I love the area. I think it's the perfect setting for the Divine series.*

Q. *Divine Match-Up* is your fourth novel in this series. What tricks do you use to maintain the character development and story lines from one book to the next? Are there any techniques you use in each book to refresh readers' memories about what happened in the previous installment?

A. *I actually have a notebook filled with notes from each book in the series. I keep a schedule of Divine's classes, her hobbies, favorite foods, etc. I also keep notes on the other characters as well to maintain consistency. I always read the previous book before sitting down to write the next one in the series to refresh my memory. I also try to weave in little details from the previous books in the event that the reader is reading about Divine for the first time.*

Q. You write so convincingly from the point of view of teenagers. Where do you find your inspiration? What kind of research do you do for each novel to maintain the authenticity of your teenage characters?

A. *I raised two daughters who are now twenty-eight and twenty-four and I'm happy to say that I survived their teenage years. WHEW! However, I have a thirteen-year-old son home with me and I mentor several teen girls in my area.*

Q. In your Author's Note, you make it clear that the novel is in part a cautionary tale in preparation for what you see as an inevitable trend in American high schools. How did you find out about *wanghun*? Do you already see something similar happening among teens today?

A. *I was on the Internet reading articles from various newspapers and came across one about a twelve-year-old boy with three wives. This same article mentioned it wasn't only the teens participating in wanghun—adults were doing it too. There was a woman who found out about her fiance's virtual bride and called off her wedding. She felt it made a mockery of marriage. My fear is that it will open the door for Internet predators, give teens the wrong idea of what it truly means to be committed to another person . . . I believe that virtual marriages can put you or someone you know in danger.*

Q. One of the biggest Internet safety concerns recently has been the rocketing growth of MySpace and the opportunity it creates for young people, especially teens, to be taken advantage of. Yet you have a successful presence on MySpace yourself. What do you have to say about how such technologies can be both a curse and a blessing? What words of wisdom can you offer teens to help them benefit from the unlimited possibilities of the Internet instead of being harmed by it?

A. *I believe the theory behind MySpace is a wonderful concept but, like anything else, if used irresponsibly it can cause serious harm. It is up to the parents to speak to their children regarding Internet safety. Make sure you have access to their MySpace or Facebook pages. I am very selective as to who my friends are on MySpace—I even have a message posted on my profile page that before I accept you as a friend I have to check out your page; if I find it questionable, I will not allow you to become a friend. Even then, I feel it's my responsibility to protect any teen who visits my profile. I want to add that I don't think you should post pictures or any personal information on your profile that will allow a predator to pinpoint your location. Also, if you don't know the person asking for the friend request—do not accept it.*

Q. Alyssa and Divine pray regularly for forgiveness for their sins, though it doesn't seem to stop sassy Divine from getting into trouble. What do you think the real "power of forgiveness" is?

A. *Praying for forgiveness doesn't keep you from sinning. We are not sinless, but it should be our goal to sin less each and every day. God loves us unconditionally, therefore, when we sin and ask for forgiveness—He forgives. However, we are to forgive others as He forgives us—the past is the past and we shouldn't look back. We have to forgive even when we feel it's undeserved. That's the real power of forgiveness.*

Q. Your fiction is categorized as Christian Fiction, and you write primarily for an African American audience. Do you think non-African American, non-Christian readers can still glean something profound from your novels?

A. *The issues confronted in all of my novels are universal. We have all loved, been hurt, been rejected, made mistakes, etc. You don't have to be African American or a Christian to get the message in my stories. I tell people all the time that I don't just write for the Christian market—I write for the wounded in spirit, the rejected, the ones needing a word of encouragement, the ones searching but have no idea what they're searching for. My novels are not preachy and I write to entertain, but I want to also include a message of hope—that God is the answer to all of life's problems.*

Q. As a Christian and an artist, what role does God play in your creative process?

A. *God is the reason that I write. He gave me this vision as a young child and when He gives you a vision, He gives provision. He has placed me exactly where I needed to be at the appointed time. All of my stories, I believe, are designed by God. I write because I love it, but mostly I write for His glory.*

Q. Divine and her mother are each seeking to improve their relationship with God in their own way. Do you ever get to work through some of your own struggles via your characters? Do you feel that any of your characters' relationships with God mirrors your own journey?

A. *Definitely. I have had those same questions and struggles during my own walk with God. I am still maturing in my faith but I've learned how important it is to stay grounded in the Word.*

Q. You must hear stories all the time from readers who associate with your characters and novels. Is there one in particular that you'd like to share with us, something that continues to inspire and encourage you in your work?

A. *I love the letter I received from a young lady who adores the Divine series and is constantly telling me that I need to write them faster. She also shared with me how much Divine inspired her to remain a virgin. She was getting pressure from her boyfriend to have sex, but after reading the Divine series, she decided to remain a card carrying member of the V Club. Since the series debuted, I've received several e-mails from V Club members and I'm so very proud of each of them for taking a stand. Even if you've lost your virginity—it's never too late to say yes to abstinence.*

"Mimi, I'm dying for you to see my dress," I say into the purple-rhinestone-studded cell phone. "It's this deep purple color with hand-painted scroll designs in gold on it. I have to be honest. I—Divine Matthews-Hardison—will be in *all* the magazines. I'll probably be listed in the top-ten best-dressed category."

Mimi laughs. "Me too. My dress is tight. It's silver and strapless and Lana Maxwell designed it."

"Oh, she's that new designer. Nobody really knows her yet." I'm hatin' on her because she's allowed to wear a strapless gown and I had to beg Mom for days to get her to let me wear a halter-style dress.

I make sure to keep my voice low so that the nosy man Mom claims is my dad can't hear my conversation. It's a wonder Jerome actually has a life of his own—he's always trying to meddle in mine.

I can tell our limo is nearing the entrance of the Los Angeles Convention Center because I hear people screaming, and see the rapid flashing of cameras as die-hard fans try to snap pictures of their favorite celebrities while others hold up signs. I'm glued to the window, checking out the growing sea of bystanders standing on both sides of the red carpet.

The annual Grammy Awards celebration is music's biggest night and the one major event I look forward to attending every year. Singers, actors and anyone really important will be present. Media coverage is heavy and I know as soon as I step out of the limo, the press is going to be all over me.

Settling back in the seat, I tell Mimi, "I'll talk to you when you get here. I need to make sure my hair is together. You know how these photographers are—they're like always trying to snap an ugly picture of celebrities to send all over the world. That's the last thing I need—some whack photo of me splashed all over the tabloids. See you in a minute. Bye."

Cameras flash and whirl as limo after stretch limo roll to a stop. I put away my phone and take out the small compact mirror I can't live without, making sure every strand of my hair is in place. A girl's gotta look her best, so I touch up my lips with Dior Addict Plastic Gloss in Euphoric Beige. I like this particular lip gloss because the color doesn't make my lips look shiny or too big in photographs.

I pull the folds of my gold-colored silk wrap together and blow a kiss to myself before slipping the mirror back into my matching gold clutch. I'm looking *fierce,* as my idol Tyra Banks loves to say on *America's Next Top Model.* To relieve some of the nervous energy I'm feeling, I begin tracing the pattern of my designer gown. This is my first time wearing what I consider a grown-up gown. I've never been able to wear backless before, but thankfully, my mom has a clue that I'm not a baby anymore. I'll be fifteen soon.

"Divine, honey, you look beautiful," Mom compliments. "Anya did a wonderful job designing this gown for you. It's absolutely perfect. Doesn't make you look too grown up."

My smile disappears. She just had to go there.

"Thanks." As an afterthought, I add, "You do too."

My mom, renowned singer and actress Kara Matthews, is up for several Grammys. On top of that, she's scored starring roles in three blockbuster movies, one of which will have her leaving in a couple of weeks to film the sequel in Canada. She can be pretty cool at times but then she goes and ruins it by going into Mom mode. To get even, I say and do things to wreck her nerves. Like . . .

"I hope I see Bow Wow tonight. He's so hot . . ." I can't even finish my sentence because the look on Mom's face throws me into giggles. My dad, Jerome, comes out of an alcohol-induced daze long enough to grumble something unintelligible.

He's never allowed me to call him daddy. Says it makes him feel old, so he insists that I call him Jerome.

Hellooo . . . get a clue. *You are old.*

It used to bother me that Jerome didn't want me calling him Dad when I was little. But after all the crazy stuff he's done, I'd rather not tell anyone he's related to me. Although I've never actually seen him drink or whatever, I've watched enough TV to know what an addict looks like. If I could sell him on eBay, I'd do it in a heartbeat. I can just picture the ad in my head.

> *Hollywood actor for sale. Okay-looking.*
> *Used to be real popular until he started*
> *drinking and doing drugs. By the way, he*
> *really needs a family because he's on his*
> *way out of this one. Bidding starts at one dollar.*

Mom interrupts my plans to auction Jerome by saying, "Divine, I don't want you sniffing around those rap artists. You stay with me or Stella. *I mean it.* Don't go trying to sneak off like you usually do. I don't care if Dean Reuben lets Mimi run around loose. You better not!"

Mom and Jerome make a big deal for nothing over me talking to boys. Period. I'm fourteen and in the eighth grade. I'm not even allowed to date yet, so I don't know why they're always bugging whenever I mention meeting guys. I will admit I get a thrill out of the drama, so I figure giving them a scare every now and then can't hurt.

"You stay away from that Bow Wow," Jerome orders. "He's a nice kid, but you don't need to be up in his face. Don't let that fast tail Mimi get you in trouble."

This subject has so come and gone. All his drinking must be making him forgetful or something. Rolling my eyes heavenward, I pull out my cell phone, flip it open and call my best friend just to irritate him.

"Mimi, we're about to get out and stroll down the red carpet," I say loud enough for him to hear. "Where's your car now?" Mimi's dad is an actor too. He's always out of town working, which Mimi loves because then she can run all over her entertainment-lawyer mom. Her dad is the strict one in her family. For me, it's Mom. She's the only grown-up in my family.

Our limo stops moving. The driver gets out and walks around to the passenger door.

"We're here, Mimi. I'll see you in a few minutes." I hang up and slip the phone into my gold evening bag.

Cameras flashing, the media are practically climbing all over the limo. As usual, my mom starts complaining. But if the media isn't dogging her, her publicist comes up with something to get their attention, which isn't hard to do with my dad's constant legal battles. I just don't get Mom sometimes.

Mom claims she doesn't really like being in the spotlight and the center of attention, but me, I love it. I'm a Black American Princess and I'm not ashamed to admit it. I take pleasure in being pampered and waited on. Mostly, I love to shop and be able to purchase anything I want without ever looking at a price tag.

"I wish I had a cigarette," Mom blurts. "I'm so nervous."

I reach over, taking her hand in mine. "Don't worry about it. I hope you win, but even if you don't, it's still okay. At least you were nominated."

She smiles. "I know what you're saying, sweetie. And you're right, but I *do* want to win, Divine. I want this so badly."

"I know." Deep down, I want it just as bad as she does. I want Mom to win because then I'll have something to hold over that stupid Natalia Moon's head. Her mother is singer Tyler Winters. As far as I'm concerned, the woman couldn't sing a note even if she bought and paid for it. And I'm pretty sure I'm not the only one who thinks so, because she's never been nominated for a Grammy.

The door to the limo opens.

Leo, our bodyguard, steps out first. He goes everywhere with us to protect us from our public. There are people out there who'll take it to the extreme to meet celebrities.

Mom's assistant, Stella, gets out of the car next. All around us, I hear people chanting, "Kara . . . Kara . . . Kara."

A few bystanders push forward, but are held back by thick, black velvet ropes and uniformed cops.

"They love you, Mom."

Smiling, my mom responds, "Yeah . . . they sure do, baby."

I'm so proud to have *the* Kara Matthews as my mom. She's thin and beautiful. Although she's only five feet five inches tall, she looks just like a model. I have her high cheekbones and smooth tawny complexion, but unfortunately, I'm also saddled with Jerome's full lips, bushy eyebrows and slanted eyes. Thankfully, I'm still cute.

"Hey, what about me? I got some fans out there. They didn't just come to see yo' mama. She wouldn't be where she is if it wasn't for me."

I glance over my shoulder at Jerome, but don't respond. He's such a loser.

I have a feeling that he's going to find a way to ruin this night for Mom. Then she'll get mad at him and they'll be arguing for the rest of the night.

I've overheard Mom talk about divorcing Jerome a few times, but when he gets ready to leave, she begs him to stay. I wish they'd just break up because Jerome brings out the worst in Mom, according to Stella.

Stella turns and gestures for me to get out of the limo. It's time to meet my public.

Okay . . . my mom's fans. But in a way, I'm famous too. I'm Hollywood royalty. Kara Matthews's beloved daughter.

I exit the limo with Leo's assistance. Jerome will follow me, getting out before Mom. She is always last. Her way of making an entrance, I suppose.

I spot a camera aimed in my direction. I smile and toss my dark, shoulder-length hair across my shoulders the very same way I've seen Mom do millions of times.

Mom makes her grand appearance on the red carpet amid cheers, hand clapping and whistles. We pose for pictures.

Here we are, pretending to be this close and loving family.

What a joke!

I keep my practiced smile in place despite the blinding, flashing darts of lights stabbing at my eyes. It's my duty to play up to the cameras, the fans and the media.

I can't imagine my life any other way.

After a few poses in front of the limo, we start down the red carpet. Whenever I can, I stand in front of my parents, grinning like the Cheshire Cat in *Alice's Adventures in Wonderland.* I love being photographed and I know how to strike a perfect pose.

America's next top model—right here. As soon as I turn eighteen, I'm auditioning for that show. Mom says I won't have to. She actually had the nerve to tell me that I could be working right now as a model. Only she won't let me because she's real big on education, so I have to finish school first. Talk about dangling a pot of gold in front of my face and snatching it away.

Stella and Leo march in front of us, leading the way to the doors of the convention center.

I'm walking in front of my parents, close enough to hear Mom's words to Jerome.

Mom hugs me. This is her attempt to soothe me but the effort is totally wasted because I'm really mad at her.

"How about we go shopping tomorrow after school? We'll go to the Beverly Center and Rodeo Drive."

At the mention of shopping, my spirits lift some. If Mom insists on switching to Mom mode, then I plan to punish her by spending as much of her money as I can. This time it's really going to cost her big. "I want to go to Gucci and Louis Vuitton because I need to get a couple of new purses. Then I want to see the new collection at Iceberg."

"We can do that too," Mom promises. "Whatever you want."

"I don't have to go shopping with Stella, do I?" The last time we were to go shopping, Mom backed out to do a radio interview to promote her album.

"No, you don't," Mom assures me. "Tomorrow, you and I are going to spend some much-needed quality time together. I promise." She glances over her shoulder at Jerome. "Daddy's gonna join us if he's not too busy. Right?"

Jerome sends Mom a strange look I can't decipher.

I really don't want Jerome tagging along. All he ever does is complain about standing around while we try on clothes, or he fusses about how much money we spend. It isn't like we're spending any of his money. Mom is the one making paper.

"I might be able to make it but don't hold me to it."

I hope that Jerome's not able to join us. He's such a loser.

Stella comes over to where we're standing. "C'mon, Divine. It's time I got you home."

I glance over at Mom, giving her one last chance to change her mind. "I don't want to leave just yet. Nelly is right over there. Can I just go over there to meet him before I leave?"

"For what?" Jerome demands. "You better just take yo' lil fast tail home."

"You need to shut up. It's not even like that. I just want to meet him so that I can tell everyone that I met him." I don't include that my friend Rhyann and I have a fifty-dollar bet to see who'll meet him first.

He leans over and plants a kiss on my forehead. "You my baby girl. I'm just tryin' not to let you grow up too fast. You know I love you."

I push him away, no longer caring who's watching us. I don't need Jerome trying to act like a father now. "Leave me alone, Jerome. You are so not related to me."

"Sugar, don't do that," Mom whispers. "Remember, we've talked about this. Be nice to your daddy. There's a photographer in the corner watching us." Smiling, she adds, "Now give me a hug."

Embracing Mom, I feign a smile. This is really going to cost her big.

"I love you," she whispers.

Whatever. Right now, Mom's entering the loser zone in a big way.

Jerome purses his lips as if waiting for me to kiss him, but he'll turn blue and green before that ever happens. I walk off toward the nearest exit with Stella following. She makes a quick call to have our driver bring the limo around.

Without a word spoken between us, I climb into the limo, turn on the small television and settle back for the forty-five-minute drive home to Pacific Palisades.

Mom's face appears on the small screen.

"Could you turn that up, please?"

Stella turns up the volume.

It's a clip of Mom's interview after her Grammy win. I smile. "She looks real happy, doesn't she?"

"Yes, she does," Stella murmurs. "I believe her whole world is going to change after tonight."

I like seeing my mom happy. Lately though, I've noticed that she spends a lot of time in her bedroom with the door locked. The few times I've put my face to the door I've smelled the putrid odor of marijuana. I know Jerome has been smoking the stuff for years. But for Mom I think this is something new.

I've never told anyone because Stella and Mom are always saying, "What's done at home stays at home. You never betray family."

It really bothers me that my parents smoke marijuana, especially Mom. Just last year, she was the keynote speaker at my school's drug-awareness program.

What a hypocrite.

It's all Jerome's fault.

His constant legal battles and a recent paternity suit have taken a toll on my mom. At least that's what I overheard Mom telling Stella a few days ago.

"Do you think Mom will divorce Jerome?"

Stella put away her cell phone. "Divine, you don't need to worry yourself with grown-up matters."

"Well, I hope she does," I confess. "Mom would be much happier if she did."

"Let's not talk about this right now," Stella whispers. "Divine, you really need to be very careful about what you say in public."

A small sigh escapes me. The last thing I need right now is another lecture, especially one from a nonparent. Just because she and Mom grew up together, Stella thinks she can boss me around, but she's nothing more than the help as far as I'm concerned. She better be glad I halfway like her because otherwise she would've been fired a long time ago.

DAU ... END

CHE ... ES!

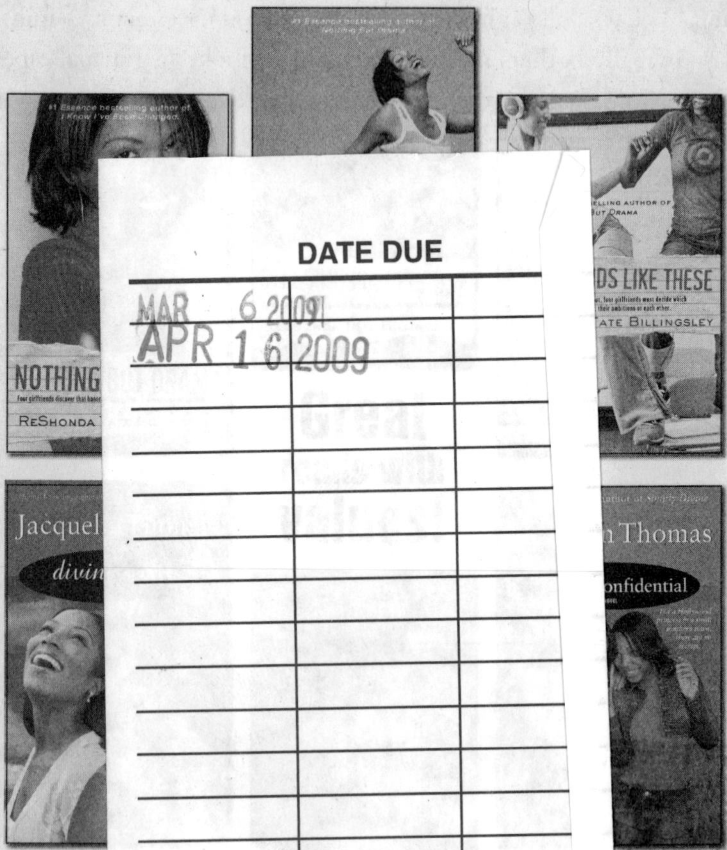

Available w
or at www.

KET BOOKS

17898

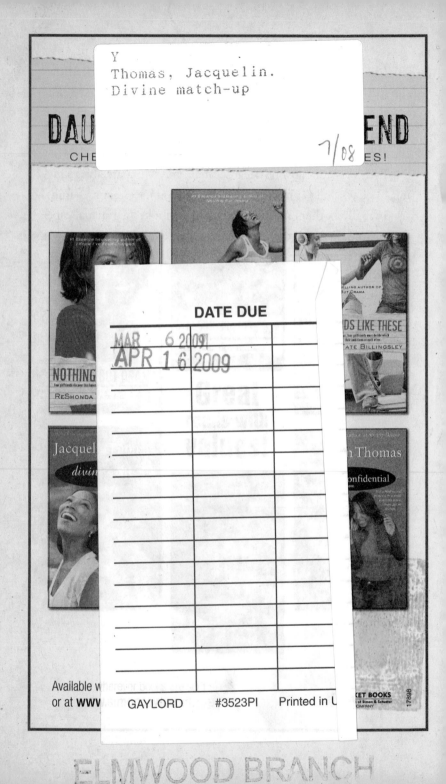